FANT

NIGHT SHIFT

0-1-1

4/18

I'm at a coffee shop getting my usual toaster oven delicacy—an egg white and turkey bacon English muffin, with a blonde veranda blend coffee and three espresso shots to wash it down. Yes, I get the weakest coffee and I un-weaken it with the molly of Arabica beans. I'm tired. I'm waiting for the caffeine to kick in so I can start my day, even though it's 7:00 P.M.

I'm still getting the hang of this nocturnal lifestyle. My friend Jimmy told me it gets easier. "After a while, you'll find it in yourself to wake up early, so you can at least get a little sunlight," he laughed, "But you'll learn to love the dark. Good things happen in the dark."

That's easy for a famous DJ to say; his dark nights are filled with people fawning over him, throwing him alcohol, praise, and promises of whatever sex he wants in exchange for his musical stylings. It's still weird to think of him like that, the dorky acquaintance from high school who always talked a big game. He actually made it. I see his name and photo on billboards all over town, accompanied by phone numbers to call for "very important" tables and bottle service. And if it wasn't enough that he's famous and adored, he makes bank for these promotions! He spent more than what I make in a month on an array of furry hand cuffs, sparkly dildos, and colorful panties.

How do I know this? Well, because I was the one who rang him up.

"That will be three thousand four hundred sixty-two dollars and twenty-nine cents."

Sparkly butt plugs of various sizes, rainbow thigh-high socks, and lime green penis lollipops line my counter, and the pile is still growing, the entourage of Tinkerbells still not done with their horny shopping spree. This had to be the most colorful pile of debauchery I had ever seen. But then again, I've only been working here for a week. It's my sixth "day" working as a cashier at Dreamz, an adult video and novelty shop located inside of a strip mall on Highway 19 in Pasco County, Florida. A scenic road known for its unusually high number of pedestrian deaths . . . and porn stores. I was hesitant about accepting the job here for a lot of reasons—one of them being the oncoming traffic. Another was that I was worried someone I knew would run into me here. It's not that I have any aversion to dildos, adult DVDs, and little booths to masturbate in, but I don't exactly have an all-consuming passion for it either. I'm not a virgin, but I can count the times I've had sex on one hand. A self-imposed friendless and sexless life, combined with a *cum laude* English degree from a state university, was supposed to lead to a dream job in academia. Yet, here I stand, behind a register, ringing up lube at the crack of dawn thanks to a shitty economy and an influx of girls who loved Jane Austen in middle school and also decided to pursue English teaching degrees. However, Dreamz does have about seventy different kinds of lube. I had no idea there was seventy different ways to moisten up your genitals. That's just not something you learn while deconstructing *The Canterbury Tales*.

My first week at the store had actually been pretty bland until Jimmy walked in on my first Friday night.

He recognized me immediately, which isn't so surprising because I'd barely changed anything about myself other than being a few pounds heavier than I used to be. Jimmy looked completely different. He used to sport a long, greasy ponytail, which was now a very well-manicured, bleached faux-hawk. He was also now covered in tattoos (one of which is a portrait of his very own face) and was wearing excessive, giant pieces of jewelry, things Joan Rivers would have called "statement pieces." A giant dollar sign necklace certainly says a statement to me, and that statement is *I can pay my rent and bills, and have lots of money left over for anything I could ever want.*

Jimmy entered the store with a group of incredibly attractive female disciples. It was 5:30 A.M. I presume the sun was rising, but there aren't any windows in the store so I wouldn't know. The girls looked like mini-me versions of Jimmy, also with multi-colored hair and tattoos, wearing various neon colored tutus, slap bracelets (*Where did they even find those? Weren't they outlawed in, like, 1986?*), fuzzy leg warmers, and platform sneakers. Their eyes were large and bloodshot; I imagine they were on some kind of designer drugs only famous people have access to. This motley crew of rainbow-bright puke skipped around the store, and swooped up anything shiny they could penetrate or vibrate themselves with; they plopped the objects on the checkout counter with glee, while Jimmy watched from the front of the store, nodding in approval. Once they were done, Jimmy strutted over to me, his focus trained on preparing his wallet for the transaction, but he immediately did a double take when he looked up.

"Taryn?!" he asked, surprised.

"Yeah! Hey!" I replied. I wasn't quite sure how to play

this off because he had been in the store for at least 30 minutes, I just didn't want to say hi to him unless he said hi to me first.

"Damn! I haven't seen you in a minute."

It had actually been about six years. But I suppose when your life is a constant drug-and-sex rush, time has a different meaning.

"Yeah! Well . . . I see posters of you all over the place. So I've been seeing you. Congrats on everything. I guess when you told everyone you were dropping out of high school to be a famous DJ, you were really on to something." A short skinny girl dressed like Betty Boop from the wrong side of the tracks interrupted this awkward reunion by plopping down a tiny, precious Swarovski crystal butt plug on the counter.

"I want this, too," she said, batting her eyes at Jimmy.

I was still new there and not entirely sure how to converse with the customers. Was I supposed to act as though I was ringing up laundry detergent at Walgreens, totally nonchalant? Or was being a slight amount of sleazy the professional thing to do? I received about forty-five minutes' worth of training for this job from the owner of the store, who happened to be drunk on her own batch of moonshine at the time. Half the items Jimmy and his minions wanted weren't tagged properly so I made up prices based on how expensive things kind of looked. So uh, $249.99 seemed about right for this butt plug. The amount of money I made in a week, going straight into an asshole.

"This looks like quite the adventure!" I said, in a very grandma tone.

"Hell yeah! We're all celebrating, 'cus I dropped a new single tonight," Jimmy said.

"Well, I hope someone picked it up for you!" I nervously replied. God damn it. Fortunately, I don't think he heard my horribly lame joke. Either that or he heard it and ignored it, which was a completely appropriate thing to do.

"That will be three thousand, four hundred and sixty-two dollars and twenty-nine cents." I said. This didn't faze him at all. He handed me a credit card. Just one credit card, without a blink of an eye. Damn. My college books were about $3,000 and I used to always spread that among three different cards along with a handful of cash.

"Oh yeah—and an hour in room four, please," he said, just before I finished ringing everything up.

In my entire week-long employment here, no one had asked for one of the rooms before. Oh wait. I mean "ROOMZ." That's what they're called here. The letter "z" apparently exudes a sexiness which I don't understand. They never taught me that in college.

Dreamz is supposed to be a store where your wildest fantasies come true. People are encouraged to purchase whatever they want in the store, and then use their purchase in one of the rooms (z). There are televisions screening adult films, giant vats of lube you can access with a pump, and plenty of tissues. On my first day, I mistakenly thought the lube was hand sanitizer, a mistake I've made sure not to repeat, since it left my hands incredibly slippery without any purpose of penetration all day.

I'm supposed to say, "Would you like to make your dreams come true?" after each purchase, as an up-sell to get people to purchase time in one of the rooms, but I haven't been. I figured if someone wanted one they would ask. Clearly, this was not Jimmy's first time back

5

there, considering he already knew what room number he wanted. At $49.99 an hour, room four was the biggest and most expensive room the store had to offer. In addition to the Kleenex and the television sets that looped random pornographic films, it had a leopard-print ottoman, and mirrors on the ceilings. It seemed perfect for the extreme types of people who came to this store. The narcissistic nymphomaniacs, sneaking spouses, self-hating, sexually deprived folks who just can't get laid elsewhere, or anyone else who has money and wants to do it in a semi-public space . Like they say—dreams do come true!

I opened the register and grabbed the key for room number four. It was a tiger-striped key, which appropriately complemented the ottoman. There was only one key per room. Not a master key or anything as far as I knew, so whoever held the key held the power to control who and what were allowed in the den of debauchery.

To give the key to Jimmy, turn to page 7.

To give the key to one of the girls, turn to page 17.

I handed the gaudy key over to Jimmy. He and his five groupies entered the room. I didn't know their names, we weren't formally introduced; I'm honestly not sure if Jimmy did either. Two of them had angel wings on and sparkly dresses, and the angel wings weren't quite holding up so well. One girl had a quadrant of feathers missing from one of her wings, and wires were poking out of the side. My OCD was high, worried that this might be a safety hazard in an orgy. I don't know if wings stayed on or off in a late-night raver orgy. Was it ok to break character and admit that you're just a girl in store-bought wings? Or is part of the fetish continuing to be a fairy regardless of the amount of existing wing? I wouldn't know. Aside from the fairies, there was a girl resembling a unicorn, and one very conventionally attractive ethnic-looking girl in a plain, beige short dress and heels, who resembled a hybrid between a less attractive Kardashian and one of the more attractive cast member of *The Jersey Shore*. The power of Jimmy's penis (and his credit card) brought together different shapes, sizes, colors, and even species.

There's a surveillance camera in these sex ROOMZ, and a monitor near my register that shows me what's going on in each room (the customers can't see it, since it faces me when I'm behind the counter). Whenever someone is in one of these rooms, I'm supposed to keep my eyes on the monitor and be on a look-out for anything that could get the store into trouble . . . however I'm honestly not sure what I'm supposed to look out for, since apparently anything goes here. Sandy, the owner of the store, explained to me that their old lease grandfathered them into some kind of privilege that allowed them to have full-on nudity and penetration in the store. The only thing Sandy told me is specifically not allowed is any kind of escorting. Or any exchange of money for sexual services (except the buying of the room). Only happy and horny willing participants can get penetrated here. A four-thousand-dollar butt plug tab that leads to sex is not paying for sex! It's just paying for sex toys.

I had never seen so many people preparing for a night of sex together. *How would they make this work?* I thought to myself. *Do they take turns on Jimmy? Does he sit and watch? Are all of these girls lesbians?* With no actual proof and a reliance on stereotypes, I guessed that the Jersey Shore girl was not at all a lesbian and would only partake in penis activities. The unicorns and the fairies were the ones who dominated the shopping spree while she did adorable little bumps of whatever drug they were doing out of a pen cap with her back turned to me. But she still followed Jimmy into the room, seeming just as eager as the other girls to get on with whatever the evening had in store. She and the other girls started to unpack some of the purchased toys, and Jimmy removed his coat.

The unicorn girl fussed with the TV remote. Apparently she was assigned to pick which porn they were going to watch, but I don't think she realized that this was not a multiple choice option. There was only one porn cued up to play—the remote's only purpose was for volume and turning the TV on and off—but the unicorn kept flipping through the nonexistent channels. I could see her getting frustrated. She was far too drunk to be deemed the IT department of the orgy.

It's part of my job to choose what DVD gets put in there—at the beginning of the evening I picked a four-hour compilation that seemed to have a variety of sex acts on it, from what I could tell on the back of the DVD. If unicorn girl could just find it in herself to push the fast forward button with the arrow on it, it could definitely solve the problem at hand. Jimmy and the Jersey Shore girl were making out in the corner while the fairies danced in the corner, waving their arms around in geometric shapes, using their butt plugs as glow sticks. Entrancing as they were, I couldn't help but notice that Jersey girl whipped out Jimmy's cock. It was semi hard, and seemed rather large for his half-aroused state.

The attractive ethnic girl pulled her dress up to reveal a beautifully plump, tanned ass and twerked it against Jimmy's cock as he jerked off. The two fairies had sparkly magic bullet vibrators against their clits as they watched and kissed each other, though unfortunately the unicorn was still messing with the TV. Sensing that the frustration would just continue, one of the fairies signaled to the unicorn, beckoning her over to them. It's nice to know that all the members of the raver animal kingdom got along so well!

Jimmy was beginning to look a little flustered. The girl in front of him just kept twerking, shaking her beautiful ass up, down, and around; it was hypnotic, you couldn't help but follow it wherever it moved. How did she get so good at this? His cock was now rock hard but she just kept twerking. What a tease! Jimmy's cock had a defined curve to it, and I could see that it had reached its true erect size. The head of his penis was also abnormally large, like a big mushroom head. This was certainly a penis with some character, which suited his personality quite well. His cock was throbbing and he was beginning to jerk it faster and faster, but the girls were simply not paying attention; the other girls were focused on their own corner of lesbian eroticism. I really enjoyed the show of masturbating and giggling and pulling on the glow-in-the-dark barbells hanging off each other's nipples. This orgy had split into two. I think Jimmy's penis was the only thing that could bring them together.

Finally the twerker turned around and got on her knees. She wasted no time at all, and immediately started licking Jimmy's penis up and down, taking periodic breaks to flip her hair around. She had beautiful big brown eyes and stared into Jimmy's with such conviction. Was she in love with him? Was she going to murder him?

Suddenly, the unicorn reached a very large and very noticeable climax from the little vibrating bullet that sat on her clit. Her hips and legs started shaking, and her eyes rolled into the back of her head. I will have to remember these effects the next time a customer asks which bullet is the best. I made a mental note that this one works pretty damn well. Somehow her unicorn hoodie thing stayed on! This must mean she was actually a unicorn, not just a girl in a unicorn hat. There is no way I could keep a hood on so gracefully through an orgasmic earthquake.

That initial orgasm changed the mood of the room. The two fairies grabbed a pink, sparkly, double-sided dildo and began sliding back and forth on it, and the tan girl with the psychotic eyes started giving an actual proper blow job instead of a half-assed hand job. The unicorn crawled over and fed Jimmy's cock into the tan girl's mouth. Like Santa's little unicorn cock helper. She tried to stick her tongue in and get a lick of Jimmy's shaft, but she was subtly pushed away by the other girl. She moved her face around to the other side of his cock and tried to get a tongue in through a different entrance, but she was blocked again. Then the Jersey Shore girl, with an expression similar to an angry mother scolding her child, pointed at the TV remote with very obvious disappointment. I couldn't hear any sounds on my monitor, but I could see expressions. And this expression said, "Bitch stay away from the dick and change the channel."

I'm not sure if Jimmy realized what was happening here. His eyes were closed—and I had no idea why. If I ever in my lifetime get the opportunity to have sex with more than one person at a time—or hell, more than one person in a week—I would for sure keep my eyes open and savor every last moment, and I would try to get enough stimulation to try to put some away on reserve in that part of my brain that I use when I am alone with my shower head.

"HEY."

I was stuck in a trance behind the register. Half of me was simply asleep standing up and the other half was fantasizing about the prospect of having more than one sexual partner at a time sometime in my lifetime. I gasped. The unicorn stood right in front of me, naked and sweating.

"Uh, hi. Can I help you with something?"

"Can you fix the TV, I think it's broken," she said. She looked as though she was going to cry. Poor imaginary creature. They probably didn't have television sets in the magical forest she spawned from.

"Well I . . . I'm not supposed to interrupt you guys. Are

you sure you . . . are ok with . . . you know, me coming in there?"

"Yeah it's fine," she said. "You know Jimmy, so you're cool. Just please fix the fucking TV," she said in a panic.

I wanted to tell her to sit back and relax and give herself another earth-shattering magic bullet orgasm, but I didn't want her to know that I saw everything. I'm just a store clerk, I'm supposed to be an impartial helper, kind of like an asexual robot.

I followed her back into the room. It was like I had the opportunity to step inside of a video game I'd been playing, or porno I'd been watching. It was surreal.

The two winged pixies were sliding back and forth on the double-sided dildo like their life depended on it. Faster and faster, with one of their wings still fully intact and the other one's feathers falling all over the floor. *I'm gonna have to clean that up later. Dammit.*

I got up on a step stool and went behind the television as if I was some kind of honest repairman. I knew there was nothing wrong with the TV. This TV was just a means to an end to play DVDs, and only one DVD could be played at a time. So I stood on the stool, pretending to work, but was really just watching what was going on.

I had been stuck at the counter for seven hours, organizing things, ringing up a few purchases. It was pretty standard, and kind of boring. Hanging out in this electro-sex haven was much more entertaining. I liked the lighting. Something about the purplish-blue mood lighting in here that Sandy prided herself on was soothing. No one seemed to mind that I was in there. I blended with the darkness in the corner as I unplugged wires that I plugged back into the same spot.

With me working on the television, the unicorn was able to focus on Jimmy's cock. She finally found a way in, and she did not take this opportunity for granted. She slobbered all over Jimmy's cock, swallowed the whole thing all the way down. Jimmy finally opened his eyes and forced his hand down on her head, squishing her horn. I wasn't sure how I felt about the unicorn not being a unicorn anymore but I was glad she got some cock.

The tan girl stuck her ass in Jimmy's face and resumed to her ass shaking. She kept repeating the same moves, but they weren't boring. Her ass was perfectly round and mesmerizing, and she knew it. The double-sided dildo fairy team made the sparkly toy disappear between their two wet pussies as they rubbed themselves against each other. They moaned and giggled. The tan girl just kept repeating "Ohhhhh, you like my ass, baby, don't you?" while the unicorn seemed to have released all mucus and saliva from her nasal passages and throat and slobbered it all onto Jimmy's cock.

The two fairy girls both had the most adorable, silly orgasms. They were incredibly loud but I'm not entirely sure how convincing they were. They definitely enjoyed themselves, though it didn't seem like they reached real completion; they may have just mutually decided that they were tired of the double-sided dildo.

The fairies spilled out some kind of powder on the table amidst the keg of lube and the Kleenex and snorted it up with some penis straws, continuing to giggle with their tits out. *Don't mind me over here, I'm just fixing the TV.*

The two fairies were technically in the same room, but after the magic powder traveled through the penis straws and into their noses they were definitely transported to a different universe. Their laughter hit a transcendent octave. The look in their eyes turned carnal. Their movements in their bodies slowed like they were walking through mud. The inhibitions they had that kept them having sex solely with members of the same species in the rave animal kingdom were gone, thanks to the magic penis-straw powder. Now they had the confidence to seduce Jimmy.

The two girls crawled over to him with a look of determination. The fairy with the intact wings pushed the unicorn away, hopped onto Jimmy's cock, and rode him. The wires from her wings moved in time with her crazy rhythm, and the feathers flew into Jimmy's mouth with each bounce, but he quickly flicked them out of the way. She slapped her own breasts and pinched her own nipples as she rode him, his giant mushroom head of a penis going all the way in and all the way out, her pussy dripping wet all over his cock. The other girls stopped grabbing at him and stared in awe. I could tell she was looking at her own reflection on the not-working TV. She was proud of her superhuman sex ability. Quite frankly, I was, too.

The other girls in the room immediately stepped up their sex game to the same level of oomph that the fairy with the good wings had. What was once a half-assed, late night, drug-infested orgy became the raver sex Olympics, sponsored by fairy penis-straw powder.

"Give me that cock," the tan girl said. She wasn't asking, she was demanding. Then she wasn't even demanding, she was just doing. The cock instantly became hers. These kinds of girls always get what they want. She kept on twerking, but this time on all fours, backing up against

Jimmy's cock. Her face on the ground and her ass up in the air and Jimmy winced, moaned, and cried all at the same time as he thrust his entire body into her pussy. The other girls furiously masturbated in a merry-go-round surrounding him.

I wasn't sure how much longer I could pretend to fix the TV. Did they know I was still in here? Should I sneak out? Should I stay? Should I turn the TV back on? What do I do?! In the midst of me fumbling and trying to figure out what to do, I flipped the TV back on, and well . . . it went on. Because it wasn't broken in the first place. What I mean to say is, I turned the TV back on.

I fast forwarded the DVD to a different scene in the film, that so happened to be an orgy. I knew exactly what time code to turn it to. This "Four-hour big boob Exxx-travaganza" had played several times in the store before. There was a particular scene in this DVD where several females had sex with one male—known as, I learned from the movie's box cover copy, a "reverse gang bang." From that I deduced what would most likely be an un-reverse gang bang, too—which I hoped to explore in other DVDs from this store. But not tonight.

"I fixed it!" I said with excitement, hoping to get a round of applause from the orgy, but no one noticed. Except the unicorn who took her four fingers out of her vagina and ran up and hugged me.

"Thank you! You rule!" she said.

"You're welcome! Enjoy!" I answered. "The TV, I mean. And everything else. Or at least just the TV," I awkwardly added.

On the TV a muscular, girthy male signaled for five females to get down on their knees, and they did immediately, and then he ejaculated an equal amount of cum onto the five girls' faces. Simultaneously, Jimmy pulled out of the Jersey Shore girl's ass, masturbated furiously, shimmied and shook his body, and let out a howl like a werewolf at the moon . . . and ejaculated a drop of cum onto the unicorn's cheek, pulled back, shook around some more, and a few more drops of sperm dropped onto the floor. The members of the magic animal kingdom—fairies and unicorns alike—scurried to lick it off the ground. The other girl casually put her clothing back on.

Jimmy then put out a few lines of mystery powder on the table for himself. He didn't use a penis straw. He used a hundred-dollar bill that was previously rolled up in his wallet. I don't know much about drugs but couldn't a one-dollar bill serve the same function? I mean, really. That was just excessive.

To go back give the key to one of the girls instead, turn to page 17.

Continue with Taryn in this fantasy, turn to page 23.

I opened the cash register and grabbed the key for room four and handed it to the fairy with the largest wings in the group. In this collection of fairytale creatures, the big wings screamed authority to me.

The fairy with the big wings grabbed another fairy with much smaller wings, along with a girl dressed like a slutty unicorn, and another girl who was not dressed as a part of the animal kingdom and looked more like a Jersey Shore/Kardashian type. They all giggled, and sprinted into room four and locked the door.

Jimmy was lethargic, and didn't realize what was happening. He was lost in deep concentration, staring at the back of a DVD box cover for a movie titled *School of Black Cock, #3*. After seventeen consecutive years of schooling, and a very large student loan eating up half my very small paychecks, I couldn't possibly ever imagine getting aroused by any pornographic film that reminded me of school. He dropped out early so I could see how he was nostalgic about classrooms and such. I wasn't sure what to do here. I pretended to be busy rearranging a display case, but then I actually realized that the display case truly did need some different products in there. These dildos looked like they were from the '90s. Was there an expiration date on dildos? Does the material erode over time?

"Hey, uh . . . where did everyone go?" Jimmy shouted. I wasn't actually sure if the question was directed at me but there was no one else here to answer. I looked away from the retro dildos to address him.

"The girls are, um . . . in the room. I'm sorry. Everything happened kinda fast. I gave the fairy the key because I thought she was in charge. I'm sorry—you paid for the room, I shouldn't have done that. I'm still new here—I didn't think . . ."

"Shit. For real though?" he replied.

I had no idea how to respond. What a bizarre fragment of a sentence.

"Um . . . maybe you can just knock and they'll let you in? Or . . . I can give you your own room if you want. No extra cost. Then they'll learn their lesson!"

I had a déjà vu of my mother who attempted to console me after I was stood up by my prom date. Coincidentally, that prom was also Jimmy's first DJ gig. I found solace in the fact that whether you're covered in acne, or you're covered in tattoos, you still have an equal chance of getting rejected.

"It's all good. Whatever!"

"Yeah! That's the right attitude. It's their loss. Really." I paused. Sometimes I feel like I just can't stop talking. I have a way of making uncomfortable moments so much worse by just opening my mouth, but I can't stop it! "Not like . . . I would know. I mean . . . yeah . . . I can just tell, you would be great in there, really, and they'll be sorry!" Again I am channeling my mother, and nobody's mother belongs at a porn store at 6 A.M.

"Let me get a peek, yo," he said.

"Oh! Well . . . yeah. I mean, I'm supposed to be keeping an eye on them. I think, technically, I'm not supposed to show customers the security camera, but since we're like

18

. . . friends . . . and, like, you paid for the room. I think it's fine," I said uncertainly.

There's a surveillance camera in these sex ROOMZ, and a monitor near my register that shows me what's going on in each room (the customers can't see it since it faces me when I'm behind the counter). Whenever someone is in one of these rooms, I'm supposed to keep my eyes on the monitor and be on a lookout for anything that could get the store into trouble; however I'm honestly not sure what I'm supposed to look out for, since apparently anything goes here. Sandy, the owner of the store, explained to me that their old lease grandfathered them into some kind of privilege that allowed them to have full-on nudity and penetration in the store. The only thing Sandy told me is specifically not allowed is any kind of escorting. Or any exchange of money for sexual services (except the buying of the room). Only happy and horny, willing participants can get penetrated here. A four-thousand-dollar butt plug tab that leads to sex is not paying for sex! It's just paying for sex toys.

I invited Jimmy behind the register and I sharpened the contrast on the old television monitor as much as I possibly could. If only I had some popcorn, this could have been like the high school date we never had.

The girls seemed to be enjoying themselves. I was tuning in a bit late, but they were all naked, aside from wings, legwarmers, a unicorn beanie, and the more conventional looking girl who didn't dress up like any mythical creature had her VIP laminated badge with Jimmy's face on it dangling between her incredibly large, and very obviously unnatural, perky breasts. I like that she showed her loyalty to Jimmy in some sort of way, even though he spent four thousand dollars and wasn't even invited into the room.

The two fairies got on all fours and faced their asses towards the unicorn and the Jersey Shore girl, and began the process of inserting their crystal butt plugs inside of themselves. The fairies helped each other out by touching each other's clit and rubbing lube on each other's asshole. The other two girls stared at them with amazement, and applauded their anal abilities. Jimmy gave his own applause on our side of the store. Butt plugs truly brought joy to people in a way I never knew!

The fairies shook their asses, and kissed each other. One fairy licked the other fairy's ass; it was sparkly and erotic and so dazzling. I had never really seen an accessorized asshole and it truly was quite beautiful.

The Jersey Shore girl appeared shy, but curious. She tugged at the unicorn's nipple rings and played around with her meaty clit ring in amazement. The unicorn's clit ring was incredibly thick—it looked heavy, like a giant silver weight dangling off her pussy. I didn't know clit rings came in various sizes like that.

The in-charge fairy with the larger wings grabbed a Hitachi magic wand—something we sold as "back massagers"—and placed it on the Jersey Shore girl's pussy. I did always find it odd that amid anal beads, dildos, and ball-gags there were devices to massage one's back. Now I get it!

Jersey girl's shyness disappeared. She relaxed as her eyes went into the back of her head. She grabbed onto fairy number two's ass for balance, and the fairy rubbed her clit with her own fingers, while grabbing onto the unicorn's tits, all still with the butt plug inside of her.

Jimmy rubbed his crotch. I could see a boner poking from the inside of his pants. I had to admit, I was a little wet, too. What an advantage we have as women that we can be so secretive with our own perversions! I don't envy a large metal-like rod that told the world when we're aroused. But he didn't seem to care. I suppose not having an erection at this moment would be worse. His eyes were glued to the TV.

The unicorn grabbed the VIP badge with Jimmy's face on it that was around the Jersey Shore girl's neck, and kissed her ferociously as the Hitachi was still on her clit. Everyone seemed so determined to make this girl have an orgasm. Perhaps once she had one, she would turn into a unicorn, or a fairy, too? Jimmy reached for his cock underneath his pants and began pleasuring himself behind the register. I'm not quite sure if this was allowed, but I don't think it was illegal. Jimmy was a local hero. He pushed buttons on laptops at nightclubs that cost over fifty dollars to get into. It was an honor to have him rub his own cock underneath his oversized pants in the middle of our store, right?

The fairy with the smaller wings lied down, and the other fairy wrapped her legs around her head and sat on her face. The unicorn followed suit and laid the Jersey Shore girl down and sat on *her* face, with the "back massager" still glued to her clit. The fairies morphed into a 69, and licked and fingered each other progressively with more and more fingers inside each other's wet pussies, until every part of their hands disappeared. It was intense. They continued, until they both started pulsating on each other's hands. Holy shit! I noticed a small fountain of squirt come out of the fairy with the bigger wings' vagina. Jimmy continued to touch himself. The Jersey girl then shook uncontrollably with the unicorn's pussy in her mouth. The back massager had broken her down and given her a greater orgasm than anyone else's. The fairies licked their juices off their fingers, and the unicorn seemed satisfied to have cum inside of such a perfect pair of collagen-injected lips.

And Jimmy . . . well . . . he rubbed himself to completion successfully without even taking his pants off. I ran to the bachelorette section of the shop and pulled out a "Tuggie," aka a fuzzy sock that fits on your cock. A sock cock, if you will. I offered it to him as a complimentary gift. I thought it would be a comfortable alternative to wear for the ride home as opposed to his stained pants. There was a neon green one that I thought suited his style quite well.

The girls laughed and poured out some various powders on the table that they snorted through a penis straw. They took their time getting ready. They had about thirteen minutes of room left.

"Do you want me to call you a cab or something?" I asked Jimmy.

"Nah," he said, "I got a limo outside."

Yeah. Of course he did.

To go back and give the key to Jimmy instead, turn to page 7.

Continue with Taryn in this fantasy, turn to the next page.

It's Saturday night. The freakin' weekend. Most people my age will be gearing up for a night of bar hopping, and one-night stands. As for me, I will be spending my Saturday among vibrators, silicone dongs, and films as fine as *Grand Theft Anal 7*. Who's to say who's having a sexier night?

My shift has just begun, and the owner, Sandy is here. My mother's mother died when I was three years old and my father's mother died just before I was born, so I never had that grandparent that baked you pies and knitted you sweaters. Sandy, however, had a unique, grandmotherly charm; she called me toots and sweetie pie and gave me kisses on the cheek, but instead of making pie she made moonshine in her bathtub. She also regularly went on dates with suitors twenty-plus years younger than her, and some time last week she fornicated with two men at the same time. (I use the word *fornicate* because referring to sex as "fucking" when you're talking about your grandma is wrong—right?) I truly never knew women in their seventies could have such a healthy sex drive, but like I said, I never had a grandma.

On this fine evening she wore bright pink lipstick, a see-through halter top with giant metallic sea-shells covering her breasts, paired with stone washed jeans, red heels, and a fur coat.

"You look nice tonight! Why so dressed up?" I asked her.

"Well, it's Saturday night sweetie!"

"Well, you've got some lipstick on your teeth on a Saturday night," I laughed. I pulled out a Kleenex from behind the counter, and she pulled out a pocket mirror and inspected her mouth.

"Oh, what a hoot!" She laughed hysterically. I had her hold still as I wiped the pink stain off her teeth. Then I continued to restock dildos.

In addition to parading around in faux fur and sea-shelled boobs, Sandy put out bowls of Cheetos and Chex Mix for the customers, and turned the music (which was a bizarre collection of orchestral versions of current pop songs; I don't think Sandy understood the origin of what these tunes were imitating) in the store up about four decibels louder than it usually is. She also made some kind of punch mix that she inconveniently placed right next to the register.

I didn't know she would be coming in. Was she here as my boss? Is there something I should be doing differently? I could have put out some Cheetos had I known that I was supposed to. Does that help with sales? I wanted to ask her, but I also didn't want to give away any sales tactics to any customers.

"I think there's a folding table somewhere in the back," I said. "Maybe we can bring it out and put the food and stuff on there . . ."

Sandy nodded, so I brought out the table, and laid out the punch, Chex Mix, and the Cheetos in as decorative a manner as I possibly could. The table looked a bit barren so I sprinkled some porn DVDs between everything.

"That looks lovely!" Sandy said as she lifted an anal DVD off the table. She put her glasses on and inspected the back of the DVD box cover, with the movie just a few centimeters away from her face. I wasn't sure what she meant was lovely—the graphic photographic images of anal sex that her spectacles examined or my on-the-fly table design skills. Perhaps it was a mixture of both.

There were a few customers wandering around the store. It was interesting to watch the way people navigated their way through aisles of sex. Certain people come in here with a very specific purpose and go directly to the product they have in mind. Others spend hours looking around, unsure if they need a dildo, a blow-up doll, a XXX movie, or anything and everything in between. I noticed that several repeat "customers" (if you can still call them that) frequently came in the store, looked around at everything diligently, and then left without ever purchasing anything.

One of them was here now. He repeated his same ritual that he usually did; he walked in, went straight to the DVD aisle, and strategically studied the back of 20 to 30 various box covers. He would then pick the same one off the shelf—*Bisexual Cuckold Fantasies*—asked me how much it was (mind you there is a large orange price tag on it clearly stating the answer to the question), and then he asked if we took credit cards. I would reply yes, we do, he would say he will be right back, then he would leave. He did the same thing today, only this time he took a few Cheetos on his way out. For Sandy's sake, I hope those Cheetos lead him one step closer to an actual purchase one day.

Even though I still felt uneasy talking to the customers, I was learning a lot from watching Sandy. She walked around and conversed with people, and filled the dead, awkward space that existed between the handful of often-confused, sexually inquisitive strangers here.

She was currently interacting with a large, bearded man who was wearing the most stereotypical lumberjack clothes I've ever seen: red flannel shirt, jeans, and a black beanie. I'd seen him pacing back and forth between the DVD and lingerie aisles, clearly looking for something, but definitely not seeing it.

"Honey, would you like some punch?" Sandy asked him. He nodded, and Sandy in her own seductive way signaled him over to the plastic table, aka our makeshift bar for the evening. Sandy handed him a red solo cup full of her mystery pink concoction in a bowl.

"Thanks," he mumbled, clutching the cup like a life-line. He sipped it slowly, his eyes still scanning the store for the item of his fancy. I thought about going to talk with him, maybe seeing if I could help him find what he was looking for, but just then, a tall, skinny man with some stubble, a large nose, and the sides of his head shaved walked into the store.

"Amir! Good to see you!!" Sandy ran over to him and kissed him on the cheek, leaving his skin stained with pink lipstick. She gave him a very warm, motherly (or grandmotherly) hug, which was reciprocated with a very stiff pat on the back.

"Hi, Sandy."

She poured him a cup of punch and offered it to him; he reluctantly accepted. The quiet lumberjack and the guy named Amir stood near the Home Depot table drinking punch and quickly glancing at one another. As the reddish-pink liquid in their cups disappeared, their inhibitions seemed to lower and they looked more relaxed. This was a magic punch, really. Sandy had been drinking it all night, so naturally, she danced in the butt plug aisle as a piano instrumental of a Linkin Park song played on the store speakers. Though I didn't have any of the punch, I too could feel some bravery growing within me, so I decided to put it to use and go talk to one of the customers. Maybe I could help them find what they were looking for . . .

To talk to the lumberjack, turn to page 28.

To talk to Amir, turn to page 38.

I decided to talk to the lumberjack; I was so curious about him. He didn't fit the "typical" profile of one of our customers, at least from what I could tell from the past seven days. Why was he here?

As soon as I moved from behind the counter, the lumberjack downed the rest of his punch and walked back over to the lingerie section of the store with determination. Where does one even wear lingerie? It was far too ruffled and textured to wear underneath clothing. It always just seemed so impractical to me. If I was ever going to spend $120 on a bra, I would want it to be a sports bra or something I could seamlessly wear underneath my clothes, and on its own as a top if I had ever decided to go to the gym. I could even wear it to sleep. But . . . everything did look really pretty. The lacework on some of the panties was spectacular, the rhinestones on the bras caught the light so perfectly, and garters with their stand-out buckles were definitely sexy—you know, for the kind of person who likes this stuff. I followed the lumberjack over to the lingerie and tapped him on the shoulder.

"Sir—did you need some suggestions or help picking something out for your wife?" I asked the lumberjack. His eyes immediately shot up to mine, though he suddenly looked so . . . hurt. Should I not have assumed he was married? Should I have said "loved one?" Does anyone really say that?

The lumberjack dropped the large lacey garter in

his hand and rushed toward the exit of the store. Sandy stopped him.

"Honey, if you want to try that on go ahead! It's ok!" She winked at him and, holding his hand, used her soothing grandma powers to calm him down.

"Thank you," he said, "I'm new at this."

"That's ok! My name is Sandy!" she said. "And that's Taryn! She's actually new here, too. Please let either of us know if you need anything." There was a terribly awkward silence in the store, even with the jazz instrumental edition of a Mariah Carey song playing on the speakers. "More punch?" Sandy said while handing him another cup. I should treat myself to some. I felt terrible.

After chugging down another plastic cup full of punch, the lumberjack retreated to the lingerie section. In all honesty, I didn't know if we had anything in his size. Most of these outfits were one size fits all, and the "all" definitely discriminated against women who were even slightly above average weight, and certainly did not take into account 200-pound men. He stared blankly at the pile of straps, lace, and spandex. It was really disorganized and that is completely my fault; I'd spent so much time arranging the dildos perfectly that I'd forgotten about every other part of the store.

"So what were you looking for? Maybe I can help you navigate through this mess," I said.

"Well, I, um, stockings. I like stockings—do you have any?" he asked nervously.

"Oh yeah! Absolutely! They're actually over here." I led him back to the register, where a display of stockings stood almost camouflaged in the corner. Whenever I do get around to organizing the lingerie in the store, I should put the stockings near the lingerie. I never realized 'til now how inefficient it was.

The lumberjack stared blankly at the different pairs of stockings, fishnets, thigh-highs, and tights, his eyes running up and down the stand, analyzing each pair and then zipping to the next.

"I . . . I don't know what would look good on me," he finally said.

"How about this one? I think this would look great!" I spotted a plus-size pair of nude thigh-highs with a black seam in the back. From the vast experience I had with the two and a half boyfriends I previously had in life (the "half" was on account of the fact that I called him my boyfriend and he didn't call me his girlfriend), I knew that men are typically terrible at picking out clothing. Whether it's a winter coat or a lace garter, it's never an easy decision.

"Those look really nice. Thank you." He seemed more comfortable now. Hopefully I redeemed myself from my earlier assumptions. He was a big guy, but he was incredibly soft spoken and timid. Like a big teddy bear.

"The stockings won't stay up on their own, so we will have to look for a garter for you!"

He followed me back to the lingerie section of the store, this time with more purpose and confidence. Who needs therapy when you have punch and thigh-highs! I pulled out a handful of garter belts from the mound of disorganized lingerie, the biggest ones I could find, but I was worried they still wouldn't fit. Would he have the same body issues I do when I try on clothing that doesn't fit? I wasn't sure how to address the fact that these all might be too small without hurting his feelings.

"I'm worried that won't fit around my gut!" He pulled up his red flannel and exposed his hairy bulging stomach. I laughed.

"It barely fits around *my* gut," I said. "Maybe I can get creative and make something work."

"I brought my own panties, by the way."

I was honestly impressed. "Oh really? Well let me see them! I want to be sure they match."

He pulled out a pair of black cotton French-cut panties with a lace trim on top that was squished in one of the pockets of his jeans. His face flushed as he rescued them from the tight space, but he looked at the panties lovingly.

"Those are really nice. I think they'll look great on you," I said. "Really, can't go wrong with a pair of plain black panties. They will match with anything!"

The garter I picked out for him was also black. The black lace garter, the black panties, and the nude thigh-highs made for a sexy combination.

"I would like to try it on," he said.

"Yeah, of course!" I walked toward the dressing room, then stopped myself. "Hey, um, I have to ring you up first. Once I take the stockings out of the box I can't put them back in. I'm sorry." I hope I didn't just ruin the moment. This was a delicate situation. Being a cross-dresser enthu-siast/motivator was a new and exciting part of my job, but doing inventory on pantyhose was also part of my job.

"Oh yeah. Sorry. Like I said, I'm new at this," he replied.

We went back to the register and a few customers were actually waiting for me to ring them up. I had forgotten about the rest of the store. Fortunately, they had punch and an assortment of porn DVDs to keep them occupied.

"Let me check these people out and I'll be right with you," I said to the lumberjack. I rang up a few people who were getting standard stuff. Lube for one person, a mix of pornographic DVDs from our $5 bin for someone else, a *Barely Legal* magazine and a Fleshlight (an incredibly popular replica of a vagina that conveniently comes in a receptacle that resembles a large flashlight—for those of you who didn't know) for another. I quickly got them out of the way so I could get back to helping the lumberjack, whom I realized I should stop calling "the lumberjack." Personal attention was the key to good business, was it not?

"What's your name, by the way?" I asked him when it was finally his turn at the register.

"Billy."

Billy. I liked this name. It was kind of unisex, so no matter which gender he identified with I could use the same name. I always thought the name Billy for a woman was hot. There was a woman named Billy (or Billie, actually) on *Days of Our Lives*, which I watched in its entirety when I was sick one week in college. And damn, that character was hot. Had I not been sick at the time, I would have definitely been aroused.

I rang up the pantyhose and the garter belt. I stretched the sides of the lace in the garter as far as it could go, and it still didn't look like it could fit Billy.

"I've got an idea."

I took the safety pins off the garter that were holding the merchandise tags and moved them to the back of the garment. I attached pieces of twine I normally used to tie down cardboard boxes that went in the recycling bin in between them. It gave the garter an extra foot of length. The twine really complimented his burly, grungy look.

My Saturday night-shift was suddenly like an episode of *Project Runway.*

"Let's get you back to the fitting room!" I said.

The fitting room was actually just the bathroom. Calling it a "fitting room" just felt fancier and I assumed he wanted to feel fancy, with thigh-highs and a garter and all. He took his purchases and went into the room. I stood nearby.

"If you need anything let me know!"

I hung around outside for a while, almost hoping that Billy would call me in to see him. I was definitely invested in his fetish well-being at this point. Several minutes passed and I realized that I just looked like a girl who desperately had to pee.

"Are you ok in there?" I knocked and asked.

"Actually—could you come in here?" he answered, after a few more minutes of silence. I was secretly very pleased, but I put on an air of concerned professionalism.

He unlocked the door and I entered. Just as I suspected, he was having issues tying up the twine in the back. He had put his pants on top of the thigh-highs and the garter was peeking out around his belly.

"I want to see the stockings," I said. "After all, I did pick them out!" I truly did want to see them. I had never seen a large man in lingerie before and I found something about the dichotomy between his personality and his outer appearance to be very . . . sexy.

He turned his back to me and unzipped his pants. He did a great job picking out panties; they fit him nicely. His asscheeks hung out of the bottom, and his ass was actually more toned than I expected. I tied up my twine concoction in a knot so the garter belt would stay up.

"There you go," I said. "Fits like a glove. I mean a garter. Ha!" I nervously laughed.

He turned around and I stared at him. His flannel was still on, and I could see a giant bulge inside his panties that appeared to be slowly growing. I had never seen a man's cock inside of dainty women's panties and I surprisingly really enjoyed the sight of it. His flannel was still on and his jeans were around his ankles. I unbuttoned his shirt, his chest was hairy and his gut was large. He was so manly up top and so delicate on the bottom, and the twine all kind of tied it together, literally and metaphorically. The few men I had sex with in my life were tall and skinny so I assumed that was my "type." I had no idea I could be attracted to a man like this and I didn't know a man like this would ever want to wear sheer thigh-highs.

"Take your pants off!" I said. "You'll see the full ensemble without anything blocking the view."

"But I don't have the right shoes," he sighed.

I looked down and realized he had cowboy boots on, which actually sort of made sense with the outfit.

"I will order some large heels for you, if you'd like. You know . . . for next time. But I think your cowboy boots look good! It's not like you're wearing construction boots or dirty sneakers."

As he took his pants and shoes off, someone knocked on the door.

"One minute!" I said. Damn it. This was the only bathroom. I thought we were in an actual fitting room for a moment. He went to pull his pants back on and I stopped him.

"Why don't you walk around the store for a bit in your new clothes? I can hold onto your pants for you; when you want them back just let me know." I could see a big smile underneath his beard, he took a deep breath and let out a big sigh of relief.

"All right, I can give it a try." I picked up the pants and we walked out the door . . . and right into Sandy, who had apparently been standing outside. Shit—was I in trouble?

"He paid for the stockings. I promise." It was the only thing I could think to say.

"Hon, I know!" She looked at Billy. "Well don't you look nice!" And she gave him a kiss on the cheek. Dreams really do come true here. An insecure, oversized man was now being admired by a woman twenty years younger and twenty years older than him at the same time.

I went back to the register, giggling. Like I was just caught having sex with someone in my bedroom by my mom, only I was really just tying a piece of twine around a man's stomach in a public restroom. Billy walked around the store, and I retreated to the register. We kept looking at each other. He flexed his muscles and made funny faces at me. He grabbed random porn DVDs and looked at them and I could see his cock grow inside his panties. He moved his hands around the upper parts of his thigh covered by stockings. He rubbed his hands up and down his legs as far down as he could reach. It sure was a good thing he wore cowboy boots and not heels, or he would have fallen over. He rubbed more and more furiously . . . and then the stockings ripped. He looked so embarrassed. I rushed over to him to make sure he was ok.

"I rip my damn stockings all the time! It's not a big deal. Seriously. When my mom worked as a secretary she went through, like, five pairs of nylons a week."

This didn't make him feel any better. He tried moving

the stockings around so the run was in the back and not the front, but I could already see more of the fibers weakening from the movement.

"You're gonna make it worse! Don't do that—the more you move them around the more they will rip," I said. "Here—I know a trick." I ran back to my purse and pulled out a bottle of clear nail polish that had been living at the bottom of my bag for about three years. I honestly don't know how it ever got there in the first place, but every time I would clean out my purse I would come across it and think, I should keep this here; *I might need it one day.* Never did I think it would be to fix a 200-pound man's pantyhose.

"You're not gonna tie it together with rope are you?" He laughed.

"No!" I answered defensively. "Here's a secret: If you put clear nail polish on the run, it will stop it." I got down on my knees and painted the run in his stockings with my clear polish. I found myself running my fingers up and down his masculine hairy legs, and I loved the way the stockings felt on top of his thighs. I'm glad we went with the nude color; it showed off his form.

"You have really nice legs," I said.

"Oh, thanks!" he replied. "I load furniture in and out of my truck all day so my legs and arms get a good workout. My gut though, that's all beer!" He laughed and patted his belly. It really turned me on to think that a man who delivered couches during the day would be trying on thigh-highs at night. Something about that made me feel free.

And just at that moment, Sandy walked out of the bathroom, her extended time in there acting as a costume change; she came out sporting her own lingerie ensemble: an all-red matching bra and panty set, with fishnet thigh-highs and heels.

"Happy Saturday!" she yelled.

Billy and I couldn't help but laugh. She continued to dance with herself, ironically to an instrumental version of Billy Idol's "Dancing with Myself" (who coincidentally was also another man named Billy who enjoyed dressing like a woman). I stood by the plastic table and Billy grabbed my hand. He looked right into my eyes and said, "Thank you." I smiled. We continued to hold hands for a bit, until we both decided to let go and eat Cheetos.

I was actually having fun.

To go back and talk to Amir instead, turn to page 38.

To keep Billy on your mind, turn to page 233.

I decided to follow Amir.

He finished his drink and headed straight to a section of the store with "male enhancement" pills. He definitely had a purpose. There were two different types of pill in the store. One kind claimed to make you last longer in bed. Essentially it was herbal Viagra. I was never good at science, but I was able to wrap my brain around the fact that different herbs/chemicals mixed together could increase your sexual stamina. I mean, if Vitamin C and echinacea could make a cold go away, then ginkgo biloba and magnesium (two ingredients that seemed to be listed in the ingredients of all the boner pills) could give you a stronger erection and libido. Right? But then there was the other category of pills—which I could not comprehend the chemistry of at all—the type of pills that claimed to make your penis bigger. It was like the magic beans in "Jack and the Beanstalk." Even as a kid I didn't believe in that fairy tale. A prince was more likely to pick me up in a pumpkin and whisk me away to a ball than having a fucking plant that grew all the way up to the clouds and led to a castle—with a harp. There was always a pointless harp in there somewhere.

"Sandy, did you order the Vaso Ultra pills like you said you would?" Amir asked my boss. What on earth was he talking about?

"No, hon'. I tried to and I couldn't. It must be off the market already. Why don't you just get one of those Extendable™ ones again? Didn't you like those?"

He rolled his eyes and anxiously browsed through the pills. He had an incredibly uneasy energy about him, and I felt compelled to help. Perhaps there was something I could do.

"What are you looking for?" I asked.

"Vaso Ultra is a new enlargement pill on the market. I've tried all the other ones here." I was shocked.

"If none of the other ones worked, why would you want to try a different one?"

"They work. I have proof that they work. But when your body gets used to the pill they stop working. The newer formulas are always more effective. It shocks the system. You know what I mean."

He wasn't asking if I knew what he meant, he was telling me that I knew what he meant—but I had no idea what he meant.

"If this one is off the market like Sandy said, it probably means it wasn't good, right? Maybe it's for the best!"

He glared at me. He was clearly not in the mood to give me a penis pill 101 lesson.

"The pills aren't approved by the FDA, so if they're really popular, they get caught, and they have to change the name and the formula right away. Usually Sandy gets the good shit before that happens because she's on top of it. I don't know what the fuck is going on."

"Well I was hired here just a few weeks ago and I'm getting the hang of things. If she lets me take over the wholesale ordering I can try to help."

Sandy interrupted. "Amir, you have a beautiful cock. I think your other method is working better than those pills!"

His face was suddenly flushed red. It's just so terrible

when arrogant men look embarrassed. It's like you see a piece of their soul that you know they don't want you to see and you don't really want to see.

"What's the other method?" I asked. I was already being annoying, I may as well just keep going. I mean, I was sitting in an adult store on a Saturday night surrounded by Cheetos and anal beads. What question could really be inappropriate here?

Sandy laughed, and walked right over to Amir and grabbed his cock. He pushed her hand away and she put it back, and this time he smiled and let it stay there. I don't know if I would ever be comfortable enough to grab a customer's genitals, even an apparent regular's, but that's Sandy for you—always up in everyone's business.

"Relax, Amir, honey. Please!"

"I've been jelking. And I have proven results," Amir said to me. He did actually seem more relaxed now. A crotch grab and some punch calmed him down. *Maybe if he loosened up his man bun that would help.*

"Excuse me—what?" I didn't know if I misheard him, or if he actually said *jelking.* And if he did, I had no idea what that meant. Was it a cute nickname for jerking off?

"Jelking," he firmly replied. "It's a certain way of masturbating that elongates your cock. You pull your shaft all the way out as you wank it and over the course of time it elongates your penis. I have proven results."

He pulled out a stack of photographs out of his pocket, with sticky notes on each picture, showing a date and the length of his penis at the time. The earliest picture in the bunch was from five years ago! And to his credit, there was a noticeable difference, and an actual mathematical difference, if the measurements on the notes were correct.

For a minute I felt proud, like, his showing me these photos was a sign that we had truly bonded, and if he was a regular I was supposed to connect with him. Right?

But on second thought, if he already had these photos in his pocket, I couldn't possibly be the first, second, third, fourth, or one hundredth person to see them. His cock was his job application and these photographs were his resume, and these penis enlargement pills were like his college degree that he paid a lot of money for because he thought he needed them to get a job.

He picked up eight different kinds of penis enlargement pills (not to be confused with the stamina pills—apparently he had the stamina department handled) and aggressively threw them down on the counter. I was starting to feel like some kind of drug dealer. Could people be addicted to penis enlargement pills?

"Are you OK?" I said. Which was probably an inappropriate question to ask in here.

"I have a date with my girlfriend this week," he replied. "The average female desires at least a six-point-three-inch penis and mine is currently only five point eight."

He had some kind of penis-size OCD, but it came from a somewhat romantic place. I think.

"Why would you go through all this work for just an average female?" I laughed out loud at my own joke. He didn't find it funny.

"She is not average. According to her dating profile, she is twenty-five years old, has D-cup breasts, a twenty-four-inch waist, and she is five feet eight inches tall."

My B-cup breasts, thirty-inch waist, and five feet three inches were mildly offended. But then again, there was a good chance he was being cat-fished by someone with completely different dimensions. Or even a completely different sex.

"Wait—is this the first time you'll meet her in person?" I asked.

"Yes. We've been talking on the phone every day and texting every night, for months. I know she is the perfect girl for me and I'm worried my dick just won't satisfy her. It's just not the appropriate size. Not yet. I can get there."

"Hasn't she seen it yet? I mean, why don't you just send her one of these photos? You have so many of them."

"She has a photo," he shortly answered.

"Okay, then, she knows, and she still has plans to see you? I mean, I will ring up these pills, obviously, but I think you're in the clear here! Cheer up!"

Sandy's positivity and happiness was contagious. I had never given anyone cock therapy before. But Sandy seemed to be the number one supporter of his cock and she was cackling in the background, and I found this laughter quite counterproductive to this remedial treatment.

"She's got a photo of a cock all right—but not his! What is that poor girl going to think when she finds out you sent her a picture of a porn star's dick?" Sandy laughed.

"Stop it, Sandy. Why are you talking about this in front of everyone? I will get mine that big. I can do it. It won't be a lie once it's the same size. I just need a few more centimeters and I can be the man that I know she deserves."

"How do you know what she deserves? You haven't even met her yet!" Sandy replied, still giggling.

"I have met her plenty, just not in person. The connection we have is beyond being physically present and being an ocean apart doesn't belittle the status of our relationship. Her voice turns me on; even just the mere glimpse of her name appearing on my phone as a missed call or an unread text excites me more than anyone I have ever interacted with."

There was dead silence in the room. This internet romance had more gusto than anything or anyone I had experienced.

"How, um, does Sandy know what photo you sent?" I asked.

"Well—I mean—she found the cock . . . for me to send. I . . . I asked her to. As a favor."

If I was the cock therapist, then Sandy was the cock enabler. Grandmothers aren't ones to practice tough love. They usually give in to what their loved ones want, to make them happy. In this case, her loved one needed a photo of a cock off the internet.

He took three of the pills that he purchased and asked for a key to room one. This was a smaller room, with plenty of lube, tissues, and a comfortable couch. I handed him the key and he rushed off to the room without any further instruction from me.

"Oh, Amir," Sandy sighed. "When will that boy gain some confidence in his penis?" She shook her head in disbelief and rested it on my shoulder. The two of us watched the monitor behind the register, and waited for him to begin "jelking" off.

He wasted no time—as soon as he entered the room he played some kind of porn he had on his cell phone. He had a large screen and a mini stand that clipped to the back of it. He came prepared!

He took his cock out and as Sandy wasn't exaggerating—it was nice! Thick and round, like the size of a ketchup bottle. The head of his penis was a unique triangular shape, which looked incredibly pleasurable. I felt like I had seen dildos the same size of his dick. It was shorter and fatter than the few that I'd seen in my life, and not the lengthiest cock in the universe, but I didn't see that as a problem. Not like I was in any position to be a penis snob, but truly, I wouldn't have been disappointed had I been presented with that.

He pulled his penis as far out as possible, like he was stretching a salt-water taffy. His penis looked red, and then he smoothed it out. Then red again, then smoothed out. Was he moving the blood vessels around? I'm not quite sure. He moaned, though I wasn't sure if it was a moan of pleasure or pain. His determination to stretch his penis was admirable. I was lucky to have men open a car door for me, let alone go through a physical mutation just for my pleasure.

He massaged his balls. He licked his fingers and massaged the head of his dick. He rubbed his chest, he scratched himself, he alternated his right hand and left hand on his cock, still pulling the skin forward. He grabbed some lube, placed one hand at the base of his cock and his other hand pulled his shaft forward in long strokes, like he was untangling a garden hose. He manipulated his skin, cupping his balls, while he stared at the girl-girl-boy threesome porn on his phone screen. This was an intense jerk-off—or jelk-off—session. It was masturbation with a true purpose. Sweat poured down his chest. He breathed heavy to the point where I could see the audio levels on the monitor peaking. He pulled his cock forward—as far forward as he could possibly make it go. I was actually scared for a moment he would wind up pulling the thing off. All the while his little bun up top of his head hadn't budged. Not one hair out of place.

He had an explosive amount of testosterone. I wasn't sure if I wanted him to throw me against the wall and fuck me, or if I wanted to watch him hit a body bag at the gym. Or maybe I just wanted him to continue jelking off his perfectly sized cock.

"It really is a nice cock," Sandy said. "He just needs to learn to love himself." From the looks of it he truly knew how to love himself quite well, at least physically. My panties were wet just watching this vehement self-pleasure.

He completed; an incredibly large and healthy, creamy-white finish, and cum dripped down his legs. He then took a finger and dipped it in his own cum, licked his finger, nodded, and smiled.

Sandy let out a loud laugh. "I added some pineapple juice to the punch. It makes cum taste real good!"

It's always nice to learn new family recipes from your grandma.

To go back and talk to the lumberjack instead, turn to page 28.

Continue with Taryn in this fantasy, turn to the next page.

"Well, I've got to go home. It's definitely past my bedtime," Sandy said. It was one in the morning and I could tell Sandy was winding down. I, on the other hand, had eight more hours to go. However, my day began with an alarm clock ringing at 6:00 P.M., so I was painfully awake, and I was also slightly aroused from seeing everything I just saw.

Sandy left and I was alone in the store, left to my own thoughts in a three-thousand-square-foot room filled with dildos. Should I treat myself to a cup of the punch? There was a bit left in the bowl, so I figured, why not? I chugged a cup. It was actually pretty good.

The customers who came in between 8:00 P.M. and 11:00 P.M. usually bought items to use for the evening. They had this air of excitement to them, like patrons at a bar in the early evening filled with optimism and confidence that they would find a person to go home with at the end of the night. Even if that "person" was a Fleshlight, a pornographic film about women in their 40s fucking their pool guys, or just some purple anal beads, it was still a happy ending to an evening. The customers who came in between 4:00 A.M. and 7:00 A.M. were usually on their way home from somewhere. They were visibly drunk or high, with a bag of mixed emotions. Sometimes they came in groups (like Jimmy), and sometimes they were just alone, but the "after-hours" customers all very much had a place to go before the after. These customers had a social life, but not a sex life; or they had romance in their life and not much sex; or they had a sex life but wanted more kink, and Dreamz was there for all their 4:00 A.M. to 7:00 A.M. needs.

However, the customers during the hours between midnight and 3:00 A.M. were different. They required more attention than others and spent less money than most. These people weren't going to or coming from anywhere. The store was the beginning, middle, and end of their night.

But who was I to judge? I, too, was the before, during, and after party. Hell, I was the entire party. I used to tell myself, this was a temporary job to hold me down until I got a real job, but I wasn't actively doing anything to pursue something "real." Was I supposed to be? Was I supposed to be actively applying for jobs I didn't really want, that likewise didn't want me either? I had the credentials to be an incredibly mediocre teacher, but that paid just as much or maybe even less than what I was making, and I had less of a passion for teaching than I did for selling keys to ROOMZ. Having a night job gave me a convenient excuse for my lack of social life. The unique debauchery that ensued ignited sexual fantasies in parts of my brain that I never knew existed. I guess what I am trying to say is that I liked it there.

The night progressed. The post-midnight lull continued, as people wandered through the store, picking up different products they had no intention of buying and putting them down.

"How much is this?" a man in a stained Hard Rock Cafe Orlando T-shirt asked. He was holding up a vibrating egg that was certainly meant for a woman's clitoris.

"$24.99," I answered.

"And what about this?" the same man asked, this time about a kitschy, bacon-flavored lube we carried.

"Oh, lucky for you that's on sale today! It's $12.99." It was on sale because no one actually wants to use a bacon-flavored lube.

"Okay. What about this?" he asked, holding up a studded dog collar, intended for BDSM roleplay.

"That's a hundred percent leather so that's a bit pricey—it's $89.99. But it's great quality!" I replied.

After a long, awkward silence he said, "All right—I will be right back."

Any time anyone ever told me they would be right back, they never came back. When I previously worked retail as a teenager, I was taught to invasively drive sales. I was applauded if I stalked a customer and made a sale simply because they wanted me off their back. But to Sandy, the sales seemed secondary to making the people—and the genitals connected to them—who walked through this door feel comfortable. So if it gave someone comfort to ask prices on butt plugs they never intended on buying, then so be it. I hope it inspired some kind of arousal in their brain, and they went back home and got themselves off by using all the products they didn't buy in their minds. Except the bacon-flavored lube. I never understood that one.

The hours ticked by, a few people coming and going, but the store was mostly quiet. It was now 7:00 A.M. Between 7:00 A.M. and 9:00 A.M. was always the slowest hours of my shift. Time moved like sludge. There was no way it was only two hours. It had to be at least six.

I grabbed a broom and swept the floor, something I usually did at this hour to keep my body moving around.

I heard the bell attached to the door ring from across the store. It was most likely Sandy coming in to take over the next shift a little early. That bell only rang once every handful of times the door opened. Sandy knew how to push it open at just the right angle so the bell would go off.

But it wasn't Sandy at the door. In walked someone who did not look like any of the "normal" customers, and someone who didn't resemble anyone I had ever seen in Tampa, either: Tall, skinny, sharply dressed in a sexy black blazer, tight black pants, a white button-down shirt with a pointy collar, and a silver watch. This clothing ensemble certainly wasn't from Walmart, and it wasn't even from Target.

She was stunning.

She had short, slicked-back black hair, and a purple rose tattooed on the left side of her neck, just barely peeking out of her suit. I stared at her as she entered; I grasped the broom handle, and it gave me a splinter.

No one ever came in here wearing a suit, and very rarely did I ever see women in here, particularly by themselves. I watched her survey the store, looking over the rows of products until she finally saw where I was standing.

"Hello! I'm Amanda. Is the manager here?"

"Hi there. Good morning. Um, it's just me here! The owner should be here in about an hour. I guess we don't really have a manager. Just me and the owner. I'm Taryn!"

I was fumbling my words. I am not used to interacting with people who wear suits. I mean, my current boss wore ruffled skirts with flamingos on them. I had never in my actual life interacted with a woman who looked and dressed like this.

She looked at the clock on the wall then looked at

her phone. "Shit, I'm sorry. I am three hours early! I'm completely jetlagged. I just flew in from Australia, and my phone doesn't know what time zone we're in."

I was so confused. Was I hallucinating? Was a side effect of moonshine punch delusions of beautiful women in suits?

"You don't sound like Australia. " I paused. "I mean, Australian. You don't have an accent," I said.

"Oh I am not from Australia. I was just there on business. I'm a sales rep for JT Stockroom."

"A what? What's that?" I asked. "I mean, I know what a sales rep is; you're here selling something for our stockrooms?" I nervously laughed. Why was I so nervous?

She grabbed the leather collar off the shelf that a customer picked up and put down earlier in the night, and she pointed to the tag. It said "JT Stockroom" on it. I honestly never paid attention the names of the companies listed on the tags on any of the items; I barely knew the names of all the items at the moment. I never gave any thought to where any of these products came from. I assumed they were all made in one giant slutty factory somewhere that Sandy went to once a week on her way back from bingo.

"Oh! I am so sorry. I should have known that name. I'm still pretty new here."

"It's ok. It's my job to travel to all the stores that carry our products and educate the staff about them. I had talked to the owner and told her I would be in at 11 A.M. But my jetlag apparently got the best of me!"

I would have offered her punch and Cheetos but that was put away. It was really sexy to see someone so corporate who professionally traveled the world and talked to people about dildos. Sorry—I mean—leather collars. I had no idea this type of "real job" existed.

"Did you work the graveyard shift?" she asked.

"Yeah! I do. I mean I did. That's me!"

"That's rough. You must be so tired by now! Not many stores stay open twenty-four hours anymore. That's cool that you guys do," she said.

"Oh, I thought all stores like this did. I had no idea. I've actually, in all honesty, never even been in any adult store, other than this one. So I wouldn't know!"

"Really?"

"Yeah, I mean, I never really had a reason to."

She smiled at me. "There's always a reason to learn more about sex."

I never thought of sex as something I had to learn about. It was just something I occasionally did. I never had anyone to talk about it in detail with and the few partners I had were definitely not adventurous. An "adventure" to my last boyfriend was to have the quietest, quickest sex we could possibly have so his roommate wouldn't wake up. I always wanted more, but I wasn't sure how to say it. Even with all the feminist literature I read and women's studies classes I took, I still very much felt like the men in my life were the ones who were supposed to initiate sex.

Amanda walked around the store, and took photos of where the JT Stockroom products were located. I noticed a common theme; all the more expensive leather products had their name on the tag. She stopped suddenly in one of the rows and pointed to a metal box that was slightly hidden behind a bunch of boxes of vibrators. Looked like a lunchbox or something that belonged to the Oracle in *The Matrix*.

"Well that's not a good place for this! Why do you have it tucked away like that?"

"I'm sorry, what is that?" I nervously laughed. I really had no idea what it was. I had never seen that silver box before, and I'm noticing now there was a $350 price tag on it.

She opened the box and pulled out this black wand with a glass attachment. There were several other glass attachments elegantly placed inside of the box inside of carved-out slots in black foam.

"It's an electric wand," she said. She pushed a button on the side of the wand and it lit up. "Looks like it's still got some charge in it!"

"What is that for? Do we use that when the power goes out or something?" I laughed. It wasn't a very funny joke. The more nervous I get, the worse my jokes get.

"It's for electrical play. It's a really neat product of ours! Here—I'll show you!" Amanda was so assertive. It truly was a new and very exciting thing for me to be spoken to with such confidence by a woman in a suit. I finally dropped the damn broom that had been in my hands (*I can deal with the splinters later*). She ran the wand up my arm and it showed a blue glowing light. It shocked me in an exhilarating way. It was like a tight pinch—it woke me up, and I wanted it more.

"Turn it up a little higher!" I said, and she did. The shock on my arm was stronger; it was so strange to feel excited by a small amount of pain on my arm.

"Wanna see something really cool?" she asked.

"Well, yeah, of course I do," I answered.

She took her suit jacket off and threw it on top of a pile of disorganized dildos in boxes. She pulled up the right arm of the most chic-looking, white button-down top I had ever seen, and revealed fishnet covered legs of a 1950s pin-up girl tattoo. She reached over aggressively and held my hand, gave me the wand, and told me to put the wand on her arm.

"I don't want to do it wrong!" I was nervous about causing permanent damage to her tattoo, which took up a lot of space on her arm.

"Literally just put it on my arm, you can't possibly do it wrong."

I took a deep breath to calm my nerves, then I ran it up and down her arm as she held my hand. She shook and smiled, and a few seconds later I felt the shock in my arm.

"Holy shit!" I said. "Let me do that again!"

I continued to hold onto her hand, and ran the wand up her arm, and it shocked me again.

"Our arms are working together as a converter."

"That is so crazy!"

"I've done demonstrations at different stores and had fifteen customers holding hands, and the shock went all the way through them all. You should try it on them sometime! It's really a lot of fun."

"Wow, so—wait—do people use that, like, during sex?"

She laughed. "Well, it's an impact toy. You can keep it light and just use it as a tease, or you can turn it up and make it more painful. I guess it's really more for kinky foreplay!"

I had never before heard the terms "electrical play" or "impact toys" in my life. It sounded dangerous. I liked it. I mean, what would you do if you were interested in that kind of thing and you didn't have this? What else qualifies as an "impact toy?" Do people stick their fingers into wall sockets to get off if they don't have this special silver lunchbox?

I thought of Amir. I thought of electrocuting his thighs as he "jelked." I bet a little sting just around his balls would have done him some good while he stretched his penis for the woman of his dreams.

"That was really cool. And I'm definitely awake now. Thanks." I laughed.

"So, what time are you done?" she asked me.

"Oh—pretty soon. About an hour. Why?"

"You wanna meet me at my hotel for breakfast when you get off—I mean—when you're done? Whatever happens first." She winked at me and laughed. I hadn't yet seen someone inside this store in the world outside this store. This was like all my lives colliding together, even though I didn't have much of a life other than sleep and Starbucks outside of here.

She didn't wait for my answer. She handed me a card and wrote the name of her hotel and her room number on it. It was a very cool and confident way to say, *I'll be here, come if you want to, or not, I don't really give a shit.*

To stay in the store and see what happens next, turn to page 55.

To meet Amanda at the hotel, turn to page 59.

Amanda left the store, and I couldn't help but watch her leave, her body swaying deliberately (I think, though maybe that was my imagination). Shortly after, Sandy came in, ready to start her day and mark the end of mine.

"Good morning, hon'!" she said. "How was the rest of your night?"

"Fine! Good morning, um, did you know you had some appointment with a sales rep from JT Stockroom?"

"Sales rep from what?"

"JT Stockroom—the company that makes all the leather stuff and this really cool electrical wand that was hiding behind the dildos over there." I pointed at the lunchbox, now sitting by the register.

"Oh, that was today? Well, anyone is welcome to come by. I will be here!"

"Do people from the sex toy companies come by a lot?" I asked.

"Once in a while. We're not a big chain so they don't go out of their way, but if I buy the stuff, they'll find me!"

Sandy spoke to me as she put on her bright red "wet and wild" lipstick that went far outside the outline of her lips.

"How do you decide what to order?" I asked.

"Well, I get sent catalogs and lists from these different distributor fellows—once a year I get invited to a whole-sale convention and I do a lot of the ordering there. I just pick what I like! Someone will buy the stuff eventually."

"That's interesting," I said. "I never knew what it took to get stuff in here."

"I just follow my heart and see where it takes me. It usually takes me to the biggest dildo!" She laughed.

"I'm gonna eat my breakfast and freshen up in the back; when I'm done you can go home!"

"All right!"

The store was now empty. Most people in Tampa were at church at this hour on a Sunday. I grabbed the electric wand, and I decided to switch up the attachment on it. One was shaped like a comb—that one looked neat. I snapped it on and pushed up the electricity level to a bit higher. I rubbed it up and down my arm, and the electric blue lights tickled me in such an exciting way. It did hurt, but not like an actual injury. It was an arousing kind of pain.

I brushed the electric comb over my tank top, over my nipples. Even with a sports bra on underneath my shirt I could still feel the sensation. I turned it up higher and it was really strong. I pushed it against my left nipple as hard as I possibly could and it felt like a sharp bite. I didn't know my nipples were so sensitive! I never paid much attention to them. I went back and forth from my left to right nipple, over my shirt. I could feel my areolas getting warmer. Each time I placed the wand on my nipple I let it stay on for longer and longer, taking it away when it hurt too much but putting it back when I wanted the pain again. I was literally torturing myself.

I felt my panties get moist. I looked around the store, there was definitely still no one there. Even though I was surrounded by sex, I still wasn't supposed to be getting off. This was work! I was supposed to be a professional.

But then again, how could I give my customers the best toy advice if I didn't know how to use them?

I took the electric wand and slid it down my pants, but over my cotton panties. I zapped my own labia; the pain was exponential down there, but so was the pleasure. It felt so dangerous and amazing, like a lightning storm of pleasure. I went a bit further down to where my body got more sensitive. My underwear and the tuft of pubic hair underneath it was a layer of protection—my security blanket in the realm of new sexual exploration—that made me confident enough to put the electric current up to the highest level there was. It was worth a try!

I turned the wand up the highest it could go, and zapped myself right above my clit. The neon blue light shined through my jeggings. Had someone walked in they could have definitely mistaken me for some kind of alien (there had been a fair amount of UFO sightings in Tampa this year so perhaps it wouldn't be so outrageous to find an alien masturbating behind the counter at an adult video store). Blood rushed through my body and I let out a loud noise that was something like a moan, a gasp, and an "ouch" at the same time. My vagina was pulsing, I felt like it was its own entity, breathing heavily and gasping for air.

I put the wand down, and took my fingers, reached inside my underwear, and rubbed my clit. It had been months since I masturbated, and I wasn't sure why. All that time I spent alone in my room watching TV—why wasn't I masturbating? Now there I was at work, trying to squeeze in a quickie with myself before my boss walked in. Time management has never been my strong suit.

I rubbed my clit furiously, as if I was trying to reach

inside myself and pull out my own orgasm. My mind flashed to so many images—I thought of Amanda and the way she unbuttoned her shirt, and the expression on her face when she said, "there's always a reason to learn more about sex." I even thought of Amir, and the way he stroked his cock with such determination. That seemed like it happened years ago. My brain scrambled through erotic channels of cock and pussy, a woman in a business suit, and a man with a bun. My clit was so swollen from electrocution and friction, I rubbed harder and faster, I pushed my pussy deeper into the chair I sat on behind my register—I think—I was having sex with a chair. I breathed in deeply, I moved my fingers slower now but with more pressure on my clit, and yes—finally—I felt it. *Lightning.* I held onto my nipples, my legs felt like Jell-O, a big wave of warmth rushed through my body.

I took my hand out of my pants and decompressed. I was definitely ready for a deep sleep straight through the remainder of the sunlight for the day. Maybe I will even masturbate after I wake up. I should really do that more often.

To go back and meet Amanda at the hotel instead, turn to page 59.

Continue with Taryn in this fantasy, turn to page 65.

I spent the last hour of work staring at Amanda's business card. I had never been with a woman, or even been hit on by a woman. She did ask me to get breakfast—did she really mean *breakfast*? How could I go? I had no idea what I would be doing. Was I really attracted to her, or to her confidence? Did it matter? And yet, even as I asked myself these questions, I knew that I was already going to go.

I hadn't been on a date in a really long time and I wasn't quite sure if I was going on one now. As soon as my shift ended, I drove to the Residence Inn and I parked; I sat in my car, and hesitated about going inside. Was she even going to be there? Should I call first? Should I text her? What should I do?

It was 9:30 A.M. and I hadn't slept yet. It was humid outside, my hair was frizzing up, and I had technically been wearing the same clothing since yesterday. The morning looks completely different when you haven't slept. Everything looks translucent. The people starting their day at this hour don't look like the same species. You feel like you're a ghost floating about the world, where you can see everyone else but they can't see you. The good thing about being a ghost, though, is that you're invisible, and invisible beings can have frizzy hair, or pretend to be lesbians and it just doesn't matter. I was so far from my comfort zone, that it just didn't exist anymore. I had lived my whole life inside of a box and now I was in a bisexual trapezoid, at an hour when most people were at church.

I walked into the hotel, and called the cell phone number on the business card. She picked up on the first ring.

"Hey there, Amanda; it's Taryn. I'm in your hotel lobby."

There was a brief silence.

"Who?"

That was definitely the worst possible response.

"Taryn, from, you know, the store. From like two hours ago." I didn't want to say "porn store" out loud. I felt like you just weren't supposed to say that in public, on a Sunday, in Tampa. There were, like, families in the lobby here.

"Oh! Hey there. Sorry. I'm good with faces and bad with names. So bring your pretty face upstairs. Room 402."

Click. She hung up. And I headed to the elevator.

Just a few moments later I was knocking on her door and she was immediately answering it. The pants to the suit she wore before were still on, but with a plain black tank-top on. I could see more colorful tattoos on her arm, one of a dagger, a few different colored roses, and a skull, and I saw fully exposed breasts, with long wavy blonde hair on the top half of the pin-up girl that I wasn't able to see before. Amanda's blazer and button-down shirt were hung on a chair in the corner of the room that I could see out of the corner of my eye.

"Come in!" she said.

I sat on the bed, since eighty percent of the hotel room was the bed.

"You must be beat," she said.

"Well, I'm kinda used to this schedule. I'll really crash around noon. Thanks for inviting me over, going home and watching morning talk shows gets depressing." I laughed and she smiled.

"Where are you from?"

"Los Angeles," she said. "But really I live on a damn airplane. I am barely ever there."

"Well that sounds exciting to me, I'm at my house entirely too much."

"I really didn't think you would show up," she said.

"Why?" I asked.

"You just seemed so—scared."

"Well, I am. But, I'm here anyways."

I found myself smiling, something I don't do often. She reached over, put her hands through my sticky hair, and kissed me. Her suit, her tattoos, and her slick hair intimidated me, but as soon as she kissed me I felt at ease. Her kiss felt soft and gentle. Her body smelled like a man's cologne, but her mouth tasted like a woman's perfume. I felt comfortable, like my body just knew exactly what to do next.

We continued to kiss, and she began to kiss my neck as her arms grasped for parts of my back. She held me closer to her, and she lifted up my striped Gap T-shirt, and unveiled my ever-so-sexy navy blue sports bra. If I had thought there was any inkling of me winding up in a bed that wasn't mine, I would have worn one of my slightly more seductive lace bras, with matching panties, but that wasn't the case.

However, my bra was torn off quickly and I don't think she gave a shit of how lame it was. She pushed me down and grabbed my perky tits (I swear, part of the reason they are perky is because I wear sports bras). She was definitely the aggressor here and I was excited about it. She pinched my nipples and kissed my skin, she sucked on the side of my neck like a vampire and grabbed my breasts with overwhelming passion. My legs kicked up in the air as some kind of possessed reflex. My entire body felt what she was doing and we were only at second base.

She let go of my neck and stared at it.

"I like leaving my mark," she said. She turned me towards the mirror and I saw a big swollen red hickey on my neck. I liked it. I felt like I was part of a gang. How many others were wandering around this earth with this same mark? It was nice to be part of something.

She continued to kiss me and her hands migrated down my body, gently but urgently. She stuck her hand inside my fuchsia panties, and in an instant knew the parts of me that would drive me wild. She knew her way around my vagina better than I did. She tickled and teased my outer pussy lips, and she gently pulled at my pubic hair. She licked my nipples and moved her fingers up and down the inside of my lips. There were so many sensations running up and down my body, I couldn't stop looking at her beautiful face and her beautiful arms. It was really an incredible feeling to stare at a woman touching my body.

Her clothing was still on, and she continued to just focus on me. I wasn't sure if I was supposed to be doing something to her too? But I really enjoyed being pleased. She was leading this, and I liked being her prisoner. I figured she would let me know when I was supposed to do something other than quiver and tremble and smile and enjoy.

Her mouth moved down my body and she spread my

pussy lips wide open. She grabbed some lube that she conveniently had inside of her hotel night table, (a water-based lube I definitely recognized from the store) and she poured it all over my vagina, and then she massaged her fingers around my clit, faster and faster. I was so incredibly wet from a mixture of natural juices and lube. I felt like I was going to burst. I had never experienced such an incredible feeling before. I moaned loudly, a part of me felt like I was going to cry.

"I—I think I'm gonna," I breathed heavy and I couldn't get the words out of my mouth.

"You're gonna what?" she asked.

"I'm," I laughed, "I'm gonna cum!"

She went faster and faster; she must have previously gotten some kind of map to my clit, because she knew her way around it so perfectly. I started to feel the beginning stages of an orgasm and she stopped.

"Wait!"

I sat on the bed with my legs spazzing and panting like a sick dog. She grabbed a leather holster with a curvy strap-on silicone dildo from her suitcase, took her suit pants off, and pulled the contraption on herself, a woman with a cock poised and ready. She thrust herself inside me, and continued to rub my clit. The dildo hit my G-spot instantly, she thrust in and out, and rubbed my clit at the same time. Fucking hell, she was an amazing multi-tasker. I could see my internal juices on the dildo each time she pulled out, I grabbed my own breasts, I pushed my pussy towards the dildo so it could get as far inside me as it possibly could, and moments later I let out a loud carnal noise, some kind of cross between a scream, a moan, and a grunt. It was a giant orgasm that lasted for several minutes, and went in different waves. It started from my inside and spread to my outsides; it felt like twelve different orgasms rolled into one. Like every part of my body just got off in its own individual way. Is it possible to have an orgasm in your toes? Because even my toes never felt this good.

She kissed me softly again.

"You're a lot of fun," she said.

"Me? I barely did anything. Isn't it my turn?" I mean, I knew I couldn't do what she did, but I could sure give it the old college try.

"Well don't you remember? I gotta go meet with your boss! And I have a few more stores to go to after that."

"Oh! Yeah, well," I couldn't really speak.

"You can stay and crash, it's cool! The beds here are super comfortable."

"Really? You sure? I seriously don't think I could drive home coherently right now. Really."

"Yeah, definitely." She kissed me again. She brushed her teeth, and I watched her put her suit back on. Before the top button was buttoned I fell into an incredible sleep.

To go back and stay with Tayrn in the store insted, turn to page 55.

To see what happens in the hotel next, turn to page 122.

My "weekend" consisted of Monday, Tuesday, and Wednesday afternoon. I worked Wednesday through Sunday night. I kept the same sleep schedule even on my days off so as to not fool my body into thinking I was a person with a normal schedule. I usually spent these days/nights doing laundry, binge-watching multiple seasons of a TV series on Netflix, and challenging myself to see what kind of gourmet meal I could come up with using whatever wasn't rotten in the fridge and whatever was lingering in my pantry. Last week I really outdid myself with a baked ramen noodle casserole, made with hot dogs and cheddar cheese.

But this week was different. Meeting Amanda made me feel motivated; suddenly, I felt that I could actually make a difference in my workplace. I never thought of the rinky-dink shop I spent half my week at as something tied to an entire industry, but it was. There were so many possibilities to explore. Should I add new inventory? Should we have a blog? Do we even *have* a website? I pondered these things to excess. Having a wonderful orgasm also greatly awakened me, like an espresso shot that was administered from my clit. I never understood how important orgasms were. I need to have more of them. I felt this new urge of wanting to leave the house and go further than the grocery store, to explore the world around me. All the crucial Netflix series I hadn't watched yet was not my number one priority at the moment. I mean, it was definitely at number two or three, but not one.

I decided to venture out and go to other adult stores for comparative purposes. I did some research and found a few in the area—I had no idea some of these stores were on Yelp. Dreamz was not found on there. I wasn't sure if that was for better or for worse.

There was a Hustler store about forty miles away. It was right in the middle of downtown next to all the nightclubs and bars. I had seen it before and never went in. I honestly thought it was a clothing store for Hustler apparel, I didn't know they had a selection of sex toys and adult videos. The outside truly looked like a clothing store—it was decorated out front like any store you would see in the mall, with nice lighting and attractive window displays with mannequins wearing fashionable Hustler branded pants and bedazzled tank tops. The outside of Dreamz didn't even have a store sign. Sandy told me there was at one point but it fell down in a hurricane and never got put back up. Instead there was a small blue neon sign outside of Dreamz that read "VIDEO, DVD, XXX." Not sure if that was intended to be one sentence, or three words, and I wasn't sure what the difference between "video" and DVD even was.

I parked my car a few blocks away from Hustler and right above my car was a billboard advertisement for an upcoming gig of Jimmy's at a nightclub in the area. All I could think was, *Ha! I saw his cock*. So weird. Go me.

I walked into the Hustler store and it was pristine. Half the store had shiny hardwood flooring and the other half had red carpeting, with intricate, repeating gold paisley designs. Life-size images of beautiful, busty models wearing Hustler branded lingerie decorated the doors of the dressing rooms, while current pop music was playing on the loud speakers. There was a fully functional cafe inside, with a cute tattooed barista girl making lattes, cappuccinos, and chai teas. There were glass display cases with rotating discs inside showing off high-end vibrators. A few of them we actually did have in stock at Dreamz but they looked completely different being all illuminated the way they were here.

I got myself an incredibly delicious latte; the foam up top was crafted into a design of a heart. It was so neat, I didn't want to drink it. I snapped a photo of it and made it the background wallpaper on my phone.

"Can I help you with anything?" A tall, thin, handsome metrosexual man in skinny black jeans and a Hustler V-neck top asked me.

"No! I'm just looking around, thank you!"

"Just so you know, all of our apparel is thirty percent off today!" He pointed at a wall filled with neatly organized T-shirts, hats, and sweatshirts.

"Oh thanks! I will be sure to check it out."

"If you want to try on anything let me know and I will start a room for you."

"Great! Thanks!"

I chuckled to myself. "Starting a room" at Dreamz is an entirely different experience. The rooms we have available are for masturbating and fucking. The only place to try on clothing is the bathroom, and that bathroom doubles as a supply closet for our mop, broom, and an abnormally large stock of paper towels.

"Be sure to stick around for Dr. Erica's seminar! She'll be here in about 30 minutes."

"Oh? Well, okay!"

I had no idea who Dr. Erica was, but I went along with it. I noticed that in the cafe area, a few more attractive staff members were setting up chairs. There were at least ten employees here! And more and more of them kept appearing.

In addition to clothing, movies, and toys, Hustler also had a large selection of books. Like, actual books, not magazines with titles like *Big and Busty*. One of the employees grabbed a stack of books and moved them over to the cafe with the circle of folding chairs. I casually picked one up; it was titled *The Female Orgasm*, written by Dr. Erica Soren. This must be the Dr. Erica who was coming to the store. I sat in one of the folding chairs with my coffee that was now cold. I had spent too long holding onto it and not drinking it because I didn't want to break my pretty foam heart.

Over the next fifteen minutes, the chairs filled up with various women, looking like they were there for some kind of paralegal or pharmaceutical conference from the way they were dressed. They were middle aged, in various suits and blazers, not at all like the ultra-stylish button-down/ jacket combo that Amanda wore. These looked like a group of upper middle-class Tampa mothers, people who definitely wouldn't go anywhere near Dreamz—or so I thought.

As I continued to study the prim women sitting around me, a woman in a red turtleneck walked into the group, her hair in a tight, neat bun, and carrying a brown leather briefcase. The mothers suddenly stopped their idle chit-chat, stood up, and clapped. I assume this must be the Dr. Erica from the book. She was led in by the same store employee who told me about the sale on clothing.

"Good evening, everyone!' the employee shouted.

"Who's ready to get down and dirty with themselves?"

Everyone laughed, including the woman who I assumed was Dr. Erica.

"This woman needs no introduction, but I'm going to introduce her, anyway. We are pleased to bring you a PhD sexologist, author, sex educator; *The New York Times* called her the principal voice for women's sexual pleasure, and she's a dear lover of three cats. Put your hands together for Dr. Erica Soren!"

Everyone clapped. Dr. Erica took a modest bow, waving her hands around as if to tell the crowd she didn't want the applause but was definitely enjoying it. She slammed her briefcase on a table in front of her.

"Let's talk about our vaginas!" she said.

From her briefcase she took out a diagram of the vagina labeled with different erogenous zones, and with no hesitation began to describe the parts of the labia and their impact on sexual arousal. The women intently listened to her lecture and some even took notes. She explained the difference between internal and external orgasms, she took out different dildos and vibrators and explained how to use them by rubbing them against the vagina diagram in the appropriate spots, and she had a recommended lube pairing with each kind of toy. The glass curved G-spot dildo paired with a silicone lube. The Cyberskin dildo paired with a water-based lube. As a bonus she showed the class some new kind of lube that looked exactly like semen and recommended for women to use it on their partners while giving them a hand job.

"Then they will feel like their load is bigger than it is and that always makes men feel better," she said. The class cracked up laughing.

She concluded the lecture by talking about anal sex.

"Let's go a little south of the vagina. Believe it or not, it is possible to have an orgasm inside your ass. For some women it's incredibly pleasurable. Don't think of anal sex as something you have to do so your husband gets you that Marc Jacobs handbag you've always wanted."

The audience laughed. This was most certainly humor that was not geared toward my demographic; husbands, handbags, and anal sex were three things that were not part of my life, at all.

However, it was interesting to hear about. She encouraged the group to use a butt plug, to have multiple vaginal orgasms before entering the butt, and she recommended breathing exercises to relax, and of course suggested yet another lube.

"And women—it's a good idea for YOU to anally penetrate YOUR MAN! It goes both ways! It's the best way for him to understand everything that's involved in the erogenous zones in the rectum."

The lecture concluded to incredible applause. They loved this sex doctor!

Then the class opened up to a question and answer session.

"I just gave birth about a month ago, and since then penetration has been painful. It's made me so depressed! Is this normal? Do you have any advice for me?" one of the women in the class asked.

"Well congratulations on your new baby, but we have got to take care of your other baby—your vagina!"

Everyone in the class laughed hysterically again. This was like a grown-up professionals' sleepover party. Where did these women come from? Did my mother go to stuff like this?

Dr. Erica laid down on the ground and got into different positions she recommended for more comfortable penetration. She also went over some breathing exercises, and she pulled out something called a "lube shooter" out of her briefcase and recommended using it to coat the entire inside of the vagina with something she called "emergency lube," which was an incredibly thick silicone gel that had a similar consistency to Drano. This woman really had a lube for every occasion.

After the lecture was over, the women got their books signed and some of them asked her more confidential questions. I decided to purchase a book myself, and I waited in the line to get it signed. I had now been in the store for over an hour and all I purchased was a coffee so, this felt like the appropriate thing to do. And who knows, maybe I could learn some new things about orgasms that could come in handy.

"Thanks for coming!" Dr. Erica said.

"Thank you!" I said. "I've been trying to explore myself a little more, and this was inspiring." I was being genuine.

"That's wonderful! Treat your body and soul with lots of love and lots of lube!" she replied, as she signed the book *with love and lube, Dr. Erica*.

This woman and her lube. She must have like, kegs full of it at home.

"Hey, so, I actually work at a different store, and—I was wondering—do you have, like, booking information?"

"Yes, my manager's information is all on my website. You can contact her."

"Oh, yeah, of course. Thanks!"

I walked to my car, and out of curiosity, launched her

website in a browser on my phone. There was a calendar with her "appearances" listed on it, and the next year was completely full, with engagements all over the country and a few internationally. This woman was apparently like the Lady Gaga of masturbating.

Well, I was not a doctor and I never wrote a book. And I didn't have a website or a manager. But I was unofficially the manager of Dreamz, (by unofficially, I mean I was the only one in the store for about 50 hours a week so I think by default that made me the manager). If I read Dr. Erica's book, and maybe some more books like this, and I tried out a bunch of different sex toys, maybe I could try to teach a class? It would be great to have a real event in the store. Cheetos and punch don't exactly count as an event. There is so much down time in the store, a thirty-minute class wouldn't interfere with my other duties.

Dreamz really did need more females coming into the store. A masturbation class just for women would be great. I had so little sexual experience and definitely wasn't qualified to teach it, but there I was, sitting in my car, staring at a giant billboard of Jimmy, who had no experience at all when he volunteered to DJ our high school prom, and look where that got him.

To follow Taryn in her class research, turn to page 73.

To attend Taryn's class on masturbation, turn to page 81.

I decided to host a masturbation seminar for women. I didn't want to call it "teaching a class," because I truly didn't have the credentials to teach, but a host merely brings people together (something I did have the authority to do). I set a date, and I made a Facebook invite for it, with a pretty cover image and everything. It was somewhat official!

The next few weeks went by quickly. I had a real goal, and a project to work on. I stopped spending my downtime at the store looking at the clock and waiting for it to change, or pretending to sweep the floor. I told Sandy about it. I didn't ask her permission, I just told her I wanted to plan an event in the store for women and she sort of patted me on the head, smiled and laughed, and said "Okay, hon.'"

Unlike the Hustler store, we didn't have ten-plus employees working at a time. It was either just me, or just Sandy. At times when Sandy gets tired, she just closes the store and goes home. We truly didn't operate like a "real" store with open and close hours. This was basically Sandy's house, and if the door was unlocked and the lights were on you could come in. And jerk off. In any case, due to the lack of staff here, I would still have to ring people up for their purchases at the register, or give them keys to ROOMZ *and* run this workshop at the same time. I'd noticed the patterns of time of when it was busy and when it was slow in the store, so the ideal situation would be to have this event go on when it was slow. The only problem was, that was usually after midnight, which was not an ideal time to have any kind of event. Mothers who wear blazers certainly weren't going to show up at that time. Who were we kidding here, though? That type never showed up at any time in this store.

Deciding to do this class was the first step. Asking/ telling Sandy was the second. Checking those two things off my list was rather simple. Then came a twofold, rather daunting issue, and that was that I had no experience teaching, very little experience masturbating, and I had no clue how to do any kind of promotion to get masturbators with less experience than me in here to learn more about masturbating. The one thing I did know here was that inside of Dreamz we had a unique advantage. Part of what scares people away is also what brings people in: While the Hustler store has fancy masturbating tools, hardcover, glossy text books about masturbation, and important masturbating lectures taught by PhDs, no one in that store was actually allowed to masturbate right then and there. That's what my class would be—immersive and hands-on (pun most definitely intended). That's what was going to make a Dreamz class a clear competitor with these fancy show-off stores.

First things first, though: I needed a lesson plan. Since I myself was newly acquainted with the world of self-pleasure, and thus what the young people would call a "noob" in this matter, I decided to skim through Dr. Erica's book for inspiration. Where was I to begin? It was a very dense 350-page hardcover book written with the sole intention for women to have stronger orgasms. That was pretty cool! I never had an orgasm textbook before. Perhaps college would have been more enjoyable had I known these existed. There was a whole chapter on the clitoris, then another on the cervix, one on female ejaculation, and another on G-spots, just to name a few. Every single centimeter of the vagina got its own special lecture in here. She really laid out the vagina as not just one erogenous zone, but a whole bunch of different compartments with their own unique ways of getting off if touched in the right way. Some of the book spoke to me, some of it got far too biological and felt like a textbook; I felt like that kind of dry language might make it harder for people to understand the sexy elements of masturbation. Writing that's too clinical tends to scare people away, like my science books did to me in high school. Some of the material was also clearly meant for women much older than me, women with children, or husbands, who had been married for over ten years. It wasn't a book meant for people who just graduated college and made minimum wage and lived in an apartment with a communal bathroom in the hallway.

The chapters of the book that affected me the most were titled "body positivity" and "body confidence." Part of learning how to masturbate was wanting to masturbate and the desire to want to give yourself an orgasm comes from loving your own body. I never thought to love my body, I actually didn't know my body so well. It was an unknown blob attached to my head I needed to get to know better.

The book said to spend at least 20 minutes a day completely naked to gain more body positivity. I thought about it, and realized I was never naked unless I was showering. Due to all my roommates, I went into the shower completely clothed, stripped my clothing off as fast as possible, showered, and immediately put clothing back on. Per the book's suggestion, I started spending five to ten minutes naked in the bathroom before my shower, just staring at my own body. I stood tall and straightened out my posture, and noticed my breasts were in fact rather perky and my butt poked out nicely.

Was I attractive? It had never really crossed my mind before, since I'd always thought the answer was *no*. As new evidence arose though, I decided it begged further research. I inspected myself to a closer degree: My skin was clear, for the most part, save for a few freckles. My tits weren't huge (they went between a B and C cup depending on the time of the month) but they were perky. My nipples were large, definitely larger than the average nipple I saw in the magazines at work. I was short, with muscular legs, and a relatively proportionate round butt, and I had a few unsettling rolls of fat in my stomach but they disappeared when I arched my back and stood with tall posture. I did some squats and invented some yoga moves that stretched my muscles and woke up my insides. I did my own little dance in the nude, a cross between the jig, the hustle, and the hokey pokey, and I shook out my insecurities. I thrust my hairy pelvis in the air, and I gave my vagina its own high-five. I felt alive and excited to explore my body further.

The subject matter was one thing; the teaching implements were another. How do I decide which toys to showcase? Do I go by brand? Should I try to show off as many different kinds of toys as possible? I started looking through the giant pile of unopened mail that came to the store during my downtime. Different companies sent glossy pamphlets that came in very official-looking folders about all their different products. I learned about the different manufacturers and materials, and I was starting to wrap my brain around why the more expensive toys were in fact more expensive. I liken it to coffee makers.

Any coffee maker could make you a simple cup of coffee, but then you also have the upgraded ones that make you cappuccinos, espressos, and can steam your milk to the exact degree you desire. So, you can stick any dildo inside yourself, but the higher end ones will vibrate, hit your G-spot, or be made out of a material that feels so much like actual penis skin you'd wonder if it was created by Hannibal Lecter. Some toys were waterproof, some weren't. Some had one speed, some had five, some had twenty plus different speeds. Some were hard, some were soft. Some were meant for an internal orgasm, some were meant for an external orgasm—and some toys were meant to go inside your ass. I wasn't even going to think about venturing over to that part of my body. I'd just barely gotten to know my vagina. Maybe if this class goes well, we could expand into a series, and then focus on the ass. Do an ass class, if you will.

At work, I spent the majority of my time fantasizing about which toy would come home with me that night. I really needed to experiment with different products before I made this class happen. In other words, I needed to masturbate more if I was going to host a workshop on masturbating.

It was exciting. Knowing that something in the store was going to give me an orgasm later made me look at the entire store differently. I felt like a really hot girl at a bar, with the option to go home with any suitor that I wanted to. Only, hot girls at a bar aren't always guaranteed orgasms and I was, so therefore I was even better off than them.

I walked around the store and let my vagina do the picking. Ultimately, it was for her, so she should get the biggest say. Yes, my vagina is a "her." Dr. Erica said to give your vagina a name (though not necessarily a gender; that was my doing), so I called her Rihanna. I mean, how could I not love my own vagina if it was channeling an inner spirit Rihanna?

I decided on a Hitachi magic wand, and a soft silicone dildo. It seemed like the combo of the two was a no brainer for an orgasm. It was like I had my own special suitor for my clit and another for my G-spot, two strapping, young pieces of plastic whose only goal was to service me sexually. This combined with my own fingers and some basic water-based lube seemed like paradise. I hoped all my roommates were out of the apartment by the time I got home so I could have loud, passionate love with my two inanimate objects. Actually, fuck it. I didn't care if they heard me or not. I paid $475 rent a month and this allowed me the right to masturbate in my bedroom as loud as I wanted! Rihanna was a star and it was time for her to sing.

As soon as my shift ended, I rang myself up for my two chosen toys and jetted home. I wasn't going to put Sandy out of business simply because I was just getting to know my own vagina. Work came first, I would come second. I ran to my bedroom and shut the door, without stopping in the kitchen and making ramen noodles. I was truly very excited.

I browsed through my different recommended Pandora

stations and decided on an '80s gothic/industrial one to set the mood. Keyboards, synthesizers, and deep voices have always been sexy to me. So sexy that I avoided this type of music most of the time because I was afraid that it would turn me on too much and then I wouldn't be sure what to do about it.

I sat on my bed and let Peter Murphy sing to me through the pathetic excuse for a speaker on my laptop. I turned it up as high as it could go and it was about as loud as your average music in an elevator. I spread my legs open and lathered up Rihanna with lube. I rubbed my fingers around the lips of my pussy; it was so hungry, so excited, and so wet. I could feel my nipples getting tighter and harder, my inner body was getting warmer, I grabbed onto my own neck—not sure why. I was listening to my body and just going where it told me to go, like Dr. Erica said. My ass sunk deep into my mattress, while I clenched all my muscles. I breathed in deep, I let my pussy direct my hand and explore. I could see my own clit swelling up. I could see the color of my labia getting red, I could feel the holes in my body loosening up. This was amazing, and I had barely just begun.

I grabbed the dildo and plunged it inside my vagina. I slid it in and out, in and out, again and again and my vagina swallowed it. I started moaning. Breathing heavy and grunting. Noises I never heard myself make! They came out so naturally and meshed with the beat of the dark symphonic music barely playing in the background. The dildo hit a spot that made me quiver; I hit the spot harder and harder. I was so wet it was ridiculous. The sound of flowing moisture coming from my genitals was certainly louder than my laptop.

This was such a deep intense inner orgasm, it felt like it was being pulled from my stomach. I grabbed the magic wand and put it on my clit, which was already swollen from my finger play earlier and YES. HOLY SHIT. WHAT THE HELL WAS GOING ON! AHHHHH!

I was vibrating and quivering, moaning, and breathing, I felt like I was on some kind of body ayahuasca drug trip in the middle of Peru. This was by far the most incredible feeling I'd ever had! I was smiling, I was thrusting my own pelvis in the air because that's just what my body told me to do. I grabbed onto my sheets even though they were terribly impractical to grab. My body was controlled by this orgasm and I let it take over. It was the boss of me. I was a slave to this orgasm and I would keep doing whatever it wanted me to do. Was this one orgasm? Was this two? How many was this?

What seemed like hours later, the feeling came to an end. My body felt like wet, overcooked ramen noodles. It was spent. Rihanna had been pampered properly and it was time for her to rest. And after that, I would begin finding other women in the area in dire need of names for their vaginas and inspiration to masturbate.

But really, I needed that nap first.

To attend Taryn's masturbation class, turn to the next page.

Today was the day. At approximately 10:00 P.M., I would be hosting, teaching, assisting, encouraging (whatever you want to call it) a group of women, in the name of female masturbation.

For the past few weeks, I'd been plugging the class like crazy. I printed up event flyers and placed them by the register at the store. "I Touch Myself" was what I called it: "A night for women to explore masturbation!" I put a happy-face symbol at the end of the tagline, to give it more of a friendly class vibe. The name and address of the store was on there, along with a list of things we'd be discussing: sex toys, lubes, anatomy, and opening your-self up to self-pleasure. It seemed like a good list to get people interested; at least I hoped it was. I wasn't actually sure who was going to show up to the class. I also made a Facebook listing for the class, sharing it with my not-so-extensive friends list. Surprisingly, the first person to "like" my post was Jimmy! He gave me a virtual thumbs up, and then he re-posted the listing on his own page, which had several thousand followers. This was exciting! I'd refreshed the page a few times after that, and so many positive replies and responses came pouring in. Okay, maybe not *pouring*, but there was, like, four replies in a matter of five minutes; not bad, in my book!

For a while, I struggled with whether I should post it on my personal Facebook page. My mother and several of my other family members were connected to me there. Would they be proud? Maybe they would find this as a nice diversion from my usual vague posts that contained photos of my converse sneakers with sepia tone filters on it, along with quotes from Morrissey songs. But more than that, no one actually knew that I'd been working for Dreamz. Posting would mean revealing myself to the world.

I kept this job a secret from most people. It was supposed to be something temporary. I applied for this job because it was two miles away from my house, and it was hiring. Posting this on my Facebook page would mark this being more than just a part-time thing, it would truly be embedded in my personality. Is that what I wanted? Was I ashamed of the sex-focused life I'd been living? Or could I find empowerment in it?

Ah, fuck it. What was there to lose, really? With a click of a button, I was promoting my new-found love for masturbation to my aunts and uncles.

Sandy told me she would be at the store to help out, but she hadn't come in. She'd actually been missing a lot lately. She'd closed the store randomly in the middle of the day, and had called me to cover for her on several occasions. I wondered what was going on. Sometimes I felt like I was beginning to care about the well-being of this store more than she did. I was a little disappointed that the night would have to go on without her punch and pretzels.

I cleaned up the shop and organized everything as best I could. I replaced the flickering and dim lightbulbs, I wiped down all the countertops, I neatly arranged all the lingerie, and I took out the toys in the shelves that, from my new knowledge of masturbation, deserved to be highlighted. A glass silicone G-spot stimulator, a Hitachi magic wand, a powerful vibrating bullet egg, and one silicone butt plug for the people who were into that kind of thing. I felt like this selection could arouse all the different vagina compartments I recently learned about.

I chose to do this event on a Wednesday because that seemed to be our slowest night. This was supposed to be a ladies-only class, however I had no way of stopping any men from coming into the store. I figured Sandy could entertain/help the men that came in while my pseudo slumber-party went on, but with her not here, I would just have to cross my fingers and hope no one would actually come in between the hours of 10:00 P.M. and 11:00 P.M. It wasn't completely outlandish; that was typically a slow time on a Wednesday, anyway.

Who would come in? What if no one came in? What if too many people came in? I wasn't sure what would be worse. I put out a mix of plastic folding chairs, office chairs, and step stools, as much seating as I could possibly find. If extra seats were necessary, I could bring out some five-gallon buckets we had and flip them over. I'd cleaned them out just in case.

There was a regular flow of customers between 8:00 P.M. and 9:30 P.M. Males who came in with a purpose, knowing exactly what DVD, what magazine, or what Fleshlight they wanted. I noticed some imitations of the branded Fleshlight were much cheaper, but they never seemed to do as well. And once a guy even tried to return it. I told him we do not have a return policy on anything, particularly things you could penetrate, and then he just threw it in the trash right in front of me to prove something. His point was made. The cheaper vagina didn't work. I still wasn't going to resell it!

I looked at the clock: 9:45 P.M. I had thought that

anyone who was coming to the class would be here by now. Maybe they'd all show up right before it started? Maybe a bunch of people were coming as a group? Or maybe, maybe this was a dumb idea after all and no one was coming and I was a complete failure as a leader in sexual education. I sighed.

After about five more minutes of my moping and hoping mix, I heard the door open—a male and female came in together. That occasionally happened here, but it wasn't often. I presumed they were a couple. They were holding hands and looked close in age. If I had to guess, they were probably in their mid-forties. They were a little on the bigger side, in mismatched sweatpants and T-shirts, however the female had on a headband with bunny ears that didn't particularly match with anything else in her outfit. She wasn't in a bunny costume, she was just a woman in sweatpants with bunny ears. I liked it! It showed a very small but evident sense of adventure.

She dragged her partner around the store, and excitedly picked out a few toys and a few DVDs. It was apparent that it was certainly her idea to come here and not his.

"Does this come in a size large?" she picked up a French maid costume and asked me.

"Unfortunately, no," I answered. "That's literally the only one we have and I don't even know how it got here!" I laughed.

"Well, that's okay. I can squeeze into a medium, right honey?" she enthusiastically said while looking at her partner, who was on his phone not paying any attention to her. She rolled her eyes and handed me the medium size costume to ring up. "He'll appreciate this when we get home."

I really liked her energy. She had me with the bunny ears but the persistence of the French maid costume despite the sizing really sealed the deal. My workshop was officially beginning in ten minutes, and as far as I could tell no one was there early to claim a seat. So, to put it delicately, no one was there yet. I remembered how that sexy employee at Hustler told me to stick around for Dr. Erica, and I did. So I decided to mimic that marketing. What the hell did I have to lose?

I leaned in, as if I was letting her in on a special secret. "Hey—in about ten minutes, I'm hosting a girls-only masturbation seminar." It sounded like some kind of drug deal. I'm not sure why I whispered it; this event was public information. I was actually striving for it to be more public than it was! I should have shouted the damn thing.

"Oh, cool! Where?" she asked.

"Right here!" I replied. And I shamefully pointed to the collection of mismatched chairs and step stools.

"Really?!"

"Yeah!" I answered. I was so nervous about her being potentially disgusted with my event, or being appalled by just the insinuation of hanging out here for longer than she needed to, though I don't know why. She was most definitely a local and she didn't seem spoiled by the foam latte-art and the doctorates of sex that existed in the world. She was just a middle-aged woman in bunny ears, for no reason, looking to spice up her sex life. She was exactly who I was looking for.

"Well that sounds like a lot of fun!" she said. Her partner guy was still engrossed in his phone. She put her arms around him and leaned towards his face.

"Babe, why don't you go watch the fights and pick me

up when you're done? They have a fun thing going on here tonight I wanna stick around for."

"What? Are you serious? Brody was saving us seats!" he said.

"I never know what the hell is going on, anyway! You're always having to stop and explain to me everything. Won't this be better?" she asked.

He sized me up and down. He was actually looking at me for the first time all night, as if he had to get a good judgement of me before he "let" his wife hang out with me. So strange. He didn't pay any attention to her when she picked out the French maid costume, why was he so concerned about her now?

"So you're just gonna stay here." He was talking to her but looking at me.

"Yes," she answered. "Me and a bunch of girls are gonna be here, talking about girl stuff." I smiled. There were not "a bunch" of girls here, at least yet. But, I still had a good eight minutes before they needed to show up.

They stepped outside, I could vaguely hear them arguing through our door that never quite closes all the way. I was sure I would never see either of them again and I felt guilty. I hadn't even started yet, and I was causing a domestic dispute, which is the exact opposite feeling of an orgasm, from my experience. But the bunny-ear sweatpants lady must have worked this out; she came right back in, with a big smile on her face! I smiled right back. She was unintentionally the first person in my seminar!

"I'm staying!" she said. "Thanks for the invite!"

"Hell, yeah!" I answered. "Um, you can have a seat? We will be starting soon!"

We didn't have a café for her to wait in. This really

would have been a good time for punch. I tried calling Sandy again, but she didn't answer.

The woman didn't seem to mind the lack of refreshments, though. She took her jacket and purse off and claimed a chair. She grabbed an issue of *Jugg's* magazine, and read it like one would read the newspaper, looking over articles and occasionally saying things like "interesting," or "Who would have thought?"

"What's your name?" I asked.

"Lucy," she answered, still entranced by the magazine.

"Well, hello, I'm Taryn!"

"Nice to meet you!" she said.

"We will be starting soon," I said.

"I know, you just said that!" She laughed. It's true. I did. My nerves were highlighting my awkwardness. I paced around the store unsure of what to do next. But, at least I had one person to teach! I went behind the register to review my lesson plan. I could change it to fit one person's particular needs pretty easily, though Lucy's appearance had heightened my hope again. There were still a few minutes until the start time; I would concentrate on more people coming through that door in that time.

Maybe it was my hard-ass thinking, or perhaps the six-time shared Facebook post, but in the next ten minutes, four more women came in! One of them, I recognized; she was one of the fairy girls who came in here with Jimmy all those weeks ago. I wasn't sure where the other three came from, but they were here and that was all that mattered. Jimmy's friend looked different in her non-fairy attire. She wore tight blue jeans, UGG boots, and a tight purple tank top, with a crop-top hoodie jacket over it. It was appropriate day-off raver/club girl wear. Two older black women came together, both in heels, one wearing leopard-print leggings, the other in a knee-length, tight pencil dress, with a large belt in the middle. They were totally overdressed, even though I didn't have a dress code at all. They were holding shopping bags and large cups from Jamba Juice. This event got incorporated into their girls' day! I found that pretty exciting. And then there was another, who reminded me of me at the Hustler store. She looked pretty young, somewhere in her early twenties. She wore Converse sneakers, black denim pants, and a flannel top. She went straight to a seat and didn't look at anyone, or talk to anyone, or introduce herself, or anything.

Five people was certainly enough to quantify as something. I suppose it didn't matter. It was go time, no matter what this was. I locked up my register, and overheard the girls chit chatting with each other (well, all except the younger one), asking where they lived, introducing themselves—it was beautiful. Different, unlikely women united under the fluorescent lighting, in the name of vaginas and orgasms and stuff.

I walked over to the group.

"Hey everyone, my name is Taryn! Thank you for coming out tonight!"

The women clapped their hands. I couldn't believe they were clapping their hands, for me!

"So I put this event together tonight, so we could all take some time out of our hectic lives and focus on ourselves. In just the last few months I have really discovered the importance of masturbating. I think this is an activity women dismiss—we get caught up in our day-to-day lives and we forget that pleasing ourselves is so important to our confidence and growth. I thought we could all just get together and talk about what gets us off, how we masturbate, and maybe we can try out some toys if we're feeling adventurous."

Everyone nodded and smiled and laughed. That came out rather naturally! I had written and rewritten my opening statement for the night and it all sounded so stoic and rehearsed. I am not a PhD; I am not any kind of sexpert; I'm just a girl from a city about forty miles outside of Tampa who just got introduced to her own vagina, like four weeks ago.

"Before we start, why don't we go around the circle and introduce ourselves and talk about our experience with masturbation?" I suggested.

"I'll start!" the fairy who wasn't a fairy this evening said. "My name's Krissy, and I love masturbating! I actually like it a lot more than having sex most of the time! I like using anything strong that vibrates on my clit! It's awesome!" She giggled. "Okay, your turn!" she said as she playfully poked the bunny-ears-wearing woman next to her with an expertly manicured nail.

"Well, my name is Lucy, and I'm so glad I found this class. My husband doesn't want me to masturbate! Every time he catches me doing it he gets angry and tells me that's his job. But he doesn't ever do the job! What the hell! Is he really jealous of my own finger?"

"Honey, he's not jealous of your finger; he's probably jealous of your dildo if it's bigger than his dick!" one of the black ladies said, after finishing her Jamba Juice through a thick, large, phallic-looking straw. Everyone laughed, except the young one, who looked a bit frightened, but I wasn't sure what I was supposed to do about it.

"And my name is Kira, and this stunning beauty next to me is Raylin." The two older ladies both waved to everyone in the class.

"Nice to meet both of you," I said. "That just leaves . . . you!" I pointed to the younger girl, whose face immediately turned red. Whoops. I definitely made a mistake; the poor thing was getting very uncomfortable.

"Um . . . you don't have to talk about your masturbation experience if you don't want. But let's get your name so everyone in the group can address one another."

"It's, it's Maya," the young girl mumbled.

"Well, hi Maya. It's very nice to meet you; and all of you! We have so many wonderful things to talk about, and I'll jump right in! Like I said earlier, I'm pretty new to masturbation, myself. I've just recently discovered how to have an internal and external orgasm at the same time. It required a lot of lube, and a few different kinds of toys. This one right here, in particular." I brought out the G-spot stimulator toy and showed it off like I was Vanna White. "It was really incredible! Have any of you ever experienced this?"

A mix of excited responses came out of the ladies gathered around me. Lucy asked to see the toy, and examined it like it was a prized artifact from an archeological dig, gently and with great reverence.

"I'll take it!" she said. She was a great customer!

"I am not forcing any purchase on anyone but if anyone does want to buy any of our toys tonight I can give you thirty percent off! And you can have thirty minutes in one of our ROOMZ for free." I probably wasn't authorized to do this kind of thing but I did it anyway. If this brought in some new repeat customers, it was worth it. If Sandy wasn't answering my calls, she obviously trusted me to make these kinds of decisions, right?

The four women all talked over each other about their clits, their cervixes, their husbands, their vibrators. Even though we were blatantly causing a fire hazard in the middle of a fully functioning store, in our minds we were in our own special locker room.

Then the quiet one, Maya, spoke. I could see her mouth moving but I couldn't hear words coming out of her mouth.

"Shhh!" I said to the crowd.

"Did you want to say something?" I asked her.

"I'm a, well, I'm a virgin. I've never had an orgasm. I've masturbated a few times but I honestly don't know what to do." She looked down at the floor and bit her lip. There was an awkward silence.

"What should I do?" she asked.

This was great! Well, it's not great that she is lost and has no idea how to masturbate. But this was the exact reason I wanted to have the class. Now what do I do? She didn't know what to do and I didn't know what to do. At that moment, we were both lost.

"You're so young! It's okay, you still have time to learn about yourself," Lucy said.

"I've been masturbating every day since I was in middle school. I just kind of did what felt right," said Krissy. "I think it's hot when girls are shy. I would love to put my hands all over you and help you masturbate!"

Somehow this girl in her mid-twenties knew more about sex than all of us. The other women laughed, and Maya blushed.

"There's a lot of toys here that I know can help you,

but I really think at first you need to just take your fingers, and really explore yourself. Maybe use some lube, if you're nervous and having a hard time working up your own moisture, it can really help. It will feel weird at first but just push through and keep going. Once you work past that awkwardness it will feel amazing!" I was repeating to her exactly what I just did a mere few weeks ago, but truly made it feel as though I was a seasoned, masturbating professional. The words naturally came out of me and I believed them as I said them.

"But . . . that can't be all there is to it, just exploring! What if I don't like anything? What if I can't have an orgasm? What if my . . . you know . . . is weird looking? Am I supposed to, like, shave the hair down there? Is it necessary? What do you all do about it?" Maya asked, unloading what seemed to be a good portion of her sexual frustration onto a crowd of strangers.

"I love the feeling of my pussy after I get a nice wax! It's so smooth!" Raylin said.

"Ouch! Doesn't waxing hurt? I just shave the sides. I don't mind if it hangs out a little bit!" said Lucy, tentatively looking down at her pussy.

"Well your hair is blonde, that's why you don't mind!" Kira replied. She and Raylin both laughed. "I used to shave it all and a few years ago I stopped. I am bringing the '70s bush back whether my husband likes it or not!" She pulled down her sweatpants and showed a tuft of pubic hair sticking out and the other women (except Maya, who stared at the older lady's hair with a mix of horror and fascination) laughed, gave each other high fives, and applauded.

"What kind of noises do you guys make? Are you

supposed to be, like, loud? Or quiet? Is this something I should do when my roommates aren't home? Or does it not matter?" Maya said.

At the exact same moment Kira said, "I'm totally silent!" while Raylin said, "I'm loud as *fuck*!" right on top of each other. They both laughed.

"I live in a big, open loft and my roommates were always angry at me for masturbating too loud. So I do it in the car, when I drive. In fact, I did it on the way over!" Krissy said.

"Please, don't masturbate and drive, Maya!" I said. "You don't have to be loud! If it makes you feel good to yell then yell, but if it doesn't make you comfortable you don't have to. Lots of women have very intense, quiet orgasms."

"Does it make a mess?" Maya said. "Do I need to like change my sheets when I finish?"

"Sometimes I get messy! But I sleep inside the wetness, I don't care," Krissy said.

Everyone laughed.

"It's not always like that, honey. I've rubbed one out at my desk at work without anyone noticing. No mess there! But, I always have an extra pair of panties on hand just in case!" said Lucy.

"Every woman has different amounts of moisture in their vaginas, and it varies depending on what part of your cycle you're in," I said. I had no actual facts to back that up, but it sure sounded right. I made a mental note to look that up later.

I noticed Maya was subconsciously rubbing her inner thigh as everyone spoke. I don't think she even knew what she was doing but her body did. This girl's pussy was aching to cum, but all she could think about was changing her damn sheets.

"What do you guys think about when you're doing it?" Maya asked.

"Oh, anything! Sometimes I daydream about the time I got gangbanged in the bathroom of a nightclub by five different DJs, and sometimes I just think about someone kissing me on the beach really passionately. And sometimes, it's about someone in a big furry panda suit." As Krissy spoke she stuck her hands down her pants and got entranced in a moment. And for the first time in my life I really wanted to be a DJ, and a panda.

"Ryan Gosling," Raylin and Kira said at the same time.

"Just go watch *The Notebook* and your pussy will know exactly what to do," Kira continued. Everyone laughed.

"There's no right or wrong thing to think about! The most important thing for you to do is relax and see where your mind takes you," I said. I always hated when people would try to tell me to relax. That's a trigger word for me, and here I am saying it to someone else. I hope it worked. Suddenly I heard, "Man, I Feel Like a Woman" by Shania Twain blaring loudly. It was coming from Raylin's large left breast. She pulled a giant cell phone out of her bra, and the song continued to play through its speaker. She looked at the name on the caller ID and her expression immediately changed. It certainly wasn't Ryan Gosling calling.

"Hello?" Raylin said into the phone; she went from angry to concerned, and then told the person on the other end she would come right home. I couldn't really get what was going on but it sounded like some kind of snafu with a babysitter.

"I'm sorry ladies, we gotta go!" Raylin said.

"We?" Kira asked.

"Yes! You're my ride!" Raylin said. Kira huffed and puffed and then agreed to take her home.

"That sucks! I'm sorry! Well I'm here four nights a week—did you want to buy anything before you left? I can give you 50% off anything in the store as a thank you for coming in."

Raylin smirked, "I can always treat myself to a new toy."

And Raylin did grab a dildo, while Kira quickly picked out a vibrating wand. I checked them out and they left.

When I returned, Maya seemed a bit more relaxed, but still nervous overall. Her questions had been answered, but I wanted to do more for her. This girl had clearly never been given any friendly lessons in terms of her own sexuality, and didn't she deserve some, finally? And wouldn't it be great if my first class completely changed someone's life by giving them an orgasm, and then the ability to give themselves an orgasm whenever they wanted?

"Maya, I know you're still testing the waters with your own body, but I'd like to help open you up a bit more. Ladies, you're welcome to join us, but you especially, Maya, I suggest you follow me into one of our ROOMZ so I can physically guide you on your new masturbatory path."

Maya's face instantly turned a deep crimson. "I came here to learn about my body. I *want* to. But, I'm scared."

I walked over to where she was sitting and knelt down before her. The other women started hollering "Wooo!"

behind me, but I pretended not to hear.

"It's okay to be scared. I promise, this is definitely going to be worth it for you."

For Taryn and Maya to go into the room alone, turn to page 97.

For all of the women in the class to go into the room, turn to page 105.

I took Maya to the back of the store, and I unlocked one of the smaller ROOMZ. I turned on the one working light. I was thankful the other one wasn't working because the sad look of the fake wooden paneling in here wasn't going to help anyone get aroused, especially a virgin. The wall opposite the paneling was painted with uneven red and blue stars. I think someone tried to go for a patriotic theme in here, then gave up halfway.

I brought along a new toy that just arrived at the store. It was neon blue, long and skinny, called the "Blue Venus Vibrator." It featured an oval poking out up top that strongly vibrated your clit. I really wanted to try this one. The color alone was seductive, but the size, the alleged strength of it that it advertised, and the fact that it was only about twenty-five bucks made it the perfect thing to try.

I was alone with Maya. I sat down next to her and did my best to be the masturbation fairy godmother I could possibly be.

"Ok, now I want you to start by jumping up and down and yelling. Seriously. You're all tense and you need to shake it out!"

She looked at me skeptically.

"Come on, it'll be fun! Here, just do what I do." I got up off the seat and began to jump up and down, shimmying at random intervals and dancing in a goofy manner. As I danced, her skepticism gave way to a smile. Eventually, she got up and joined me and we jumped around the dimly-lit Star-Spangled Banner-ish room. She began to giggle.

I grabbed her hand; she blushed, but this was no time to let her give in to embarrassment. I looked at her sternly and said, "Now, start touching yourself. It doesn't have to be your vagina yet, just feel around your body and get to know yourself better. You don't have to get naked, either. Just literally feel yourself up!"

She held up her hands, staring at them and taking deep breaths. Then, tentatively, she put her hands underneath her flannel top, and rubbed them around. It was very mechanical, like she was checking for lumps in a breast cancer examination. I understood her distress; I'd been like that not too long ago, after all.

"Relax! Get to know your own skin, feel all the different bumps and crevices in there. Get comfortable!"

She rubbed in a more sporadic pattern. Her plaid flannel was completely buttoned, even the optional top button was closed, and no one did that! I could see the outline of her arms through her shirt moving around like a ghost possessed her torso.

"Think about anything that you find sexy. Anything at all. You don't have to tell me what it is. Anything or anyone that might turn you on—just close your eyes and think about them."

She stopped rubbing and closed her eyes. There was a very subtle smile on her face. I could just barely see it. I was worried that I was sounding like a meditation instructor; I had to shift directions so she would actually have an orgasm and not just fall asleep.

I took it upon myself to unzip her pants and pull them down a little. Her half smile turned to a shocked full smile. She kept her eyes closed, focusing on the object of her sexy desires.

I took the bright blue skinny wand and turned it on. In this dark room it shined like a glow stick, bright and artificial. It vibrated intensely—this thing was powerful! I lightly brushed it on top of her cotton underwear. I wedged it lengthwise between her pussy lips, with her panties still on; it just instinctually felt like the right thing to do. I kept the vibrator there, and I could feel her breathing getting heavier. She resumed touching her breasts underneath her top. The very top button of her flannel was now undone, a small sign of progress.

Her pants were around her thighs, and it was restricting her from moving. I delicately slid them down to her ankles; her eyes were closed and she was concentrated on the vibrations. I wasn't sure if she even noticed. I could see her thighs start to shake, and the muscles inside of them tighten up. I took her right hand, and I put it on the toy.

"Take this and make yourself feel good," I said. "Just see where it takes you—there's no wrong way to do it! You can stick it in your damn ear if you want!" I said. Before I said that I probably should have checked if sticking it in your ear was actually hazardous or not. I would imagine the buzzing noise would be intrusive but not an actual medical risk.

Thankfully, that didn't seem to be the area where she wanted the toy. She pulled her panties down just barely below her pussy. She had a healthy amount of pubic hair, so between that and the dark light I couldn't exactly see the details of what her vagina looked like, but I enjoyed the mystery. Her body was telling her to do things; I could see it in the change of her expression in her eyes and her face. She moved the vibrator up and down her lips, searching for the right spot. She shivered and giggled like she had a sexy case of the chills. She opened her eyes wide and looked directly at me.

"Thank you," she whispered.

I have to admit it was pretty hot to see the way this inexperienced girl submitted to me, like I invented orgasms and I allowed her to license one from me for a short period of time. If only she knew I was only slightly less confused about it than she was.

She parted her thick brown pubic hair, and spastically moved the vibrator around her entire crotch region. Her pussy was uncharted territory, completely off the map, and she was just going to have to keep driving around until she recognized some roads and figured it out. Or, well, I could step in like a good Samaritan and try to give some directions.

"Here, try this!" I grabbed the wrist of the hand that held the wand and started to guide her. I slowly tickled the top of her pussy with the blue mini wand. I could see the inside of her lips getting increasingly more swollen. It was talking to me, sending me a signal that it was slowly waking up. *Hello pussy, and good morning, I am coming for your orgasm!*

She breathed more heavily. I thought of unbuttoning her shirt but I actually thought it was incredibly cute the way she had a buttoned flannel on, with her underwear and pants slid down to her ankles. It looked like an uncensored version of a Gap commercial. There was something so intimate and seductive about a girl in a man's shirt and her pussy exposed. In addition to my own new-found fetish for it, I think it made her feel safe. I moved the toy slightly to the left, then slightly to the right; she started shaking a little more vigorously, but I knew I wasn't quite there yet. I was getting close.

"Tell me when you feel, like, just, total insanity—okay? You'll know when I get there." She nodded and looked right at me.

"Yes, yes, okay, okay," she said. This was just so cool! I don't know when the next time in my life I would have penetrative sex would be, but whenever that does happen, I will be so much better at it than I ever was. I understood arousal and connection in a whole new way that I never did before. But that's not important right now. The task at hand was finding this virgin's clit.

I moved the wand slightly down and she grabbed onto my hand. She led out an adorable moan, sneaky and soft, but it was a sound of pleasure for sure. I nestled the oval directly on that spot and held it there. She trembled and held onto my arms for support. Her breathing became faster and faster. I couldn't stop smiling. The only thing better than having a great orgasm yourself, is helping someone else have one.

"Just take it all in. Enjoy it," I said, like I was a drug dealer and she was a customer sampling out some of my new stash. She kept repeating "please, please, please."

"Please what?" I asked.

"Please don't stop!" she screamed.

Hmmm. That gave me an interesting idea. The nice teacher in me suddenly wanted to become a little bit mean and toy with her just for a minute. While she was exploring her first orgasm I was introducing myself to a new, more dominant side of my brain.

I took the toy away from her clit and stood up with

it in my hand raised above my head, like she was a dog who didn't deserve her treat. She looked at me completely shocked and whimpered, and I steadily remained true to this new character.

"How bad do you want this?" I said.

"So badly! I want it, I need it," she said.

"I don't believe you. Touch yourself and prove it to me," I said firmly.

I wanted her to feel good, but I wanted her to work for it. I figured a tiny bit of distress now could lead to a better orgasm later, right? And this would be her first orgasm. We may as well make it count.

She took her fingers and furiously rubbed her pussy in the same exact spot I had found before.

"Now, stick your finger inside yourself slowly and use the moisture from there to lube up your clitoris." She followed my instructions. She could barely fit one finger inside her vagina—she slowly inched her way in there with just her index finger.

"Take your time! It's okay!" I said. She got about half of her finger in, and she remained still for a moment. This was such a new feeling for her; she was overwhelmed. After a pause, she went deeper inside with her finger, and she smiled. Then she did a very slow in and out motion, ever so lightly and softly. I believe I was watching her lose her virginity to her own finger.

"Good girl," I said. She took the finger out and slid the slippery juices from her inside to her outside. Then her body discovered the power of multitasking, and she took her left hand and rubbed her clit, and put her right index finger back inside her vagina. Apparently she liked it in there!

I still held onto the toy. I would sit here and decide when I felt as though she deserved it to return. She stared up at me with her big, inquisitive eyes. I kept my face looking sharply rigid, or at least, I thought I did. I sure was smiling on the inside and I hope I wasn't giving it away because I didn't want to fuck up this interesting dynamic. I was getting off on it, and I could tell she was, too.

"Please!" she said again.

"More!" I said. She finger-fucked herself faster and faster now. She continued to rub her clit as well. Her flannel shirt still covered her top half. I could see the inside of her pussy but I couldn't see her nipples. The curiosity killed me, but for some reason I just wanted her tits to remain a mystery.

"Close your eyes," I said, and she obediently closed them tightly. It was cute! She continued to rub and finger-fuck herself as well as she could without looking. I came up from behind her, I put my fingers through the back of her hair, and she moaned, loudly this time. Her moan sounded more adult like, more guttural, and more natural than before. I slapped her hand away from her clit; she was ready.

I returned the blue wand directly to her clit, pressing down with great pressure. She squirmed around and I held her in place by firmly pulling the root of her hair. She breathed in and out loudly.

"What do I do? It feels so weird!" she said.

"Let it out. Come on, do it, just let it all out—for me," I said. I mean, this was all for her but I felt like she would put a little more effort into it if it was intended for me.

She quivered and shook, she moaned and breathed heavily, she started hitting the floor and she wedged her one little finger as far in as it could possibly go. I held onto her long brown hair, and I gently kissed her neck. She continued to shake and cum as I held her. It was incredibly beautiful.

"Thank you," she said, as she collapsed, her body too wobbly to support herself at the moment. She was in a smiley daze.

"No, no. Thank *YOU*," I said. And I truly meant it. That was amazing.

To go back and see what happens with all the girls in one of the Roomz instead, turn to page 105.

To see what happens next in this fantasy, turn to page 115.

I grabbed some lube and anything that I thought vaginas would want inside of them or around them. It was time for some hands-on learning.

I led my small but powerful group of women into one of the smaller ROOMZ. I figured it would be a little more intimate that way. There's one particular room that has really grown on me. It's in the corner; the walls are painted red, there's two red leather couches and the light bulbs had a red tint to them, and in the middle of the room was a thick, metal stripper pole. It was like the Devil's personal strip club, or a retro Valentine's Day explosion of sorts.

Lucy immediately gravitated toward the pole, and began spinning around it ungracefully.

"Why don't you change into your new French maid costume?" I said. "I'm sure we could use some cleaning around here." She giggled, got excited, and quickly vanished into one of the darker corners of the room. Soon she emerged from the shadows, transformed into a voluptuous but sexy maid. It was a little off-putting to see her without the bunny ears, but they were replaced with a black headband surrounded by white lace. It was fascinating to see the way her facial expressions and even her entire body composure changed after she put on her outfit. It was like she was an entirely different person.

I laid out the toys, announced, "Everyone, take what you want to use!" and put a big bottle of this "mix" lube— half silicone and half water-based—in the middle of the table. It was like a lube cocktail. I tried it a few times and I was pleased with the results: not too sticky and not too watery. I'm new in the lube market, but for whatever reason this spoke to me and it made me sound very much like I was on the cutting edge of lube technology, so I felt very progressive recommending it.

"I don't know what I want to use," Maya quietly stated.

"Use this!" Lucy picked up the Hitachi and waved it in the air. "We can share if you want," she said as she smiled and giggled. She really was some kind of sex fairy. She gave off this relaxed, happy, horny energy and we were all getting super high off it.

Krissy chose the G-spot stimulator. She grabbed it and grinned—she apparently had a plan!

And what was I going to do? I wasn't so sure. I never masturbated in a room full of people and I had to be the trailblazer here. I let my body guide me to the direction of my pleasure; that's the advice I wanted to give to Maya, and I suppose it's easier to show than tell. I reached out my hand, and surprisingly, my inner horniness told me to reach for the small glass butt plug. How did that happen? I was clearly possessed by an anal ghost. It was a month of exploring, so this seemed to make sense. The other girls cheered for the butt plug, and I grew more excited by their shouts.

We all sat in our self-chosen areas of the couches. There was a moment of silence wondering who should start. Like, we needed an official starter to wave a mastur-bation flag, shoot a pistol, and say, "On your mark, get set, go fuck yourselves!"

Krissy, of course, started it off. She raised her buzzing Hitachi in the air and ever so daintily brought it down against her pussy lips. It set us all off. She was like, my hype woman. My second in command. I was Santa and she was Rudolf, leading the way with a bright, red, LED pulse-setting button.

The room became scented with the smell of our collective mounting desire. If there had been any mirrors in the room, they would have fogged up immediately.

I pulled my spandex down to my ankles, I took the lube and massaged it around my vagina. I knew I needed to work my way up to the butt plug; I'd never done any anal insertion before, so it was prudent to go slow. I felt like I was transported back to my bedroom and I surprisingly had no anxiety at all being in a room with strangers and no pants on.

Lucy wasted no time; she didn't even use any lube. She took the G-spot stimulator and harshly jammed it up inside her. She grunted, spread her legs out, and took up most of the couch. She thrust the toy in and out and in and out of her and very deep *ohhhs* and *aaahs* came out of her mouth. This was definitely a mature, horny woman masturbating and not a younger girl. She knew exactly what spot in her vagina wanted nurturing. Her masturbation was so carnal, so gut wrenching, and so necessary. She was a maid on a mission. Her body elongated even further on the couch and she reached out her unoccupied hand and grabbed mine. She squeezed my palm as she pounded her own pussy. I barely knew her, but I felt so connected. I paused my own personal stimulation, I held her hand and simply watched. This was pure female connection, the formation of both pleasure and friendship.

Meanwhile, Krissy and Maya had their own incredibly angelic moment going on.

"Stand up and just jump around for a minute," Krissy said. "I know it might sound silly but just loosen your body up! That's why I go out dancing at clubs so much. It raises my endorphins! It makes my body feel like a gummy-worm," she giggled. She was just so cute. A younger, bitterer me would have hated her in high school.

Maya awkwardly stood up and jumped. Her body was not even close to gummy-worm. She was frigid.

"Again!" Krissy demanded. Maya jumped again, this time with a bit more fluidity but not that much. "Breathe in deep and breathe out!" said Krissy. "Now yell! Scream! AHHHHHHHHHH!" She let out a high-pitched howl. Maya echoed back with what seemed like a slight cough. I wonder what this scene would look like to an outside spectator—a woman in her mid-forties, masturbating, and a girl in her mid–to-late twenties jumping up and down and screaming next to a nervous young virgin. It was definitely quite a sight.

"Here! Take some lube and just stick it down your pants!" Krissy squirted a dollop of oozing liquid into Maya's hand. She took a deep breath and stuck her hand down her pants without even unzipping them.

"Now just relax! Feel around a little." Maya jerked her hand around, she sort of looked like she had a nervous twitch. But she was gaining more comfort in her own way, and at her own pace.

Krissy left Maya to her business and quickly stripped off all her clothing. I don't know how she did that. Were they Velcro? She was definitely an exhibitionist, so maybe it was all practice. She bared her nakedness proudly, her perky, small boobs, tight stomach, and creamy-white skin gleaming enticingly under the soft lights. Her mess of pastel, multicolored hair was pulled up into a chaotic bun; she was art erotic. She sauntered over to the stripper pole, and began to dance around it to the tune of her own drum and bass song in her head that was most likely mixed and remixed by Jimmy. I hoped that lucky bastard appreciated what he had with her.

Meanwhile, Maya worked up the courage to pull her jeans slightly down. Not down to her ankles, but to her thighs. I could see her fingers move around like bugs underneath her cotton panties. Her dark pubic hair stuck out from the sides. Her glasses were beginning to fog up. She breathed quickly in and out and in and out. Krissy stopped pole twirling for a second to check on her, and clapped in approval at the sight, like a proper masturbation elf helper. On the other side of the room, Lucy continued to thrust away, hitting her inside with the round side of the toy. I could hear the wet moisture coming from her vagina. Her pussy lips looked so hungry; so many layers of meaty flaps clenched onto the silicone steel toy, swallowing it like a straw. It was so hot to watch.

Suddenly, Krissy stopped dancing, grabbed her Hitachi wand, and walked over to Maya, a devious look in her eyes. She grabbed Maya's hand and pulled it out of her underwear, replacing her manual stimulation with the whirring Hitachi. Maya's eyes lit up, she let out a loud noise, and I could see drops of moisture sweating through the cotton. Finally.

Elated, Krissy confidently wrapped her naked legs around Maya's crotch, so that the Hitachi wand suspended between them, vibrating them both. Krissy took Maya's hands and placed them on her tiny nipples.

"You can squeeze them, bite them, slap them, do whatever you want," Krissy said with a smirk. Maya smiled; she was on a sensory overload. Their legs tightened up around each other; Maya's panties still on. Krissy hit a button on the wand and upped the speed on it, making it stronger and stronger. Their moans got louder and more simultaneous. They were beginning to morph together into one orgasmic creature.

I watched everyone and got lost in the entertainment, forgetting about my own pussy for a moment. Or so I thought. My hand reached down and I was incredibly wet, and it wasn't from the lube. I was aroused. The mixture of different personalities coming together and cumming together was just so sexy.

I grabbed a rabbit masturbator. I learned that my pussy was a bit stubborn and needed both clitoral and internal stimulation at the same time, so those rabbit toys were perfect for me. The little tentacle at the end tickled my clit and then the vibrating dildo pulsed against my G-spot. It was a multitasking toy that paired perfectly with lube and some imagination, but today I didn't need any imagination because I had a fantasy happening before my eyes. I still held onto Lucy's hand, I whispered to her, "Cum for me. I want to see you cum. I want you to cum."

I could tell she was getting close. Perhaps, with her marriage situation being what it was, she wanted someone to give her permission or encouragement to climax. I don't know. I really did want to see her cum, her body was so thirsty for an orgasm. Her pelvis shook, she thrusted the toy so deeply and strongly inside herself I was worried it might break in half. She held my hand tightly. My own vagina got looser and looser and welcomed my rabbit masturbator deep inside me. Harder and harder she went on herself, her legs began to shake and her toes wiggled around. Her large thighs were wet with sweat and pussy juices dripping down from inside her. She let out a loud, deep moan, her eyes rolled into the back of her head, she held my hand tighter and tighter, and, yes! She was cumming. It was a long climax, I think this was multiple orgasms. She jolted and quivered, again and again, and finally melted into the couch. She slowly took the toy out of herself and it was covered in thick, beautiful juices. I was so happy for her. She smiled, and said, "Thank you." She rested her eyes, and sat in a post orgasm coma, in her frilly costume.

Meanwhile, I was inspired. I took some lube and put it all over my vagina and ventured further down to my other hole. It was uncharted territory. There was an unflattering ring of hair around my butthole. I never noticed it until now. It wasn't terrible, I suppose my razor just needed to go further than it was.

My vagina felt incredibly relaxed, like it took its own tab of acid and was in a lucid state. The rabbit toy really heightened the erogenous nerves all over my lower area. I felt like I could touch the side of my thigh and it might work me up to an orgasm. It was like I plugged my body into an erotic wall socket and I was one wet vagina from head to toe. That was perfect; it was time. I took the little butt plug and placed it at the entrance to my anus. I pushed, just a little. To my surprise, it slid right in! Krissy glanced over at me and cheered, like she had some kind of Jedi anal super powers, with the ability to know when anyone anywhere was sticking something inside their ass. I enjoyed her encouragement.

It was a neat feeling—with a dildo in my pussy and a butt plug in my ass, I felt stuffed in a wonderful way. They felt like special gifts inside me. My clit, my G-spot, and now the inside of my ass were all being massaged at once, and I felt wonderful. The butt plug fit so nicely inside! It was snug and stayed put while I pampered my pussy.

I looked over at Maya, who had taken possession of the Hitachi all to herself! She still wasn't confident enough to take her panties off but you could see parts of her pure pussy sticking out from the sides of her panties. I wish I had come to something like this before I had sex for the first time. I would have been so much better at it. I don't know when the hell I will ever have sex again or who it will be with, but I know it will be entirely new next time it happens. I'm basically a born-again virgin, who recently found dildos and lube instead of god.

Krissy was vigorously using her fingers. She clearly knew what to do. We were all hard at work, touching our own respective pussies in our own ways, and I was getting to understand my ass a bit. Maya looked so doe-eyed. She was getting close, I could tell, but she panicked and took the Hitachi off her clit.

"Don't stop!" Krissy yelled. "You're scared! Just keep going, it will feel so good!"

She grabbed the Hitachi and raised it to the highest decibel it could go, placing it back in Maya's hand. A devious smile appeared on Maya's face; she had definitely never felt anything like this before. She breathed in and out, and adorable, high-pitched moans came out of her mouth.

Krissy rubbed her own clit with one hand, and used her other hand to stuff a few fingers inside her pussy. I let the rabbit do its job inside and outside of me, while the butt plug filled up my asshole.

It was like the ending of a magical fairytale; we all looked at each other, and motivated each other. Even Lucy woke back up and rubbed her clit, too, for good measure. It was so beautiful. And one, two, three, like someone conducting an orgasm orchestra, one after another, we finished.

I was first, a giant amazing dual orgasm on my inside and out. My pussy loosened while my ass tightened up on the little plug. I looked down and loved the way my decorated ass looked. It was so cool! Like a big crescendo, my body built up and let go. Lucy held my hand as I came.

Then was Krissy's turn. Her masturbation reminded me of the men I had spied on in here. It's like she was jerking off, and then came when she felt like cumming. Men asserted a sense of control over their orgasms in a way that women didn't—except Krissy had this control. She was cumming because she wanted to cum, while for the rest of us the orgasm came when it was ready. It was like she could push a certain button on her clit and let out an orgasm.

She shook her fingers furiously at the top of her clitoris, and shook and shook and let out incredibly glamorous sounds from her mouth. She was truly sexual. She stared at me, she stared at Maya, she continued to climax and her eyes went to the back of her head.

Finally, it was Maya's turn, the climax of our climaxes! She wasn't nearly as graceful as the rest of us, but it was just so damn exciting! Her very first orgasm and she was giving it to herself. Such a wonderful, powerful thing was happening before my eyes. The Hitachi vibrated on her so strongly, and she thrust herself against it, pushed herself into the white pulsating ball as hard as she could, and let out a big cry. It was so raw and innocent, she looked like she was in pain and pleasure simultaneously. It continued for several minutes, while we all cheered her on.

"Let it all out!" Krissy said. She was so horny for her innocence. It was incredible.

We came and we came. It was an unforgettable experience of mere strangers coming together. It was like we entered some kind of sweat lodge and were blessed by a shaman, only we were actually in a working-class city forty miles outside of Tampa in a sex shop. But everything is relative. This was my own kind of spiritual awakening.

We laughed and looked at each other. We gathered our clothing, speechless for the moment, all reveling in the power of pleasure we shared.

"Good job, ladies!" I said. We all couldn't stop smiling. My orgasm summer camp experience turned out better than I expected.

Now it was time to go back out into the "real" world. My real world isn't quite like everyone else's—it consisted of lingerie, fluorescent lighting, and sleep during the day time. Everything was pretty surreal at the moment. But regardless, the night turned out to be a success!

To go back and follow just Taryn and Maya into one of the Roomz instead, turn to page 98.

Continue with Taryn in this fantasy, turn to the next page.

A few hours later the store was silent. Krissy went home, to meet Jimmy probably, and I'm sure they were doing some kind of uppers and engaging in incredibly acrobatic sex. Lucy reunited with her grumpy husband. Maya went home happy, having purchased two Hitachi wands, along with a porn DVD that caught her eye!

With the seminar/workshop/whatever over, my brain had climaxed. My big project that I had been thinking of for so long was done! Not only that, but it was a roaring success.

So of course, the question started looming in my mind: What do I do next? Start planning the next class? Should this be a monthly thing? I had no idea. My boss hadn't been around in a while so I didn't have anyone to pat me on the back, or scold me. I wonder what Dr. Erica would have thought of this class. Would she ever masturbate with her students?

It was 3:30 A.M. I had about five more hours of work left. I began looking through some wholesale catalogs that I took it upon myself to request. I looked at the prices of different products; I now had a vague under-standing of which sex toys were worthwhile and which were a rip-off, so it was easier to pick out new items. If I ordered some different products there was a chance that could trickle into different kinds of customers coming into the store. If I had more of these classes, I bet it could lead to more sales for women's toys. From seeing what products customers spent money on and what prices they had shear panic attacks over, I had a pretty good idea on what price range we could be comfortable with. I realized some of the products in the store were marked up too high from the wholesale price and some products weren't marked up high enough. Sandy had to be losing money off some of these products—and it was probably just due to mislabeling the prices or forgetting what she paid for them or something. I mean, the "Orgasmic Thrusting 7-Speed Rabbit Vibrator" that just a few hours ago got me off so nicely was being sold here for thirty-four dollars and its wholesale price was thirty-two. That makes no sense! We should be making more than a two-dollar profit when someone wants the option to masturbate at seven different speeds. I took it upon myself to reprice it at sixty-four dollars and ninety-nine cents.

I wasn't making a commission off the novelties so why did I care so much? I don't know. But I did. I had this new, deep concern for the lack of orgasms in Pasco County, Florida, and I think this store could solve the problem.

I began my routine floor sweeping around 4:00 A.M. I felt like I mostly just circulated dust around the store as I did it, rather than actually pick anything up; my mind was on so many other things. At 5:00 A.M. I decided to re-lace up all the corsets in the store. They were looking a bit sloppy. I couldn't help but imagine Lucy stuffed into one of these bad girls, her breasts puffed up beneath metal boning and lace; an alluring thought, for sure.

Around 6:00 A.M., the doorbell rang and in walked Sandy wearing a tight black top, bright red pants, black patent-leather heels, and fuck-me red lipstick.

"Sandy!" I ran over and gave her a hug. "Where the hell have you been?!"

Before she had a chance to answer, Amir walked in behind her, grinning stupidly. He put his arm around Sandy and gave her a peck on the cheek.

"Well hello, Amir." I paused. "Good to see you! Your pills haven't come in yet. I'm sorry."

"Oh, that's okay. They're not even available anymore. They were already pulled by the FDA."

"Oh, I'm sorry about that."

Before I could register what was happening, Amir pulled Sandy's face toward him and planted a sloppy kiss on her lips—one that would have definitely qualified as "first base" in middle school. After a few seconds of aggressive tongue, Sandy pulled away.

"Well Taryn," she said breathlessly, gesturing at Amir. "This is where I've been."

My shock manifested in the form of an open-mouth, wide-eyed stare, and too many questions that caught in the back of my throat.

Amir looked like a cross between a rapper and a forest ranger, with baggy pants, high-top sneakers, gold chains, a green khaki drill sergeant hat, and a flannel top, with his little bun on the top of his head. He had lipstick all over his face, his man bun, a collared shirt, and black pleated pants. He was about a foot taller and twenty-five years younger than Sandy, who firmly stuck to her own style of skin-tight clothes in black and bright colors. They were completely mismatched.

"We're in love!" Amir announced, putting his arm sweetly around Sandy's shoulders.

"After thirty years of dating and two marriages," said Sandy, "I've found my soulmate."

"Wait—how did this happen?" I asked.

"Well," Amir started explaining. "I showed up to my 'date' and—it was Sandy."

"Holy shit!" I couldn't stop laughing. "Sandy, you were catfishing him?"

"I'm not really sure what that even means."

"It means you tricked him online by saying you were someone you weren't. Sandy, that's pretty sneaky. You must have spent a lot of time on this!"

"For a while I thought I would never blow my cover. I thought I could just keep coming up with excuses not to meet him. It wasn't something I planned, honestly! I just wanted to give him some confidence in himself. He was working so hard, and so selflessly, and I thought he deserved it, a nice, pretty girl giving him attention. But then...we started talking, actually talking, about life and plans and dreams. Taryn, Amir is amazing!" Sandy snuggled against her beau, showing sugary sweetness I'd never seen from her before. Amir blushed.

"We formed a true connection over those chats; I knew I loved him and I had to let him know. I couldn't keep waiting anymore. We made plans to meet at the county fair. I got there and I saw him looking around for the girl in the photo, and I just walked up to him and..."

"She kissed me right there, didn't even say hello," said Amir. "But at that moment, I knew she was the one I'd gone there to meet. She was everything I'd ever needed, and everything I'll ever want."

"And so, you know, we kind of disappeared for the last few months. The sex is—"

"Okay, I get it!" I interrupted.

Sandy started sliding her hand down Amir's chest. "His cock is just so perfect!" Amir grabbed her hand before she could go further.

"I know!" I laughed. "I've seen it. So, Amir, are you still, uh, what was that called again? Jocking?"

"Jelking!" He seemed offended. I had been so focused on vaginas the past month, I kind of forgot that penises existed. Amir's was actually the only cock I had seen in the past few months, aside from ones that plugged into the wall or attached to holsters. I had to agree with Sandy— Amir had himself a nice cock.

"I help him with the jelking!" Sandy said excitedly.

"She's got all the right moves," Amir gushed. "It's grown two quarters of a centimeter since she came along."

"Wow. That's true love right there!"

They kissed again and he grabbed her ass. They looked so wrong, yet so right.

"Well, Sandy," I started. I finally had her here, and needed to tell her what I'd been up to. Would she be mad? "I wanted to catch you up on some things I've been doing with the store."

"Yeah, sure," she said distractedly, rubbing Amir's chest.

"I just—sales are good. I organized a workshop and it brought in some new customers; I hope that was ok! It went really well, and I got some sales out of it. I think it would be great if we could order some new products, like these." I picked up the catalog with Post-it notes poking out of a third of the pages.

"Actually Taryn, I wanted to talk to you." She briefly tore herself away from her lover and looked at me hopefully. "I've been running this store for over thirty years. It's the love of my life. Well, it was the love of my life, until now. I can't imagine where I would be without it."

"Of course."

"But I could use a break, to be honest. I kind of can't focus on anything right now but Amir's growing cock."

"Oh! Well, I guess I can pick up more hours, but honestly, I think we'd need to hire another person, so I can at least get some sleep. But I do have ideas on that front—"

"Taryn, I meant do you want to take over the store?"

My breath caught in my throat for the second time in the past few minutes. "Are you serious?"

"Yes, I'm serious! Look at you—you're already running the store and it's thriving. You know how to make the customers feel comfortable, and that's the most important thing. You're way better suited for this than I am right now. What do you think? You want to make dreams come true?"

Was this for real? I mean, I could do it. She was right, I'd been running things here pretty well. Was I about to take on a huge life commitment, right here in a sex shop at 6:00 in the morning?

"Yes!" I said—it just slipped out of my mouth. I hugged Sandy. "Thank you, I'm so honored!"

Just a few months ago I was unemployed, and now I was about to run a business. I didn't know if I was totally ready for something like this, but still, I couldn't wait to get started. I have so much to learn, so much to explore.

"Now, I have something very important to give you," Sandy said. "You can't keep this store alive without it."

"The master set of keys . . . ?"

"Here," Sandy reached into her purse and handed me a folded up piece of paper. I opened it up and saw some scribbles, numbers, and arrows. It looked like a math equation. I studied the paper, trying to decipher the symbols.

"Honey, it's the recipe to my punch!"

The punch. Of course. The potion that brought Sandy and Amir together. Was there a recipe for Cheetos to follow?

"Well, I'm going to need some help figuring out this recipe. I want to make sure to get it right. Can we make a batch together?"

"Of course!"

In the past month I had learned all about the erogenous zones in my vagina, which toys women love, and how to host fantastic masturbation sessions. Now I just had to master the art of making moonshine in a bathtub and mixing it with the right kind of juice.

I had come to work that night nervous about running a workshop. Now I'd been handed the keys to a family heirloom of dildos, blow-up dolls, and porn. I thought about all of our customers: the moms, the old single men, the gay and straight couples, the husbands, the virgins. I loved them all. People came to Dreamz to learn about sex, to have sex—with themselves and with others—and I was thrilled to be a part of that. I would sell them porn films, dirty magazines, naughty nurse costumes, and the seven-speed thrusting pink piece of magic that made me find god in my vagina. This store was a very special place—lube and body fluids oozing from the cracks of the walls. I wasn't going to let Sandy down.

Here dreams would always come true.

The End

Go back and find a different fantasy, turn to page 59.

121

I woke up around 5:00 P.M., not remembering for a moment where I was or how I'd gotten there. I was used to being awoken by the sounds of my roommates scuffling around as they just got home from work, usually discussing with each other and various random people on the phone about how to get weed. But this evening I awoke to complete silence, in a bed with fluffy white pillows, and what felt like sheets with an insanely high thread count. The memories were coming back to me, visages of Amanda seductively fucking me suddenly invading my head. Amanda. I looked around for her, but it appeared I was alone. The television was on but the volume was muted, showing a loop of a commercial for the hotel I was in with montages of food from the restaurant, families swimming in the pool, and proper adult couples lounging by a fire pit. Sadly, the ad didn't show anyone getting fucked by a hot dyke with a strap-on. This hotel had no idea what the real magic in this building was.

Was I still welcome here? Should I leave? I sat back and recounted the series of events that happened last night and I couldn't believe they did. I was hoping I could see her again before she left town. I never actually had a one-night stand, and I'd never slept with a woman. Wasn't something supposed to happen after this? Wasn't it proper to at least eat a meal together, or have a kiss good-bye or something?

I stepped into the shower. It was so refreshing to stand

in a bathroom that wasn't littered with so many different people's toiletries. Just perfectly sized compact bottles of fresh-smelling shampoo and an individually wrapped mini bar of soap. I watched the suds fall down my body, circulate around my nipples, and I scrubbed the soap into the tuft of pubes above my pussy. As I slowly washed away the smell of sex on my body, I heard the door open. I smiled.

"Hey! I hope you don't mind I used your shower." I opened the curtain and let the water drip down the sides of the tub.

"It's okay! I don't have to pay the water bill here," Amanda smirked.

She was in her black blazer, with a slightly more casual soft black T-shirt under it. It wasn't your average cotton shirt; it was thin, and fell on her body in an intentional way. This was a shirt made to stand on its own.

"I've got a few hours before I head to the airport, wanna grab some food?"

"We did never actually get that breakfast," I said.

I thought that was a rather smooth, clever, and cool way to say *Oh my god, we had sex, isn't that crazy*! But she wasn't enthused. Actually, she didn't respond at all. Maybe she didn't hear me. I closed the curtain, quickly finished my shower, dried off and dressed, my clothes from yesterday still carrying the scent of arousal.

We hopped in a cab, and went to a restaurant she recommended, a place I have never heard of even though I had lived here my whole life. It had large windows and exposed brick, leather seats, and chandeliers made out of wine bottles.

"I didn't know we were going somewhere fancy," I

said. "I feel underdressed." My Converse sneakers and Target blue jeans were just as unfashionable last night as they were now.

"Oh, it's cool, it's just a little gastropub I like out here. You're fine!"

She ordered us drinks with ingredients like "hibiscus" and "jalapeño infused mescal" that sounded like they belonged in a salad, and I did a quick Google search for "gastropub" on my phone. *A bar that specializes in serving high quality food* was the definition. I don't get it. Doesn't that just make it a restaurant? I nodded, smiled, played along, and pretended this was all very routine for me, to drink alcohol with plants in it and sit in leather chairs in "gastropubs." The drink sure was delicious, though.

"So, did you go and see Sandy today?" I asked.

"Who?"

"My boss! You had said you were going to meet with her."

"Oh, right! Actually I stopped back there and the store was closed! Are you guys closed Sundays?"

"Ha! No? We're never supposed to be closed. But it's just me and Sandy on staff right now so—maybe she had to go somewhere. I try not to think about the store when I'm not there," I said. That was strange that Sandy wasn't around. I wondered where she went. Since she was my boss and I was not hers, I guess it literally wasn't my business.

"So, did you do anything else?" I felt like I was pestering her, but I didn't really know what else to say and I did genuinely want to know what she was working on.

"I stopped at the Hustler store downtown; they were doing a workshop today and used a lot of our products, so I had to make sure they were being used properly, you know what I mean?"

"I don't, actually. What do you mean by a workshop?"

"This pretty well-known sex educator—she goes by the name of Dr. Erica—she had a couples' workshop in the store today mostly targeted toward married people who just don't know how to have sex anymore. She shows them different toys and how to use them, plus demonstrated new positions on this giant foam thing. Her classes are really informative! She's written several sex therapy books, and does a ton of lectures."

I had no idea there were so many kinds of people out there who made their living with dildos and orgasms. So crazy! I'd never considered the educational side before, but it made a lot of sense that there would be sex classes.

"That's interesting! I never heard of her. Do people actually show up for that?"

"Oh yeah, there were about seventy-five people there. Her newest book had a few chapters on introducing BDSM play to your relationship, so I did some demonstrations on people with our floggers, cuffs, and hog-ties. It works out well! It's like a cross promotion with her book and the Hustler store."

"So you stood in the middle of the store and whipped people?" I laughed.

"Well, I showed people how to whip their partners properly if that's what they were into," she explained.

"That's so interesting. I wish I could get a famous sex author to come to our store to talk to anyone about anything. It's usually just a bunch of horny old men looking to jerk off. That and drunk people. We sure do get a lot of those at 4:00 A.M.!" I replied.

"Yeah, but the fact that you're in one of the last few remaining shops outside the adult use zoning jurisdiction is pretty cool. You gotta keep that going."

"What do you mean?"

"I mean, like, it's great that people get to come to an upscale shop like Hustler and talk about sex, but people can actually have sex in your shop. There's not a lot of those left."

"Yeah, I don't really know much about it but I know Sandy is grandfathered into some old law because of the lease. But when I'm cleaning up semen on the floor at 6:00 A.M., it doesn't exactly feel like much of a privilege!" I said.

"As someone who definitely doesn't like semen, or cleaning for that matter . . . I'm telling you, it is."

We both laughed. A waiter came and delivered a very large plate of French fries that looked more like baked potatoes cut into slices, with various colored sauces. Amanda ate one, multi-dipping into every sauce cup. I would have feigned disgust if she didn't look so goddamn sexy dipping that fry.

"They really have the best fries here," she said. "Try one!" She dipped one into the red sauce, which looked the most basic out of all the sauces. She probably assumed I was a standard ketchup-and-French-fries person, which was accurate. She reached over the table, slid the French fry in my mouth, and gave me a kiss to seal it in. The sauce was tomato-based, but more than ketchup; it was spicy, and vibrant, various flavors that I couldn't name melding into a unique whole, much like the kiss Amanda left on my lips. The combination left me ravenous.

"Come over here!" she said. She signaled me to sit on

the same side of the table as her, and I obliged without hesitation. I wanted to be closer to her. And to the fries, of course.

"You know, you could probably do your own kind of workshop at the store. If your boss isn't even there half the time, I'm sure she wouldn't care," Amanda said.

"What do you mean?"

"Like, if you just put the word out that couples and single women, or whoever, could come play with each other in the store, you would get a ton of people in there and probably sell a whole bunch of products. I bet a lot of people in the area just don't know what you really have going on in there."

"Or a lot of people in the area know *exactly* what we have going on and that's why they stay away!" I answered.

"Well, you have the foundation there because of the store's incredible position. Some younger blood like you could really change things up if you tried."

She had a point. If our store really was in such a unique position, shouldn't we try to use that to our advantage?

"Okay, let's say I did do an event," I said. "Would you help me? I don't know what I'm doing!"

"Yeah, sure!" she said.

"How can you help if you don't even live here?" I asked.

"I have an unlimited data plan on my phone, and I am really good at using airplanes," she smiled.

Was she telling me she would come? Were we making future plans? I honestly couldn't really tell. She spoke in these very fragmented sentences, always hinting at things but never stating them. I felt both anxious and inspired at the same time.

"So really, you'll help me?" I asked. I wanted to latch

myself onto her like a koala bear to a tree and make her stay for a couple more days. Or weeks. Or years. I wasn't sure which one yet.

"Don't do this for me," she said, "do it for your store!"

I had worked at Dreamz for about two months now. The decision to work there was not much of a decision. It was the only place hiring that was less than a mile away from where I lived. I was, however, beginning to like it. I had known Amanda for about twelve hours, and I was smitten. Putting more effort into a part-time job logically made just as much sense as putting more effort into a twelve-hour lesbian relationship, when I never even identified as one. But logic doesn't always apply when you're still drunk off an orgasm.

"Why?" I said. "Maybe I want to do this for you." I pouted like a little doll. I think I was flirting? Not sure if I was doing it successfully.

"Well, don't," she sternly said, "but do it," she added, also sternly. I wish she would have shocked me with her fancy futuristic-looking electric wand while saying that.

"All right. Maybe I will." I grinned. She fed me another French fry, like I was a good dog who had properly followed a command and earned a treat. I think I subliminally just agreed to not have a crush on her and to care about my job more, and I wasn't quite sure how I felt about that. But I was under her spell, and I was high on hibiscus drinks, perfect fries, and stunning lips.

We kissed, and kissing in public felt very official to me. I had never been kissed at a fancy restaurant before. I know, Amanda doesn't consider this a fancy restaurant, and perhaps every restaurant in Los Angeles looked just like this one. Maybe there were spices and herbs on the

McDonald's burgers there, but I considered this quite fancy and I considered this a date.

After a few more courses of decadent burgers and a velvety dessert, she slyly slipped her credit card to the waiter. The check hadn't even come yet! How could she be so confident that she could take care of the bill without even seeing it? I tried to do the math in my head: between the drinks and the food, this meal definitely cost over $150. Maybe more than that. I can't remember how many plant cocktails I'd had. Was it two? Was it three? I was lost in a blur of lust and decadence. The waiter swiftly took her card and returned it hastily with a receipt. She signed the bill without even looking at it. I had no idea what to even offer to pay, since I had no idea what the bill cost. I was in a panic and at a loss for what proper lesbian date etiquette was.

"I got it, don't worry," she said. Apparently I was not subtle about my panic. She smiled at me, which calmed my current nerves, but a whole set of new ones were beginning to arise because I knew our date was coming to an end.

We stepped outside and she hailed two cabs, one for me and one for her. I don't know why we couldn't have shared a cab back to the hotel; my car was still there. Wasn't it on the way to where she was headed next? It must not be. Right? That had to have been the only reason to separate us, after such a lovely date. A few extra moments with her would have been nice. Of course, maybe it was better to just tear off this Band-Aid and say goodbye.

She kissed me outside, I slipped my hands underneath her suit jacket and felt the softness of her T-shirt. I loved the taste of her mouth, I loved the softness of her skin, and

I loved the feeling of her breasts pressed up against mine when she came close to me. It was a new feeling, but it felt like a complete natural extension of my sexuality.

"Bye, Taryn," she said as she opened her cab's door.

"You mean 'see you soon,' right?" I countered. I couldn't help it. Maybe I was coming off as needy, but I didn't want to let her go without knowing for sure whether I had a shot with her or if this day would become one lonely but cherished memory.

She winked at me. "Yes, see you soon." Then she slid into the cab. I watched the car carry her away, the end to our first, and hopefully not last, adventure.

I sat in the cab on the way back to my apartment, pinching myself. I couldn't believe the last tenty-four hours of my life had happened; sexual surreality clouded my mind.

It was 10:00 P.M. when I arrived at my home, and I had been awake for a mere five hours. I laid on my bed and couldn't stop smiling. I was a little bit drunk. I reached for my phone, but then realized that I shouldn't grab it; if I did, I'd want to call Amanda. It was much too soon to do that, right?

I drifted off and recounted the events of the night in my head. I thought about the way that thick dildo came from her crotch and penetrated my pussy so firmly. I wish I had done more. I should have tasted her more while she was next to me. I wish I could go back in time and do it again and do it longer. I was so lucky to have been ravaged by her just several hours ago. I touched my pussy and it wasn't nearly as good as the way she touched it; how did a stranger know my body better than I did? I thought of her face, her kiss, her suit, her tattoos, and my pussy got more and more moist. I spread my fingers around, rubbing myself, then penetrating myself deeply, yearning for her to come back and in dire need to cum again. I rubbed and flicked and went as far into my vagina as possible. I spread my lips open and I pushed on my throbbing clit, harder and harder, deeper and deeper. I closed my eyes and imagined her kiss, her thrust, found myself pulling my own hair and pushing myself against my own bed as far as I could. I reached a soft but intense climax, and suddenly felt relaxed. I put my fingers in my mouth and tasted my own juices, something I had never done before, but with my recent discovery of having a penchant for the taste of vagina, it felt appropriate. I still tasted like a tiny bar of soap that came individually wrapped from an elegant hotel. Remnants of the night were still existent and I didn't want it to end.

I knew I had to plan an event. For myself. Not for Amanda. Possibly with Amanda, but not for Amanda. No. Definitely not. This is all for the store. Of course.

Continue on with Taryn in this fantasy and turn to the next page.

It had been a little over twenty-four hours, and I still hadn't heard from Amanda.

I spent several hours attempting to craft the perfect, witty text message. It consisted of a lot of writing and deleting.

"I miss you more than those French fries."

No, that was too needy.

"How was your flight?"

Too generic.

"I wanted to talk to you about that class stuff! Lemme know when you have a sec."

Too annoying.

"Heeeeeeeey."

Too stupid.

"Thinking of you," with a naked photo attached. Maybe? If I took the right photo. That could potentially work. I tried it out—boob shots, from the hip up shots, pouty kissy faces. Nothing was working for me. I retook the photo multiple times and simply couldn't find the proper angle. I put makeup on, and then it looked too much like I put makeup on just for the sake of taking a photo. Which I did. Argh!

So, I gave up on that, and decided not to write her after all. She could be on another plane by now, or even with another woman already. It was exciting and so agonizing to crush over her. Our encounter was so brief, and I had been so sleep deprived, there was a sincere possibility that my whole tryst with her had just been some kind of hallucination.

But whether she was real or a sexy, imaginary hologram who gave an amazing orgasm, I did make a promise to her to create some kind of event in the store, because apparently having private ROOMZ that allow penetration is super unique. I loved the way Amanda referred to Dreamz in comparison to the other stores she visits as part of the "sex industry." Like my job was part of something bigger, and not just a minimum-wage thing that kept me nocturnal.

Amanda spoke about sex in this ultra-professional way. It was more than just an urge that needed to be fulfilled, it was a lifestyle. I wasn't sure how to get to that level of professional knowledge of sex without having anyone to have sex with. Well I possibly had one, but I wasn't sure when it would happen again.

I started searching on my laptop various keywords I remembered that Amanda had said, like "couples," "play," "BDSM," "sex education." I found Dr. Erica's books, the woman that Amanda told me about. I also came across some instructional pornographic videos, a genre of adult movies I had no idea existed. We didn't have any of these in our store.

Several of the scenes contained a striking blonde woman named Nina Hartley. In one of her videos, she had this giant inflatable pussy, and talked to the viewer about what areas to touch, and how to properly lick it. She explained all the different erogenous zones, moved her fingers around everywhere, and described what each different part of the vulva did and what kind of orgasms were achieved in the various zones. I felt like she was speaking directly to me, my own hot blonde teacher, ready to guide me toward an A in sexual exploration.

Then a mysterious, handsome man walked in the room and followed her instructions, licking her pussy in all the proper zones until she came in his mouth. Then, she instructed the viewer on how to properly suck the man's giant, rock-hard penis, using a corkscrew motion with her hands, with lots of spit from her mouth, licking the balls and the shaft and using a balance of tongue and hand. Then she gave him a blow job very matter-of-factly and professionally, following all of her own instructions.

Next, three other women randomly came into the room, joined in, got naked instantly, and took turns on the man's penis. They all looked so happy, horny, and confident, switching back and forth from cock to pussy, knowing exactly what to do with both of them. It was admirable! I guess the instructions were over at this point in the film and it was the time for couples watching it to practice what they learned. If I ever had a penis or a pussy in front of me again, I now had some new things to do with them.

I continued my research, which is an odd term for looking at porn, but I've heard worse euphemisms. I typed in my zip code along with a bunch of other sexual terms, I clicked on link after link, exploring possible event topics. Bondage? No, I feel like someone could get hurt if I tried to tie them up with too little experience. Erotic massage? Nah, then I'd need to find a bunch of beds, and those wouldn't fit in the store, even if I moved all the shelves. There were so many choices out there, but none of them seemed good enough. Ugh! There had to be a perfect event for me to host!

Soon, I found myself on a Tampa "Lifestyles" website, which I shortly learned was another name for swingers (married couples who have sex with other people). There was a very active message board, with photos of various couples, girls and guys, listing what type of sex they wanted to have. Some of the couples were younger, some were older, one had a photo completely clothed, decked out in hiking gear, in front of a Jeep with mountain bikes and boating equipment strapped to the top. One couple had bars over their eyes in the photo, and were decked out in leather gear with studs all over it. One couple was at what looked like a kid's birthday party, with pastel Mylar balloons, picnic tables, and cake in the background (without any actual kids showing in the shot).

This was just so intriguing and arousing, honestly. To think of all these random couples in the area looking to fuck strangers? To think of parents that took a moment at a birthday party to snap a photo that put them in the market to find a third person to engage in role-playing with—I had no idea this happened. I thought I was so subversive because I was a registered member of the Green party, and I wore black nail polish, and didn't listen to pop music on the radio. But it turns out there were "regular" grownups right near me doing way more exciting things than I was. I sure hope I didn't find my parents on here.

Is this what Amanda meant when she said I could find couples who wanted to play in the store? Where did these people usually go and why weren't they already coming to Dreamz? Did we have a reputation that only solicited the sexually depraved? Did we even have a reputation at all? If we did, it was time to change it. Dreamz needed to be the go-to place for the sexually curious in Florida, and my event—whatever it will turn out to be—was going to make it the hot spot it deserved to be!

For Taryn to host a porn star event in the store, turn to page 137.

For Taryn to host about a swinger party in the store, turn to page 154.

I was back to work a few nights later. There was still no word from Amanda. I'd been ghosted by guys before, hooking up with a few of them, then never hearing from them again, but I couldn't have possibly imagined that Amanda would do that to me. Just goes to show, women can be just as cruel as men, which my gender-equality brain can't decide is a good thing (*yay, equal gender acts!*) or a bad thing (*but—I'm heartbroken*).

It was 8:00 P.M. and I was ready for another ten hours of slinging dildos, recommending lube, renting jerk-off rooms, and anything and everything in between. Part of me kept thinking about possible events to do and part of me was too hurt to even think about it. I wanted to take Amanda's stupid electrical wand and stick it inside my heart. Maybe that would numb the pain. I couldn't even go near the strap-on selection in the store; every time I walked by it my eyes welled up with tears. I was an embarrassing mess. If Amanda saw me like this, she would never speak to me again. But since it didn't look like she was ever going to speak to me again anyway, I may as well just keep wallowing in a sea of leather holsters and suction Cyberskin.

A few customers came in. I was being really snippy with them; I didn't mean to, but my sour mood was controlling even my professionalism. A young couple about my age came in holding hands—the girl had cute freckles and red hair, the guy was tall and skinny, wearing corduroy pants and a striped top. They politely asked me to recommend the perfect adult movie for them to watch. I curtly interrupted their excitement for each other and replied that porn movies were mostly meant for men to watch alone and this was a pointless endeavor. The couple slunk away, but not before the guy whispered "bitch" under his breath, like it was *my* fault. It wasn't my fault! How *dare* people come in my store and be infatuated with one another in front of me. They had no right! I was in an environment specifically meant to satisfy the sexual voids in people's lives and nothing here was doing it for me. I really just wanted to go home and obsessively refresh the incoming text message screen on my iPhone.

Sometime around 10:00 P.M. an extremely large man came into the store. He wore a T-shirt that said "Fantasies" on it, with a stripper pole and a trucker silhouette of a busty girl with long hair. He looked around the store frantically.

"Is Sandy here?" he asked. "I tried calling her and she didn't pick up."

"No, she's not here. She worked earlier today. She might be asleep by now. Can I help you?" Was this one of Sandy's boy toys? The mental image of Sandy and this obese man engaging in sexual contact was too much for my already weak mental state at the moment. However, I did my best to feign a smile, since he was either some kind of acquaintance or perhaps even a lover of my boss.

"I got this porn star doing a feature show at my club. We're having electrical problems, and the music won't play. The club is packed with people, I need somewhere to put them—you guys have rooms here with a pole in it right?"

"Um, we do, but I don't know if I can just give them to you. Have you done this sort of thing before? What's your club?" I asked.

"Fantasies—it's a gentleman's club down the road. I've known Sandy for years. We go way back. I'll split the entrance fee with the store and I'll bus all the customers over here."

"Um, I'll say okay for now and try to get a hold of Sandy. If she says no, you guys will have to leave; is that all right? Do you want to see the room first?" I asked.

"Can I fit about 150 people in there?" he asked.

"No. Not even close, but I can open up the door maybe and people can kinda spill out in the hallway?"

He picked up his cell phone, a Motorola flip phone. I can't believe those things still worked with any current phone plan. His palms were sweating and he had a bit of trouble holding on to it. He swiftly but carefully dialed a contact.

"Hey—I'm at Dreamz. Just bring the feature over here and she can start getting ready . . . Oh, I don't know." He put his hand on the phone and looked up at me.

"Do you guys have a dressing room?"

"I mean, we have a bathroom, but that's it," I answered.

"Is that the only bathroom?"

"Yes. It is, but I just peed, so I should be fine a while."

He grumbled and didn't seem to like my answer or care about my bladder's schedule.

"We also have other smaller rooms—who needs a dressing room? Is this for you?" Was he going to change out of his sweatpants and strip-club T-shirt, and into some kind of superhero outfit?

He then yelled into his phone, "Yeah, they got rooms."

He listened to the voice on the other end of the phone then looked back up at me, incredibly annoyed.

"Does it have an outlet?" he asked.

"Yes, it does. I can unplug the TV!" I said. "Or, I might actually have a power strip somewhere."

"Yes, there's a fucking outlet. Is that good enough for her?" he yelled back into the phone. I have to admit this stress that just came over the store was kind of exciting and keeping my mind away from the lack of activity on my cell phone. "Bring the feature over so she can get ready. Feed everyone some free booze in the meantime so we don't lose them." He hung up.

"So, what's going to happen exactly?" I asked.

"The store is gonna be packed! Don't worry about it. I got some of my security guys who will help you out. Sandy can thank me for this later," he said, not really answering my question at all. I was still equally as confused, if not more. But I was anxious and excited to see what would happen.

"All right!" I nodded in agreement. Seemed like this was happening regardless of whether I consented to it or not.

About fifteen minutes later, a short girl with pink and black hair and a multitude of tattoos came into the store, escorted by another guy in sweatpants and the same strip-club T-shirt, but this guy was a lot smaller than the prior one.

The guy ran frantically right up to me while the pink-haired girl was engrossed in her cell phone and didn't look up. "Dennis said he talked to you? Where can we get her set up?"

"Hey! Yes . . . yes . . . um . . . lemme show you guys the uh, dressing room."

I grabbed the key and walked them both to one of our smaller ROOMZ. The guy was holding a giant suitcase, the girl was holding nothing but her cell phone that she didn't look up from at all. I unlocked the door.

"Does this work for you?" the guy said to the woman, though she still wouldn't look away from her screen.

"Yeah, I guess. Whatever. Where am I even dancing?" the girl asked.

"Where's the room with the pole?" the guy turned to me and asked.

"Right this way," I said. I took them down the hallway and opened our biggest room, the one with the stripper pole in it. It could comfortably fit enough people to have a proper late-night raver orgy but I wasn't so sure that it was big enough for what they were looking for.

"Are you kidding me? I have to dance in *here*?" The girl looked at me, I guess expecting me to tell her it was all a joke and that there was some kind of incredible stage elsewhere built just for her performance.

I could see why these security guys were stressed out; this headliner was a piece of work! I looked to the security escort for a clue about what to do next, but the sweatpants guy was on his cell phone yelling at various people about confusing logistics. I addressed the woman instead.

"I mean, I was asked to bring you to the room with the pole. I don't exactly know what you're supposed to be doing. I'm Taryn, by the way! What's your name?"

She glared at me. "Joanna," she said. "Joanna ANGEL." Her emphasis on *angel* was fierce and comical, as if stating her last name would help me remember who she was.

"Do you work at, um, Fantasies?"

"I'm a FEATURE," she answered.

What the fuck was a feature? I didn't know people could be features. I thought it was a noun that described some kind of a column in a magazine, or a verb that implied something was an attribute. Like: *This room features a box of fine tissues, a television, and a stripper pole.*

I stared at her blankly without a reply. She scoffed and rolled her eyes.

"I'm a porn star and I get hired to dance at strip clubs around the country as a *featured* performer. I'm not like a house dancer at a strip club," she firmly stated. And then she buried herself back in her cell phone. I had no idea that there was a hierarchy of strippers.

"That's so cool! Congratulations!" I replied. "Well, let me know if I can get you anything."

"Yeah—a bottle of water, please," she said. "Oh, and here's my bio and my songs. Please hand this to whoever is in charge of the music." She handed me a typed up sheet of credits for herself that read a handful of things like "AVN Hall of Fame," "winner of over 40 AVN awards," "Owner of BurningAngel Entertainment," and "First Tattooed Centerfold of *Hustler* magazine." I had no idea what to do with this—did she just want me to know more about her? Was I supposed to memorize this so I wouldn't forget? She also handed me a flash drive. I was utterly confused, though under the context I guessed that the flash drive must be full of the music she planned on dancing to.

"Great, I'll just . . . get this plugged into the speakers then."

"Uh-huh, thanks." She snapped her phone off, sighing,

huffing, and puffing loudly as she opened up her giant suitcase. I couldn't help but peek inside: it seemed to be filled with sparkly outfits, large patent-leather boots, and multiple cosmetic bags. She pulled out a giant, plastic makeup case with skulls all over it and began putting various powders and creams all over her face. I had no idea what I was to do here but I enjoyed the challenge, and whatever it was that I had to do here I was going to execute it as best as I possibly could.

I walked out of the room, leaving Joanna to change in peace, and headed past the sweatpants guy, with the piece of paper and the flash drive crammed into my hand. He was still on the phone yelling about outlets and electricity and entrance fees and a barrage of other things. He looked up at me as I passed him.

"Oh, great, you're taking care of her music? Thanks so much!" he said. I nodded and smiled. I guess I inadvertently accepted the challenge.

So I pieced together the fragments of information I received this evening and deduced that this store and this room was going to turn into a strip club. This pink-haired girl was a porn star, and she did some kind of special show that required special music that was on this flash drive. We did have a speaker in the store, and I had a laptop in my backpack. I was sure I could get creative and figure out how to make something work.

As I finagled with the sound system, trying to find the best way to get the music files from the flash drive out through the store speakers, the place began to fill up with lots and lots of people; I hadn't realized they were letting anyone in yet! I wish I'd had time to move some of the shelves out of the way.

The crowd was as varied as they come, though not in terms of gender. It was mostly men, but a wild selection: some looked like bikers, covered in leather jackets with cycle gang insignias on the backs, while others looked like hipsters, covered in plaid and knitted beanies. There were frat-looking guys; nerdy guys in graphic tees. A handful of couples came in as well. The only thing that really brought everyone together, from what I could see, were their tattoos. Everyone had tattoos! Big ones, small ones, colored and black and white, animals of all kinds, and artsy renderings all showed up on the customers' skin. I wondered if people with tattoos really preferred to see tattooed people in their porn. At least some of them did, right? The hoard of people all meandered around the store, exploring the products, but looking incredibly confused. It was completely chaotic. There was an impromptu doorman who set up a chair in the entrance of the store and was charging people to get in. Was that legal at all? He also coincidentally (or not?) had sweatpants and the same "Fantasies" T-shirt on as the others. Was I going to be rewarded with this official wardrobe as well, if I completed my job?

The original man who came to the store—the alleged friend of Sandy—took it upon himself to just climb up on top of the front counter to make an announcement. I was desperately afraid of it breaking, and watched him nervously.

"Sorry about the confusing space, everyone! Don't worry, Joanna will be doing her special LIVE SHOW in about fifteen minutes! Follow Dennis," he pointed at the second sweatpants guy, "he will show you where she will be performing." The store full of people clapped and cheered. Some of them had open containers of alcohol. In unison they all repeatedly chanted "JO-ANN-A" in three equal syllables.

There was definitely a severe lack of communication among the various men in the sweatpants. Every time I asked any of them a question they went to yell at someone or something on their cell phone. I went to the storage room in the back and pulled out my laptop. I plugged the flash drive in and downloaded the songs onto my computer. There was a mix of Slayer, Metallica, Mötley Crüe, and then a slew of other bands I'd never heard of that loaded up images of black albums with complicated dark script titles, and hand-drawn pictures of burning churches and upside down crosses. I guessed it would be kind of a dark show.

When all of the files had transferred, I brought the laptop over to the speaker system behind the counter. There were a ton of wires in the back of it and there appeared to be a USB port. I took an old spare Android phone charger that Sandy kept in the store, I dismantled the cord from the square thing, and attached it from my laptop to the speaker. I crossed my fingers and pushed play; loud, brash metal music started filling the front of the store, eliciting cheers from the patrons who hadn't gone to the stage yet. Success! It worked.

I asked the least busy-looking sweatpants man to carry the speaker and my laptop into the stripper pole room. The room was awkwardly packed with a bunch of people waiting around with no music on at all. They seemed pretty restless. He found a proper corner to put it in, on the table that displayed the lube and the tissues. It seemed good enough.

I rushed to return to the "dressing room." Shit. I completely forgot about getting Joanna a water. I didn't want to go back in there without it. I ran back to the register and grabbed a bottle of water I happened to have in my purse. I had drunk only a few sips out of it. It was better than nothing.

I ran back to the "dressing room." Though the door was closed, I knocked. Joanna opened the door, looking like a completely different character than the short girl who entered the store in leggings and a cut-up T-shirt. She was in a black latex nurse costume, with glittery red eyeshadow and lipstick. She had a stethoscope and a giant syringe that glowed in the dark, and she towered over me in incredibly high stiletto boots.

"Hey!" I said. "Is, um, everything okay?" I asked. "I got you a water!" I slyly pretended to open the bottle of water for her before I handed it over, even though it had already been opened. I turned an embarrassment into an act of magnificent chivalry.

"Thanks so much!" She took a sip. "Did you give my music to the DJ?"

"I think I'm the DJ, actually. But, I got it!" Joanna seemed annoyed, but she smiled.

"A cute, young, girl DJ—that's a first for me!" She giggled. Then she frantically looked through her suitcase, throwing numerous thongs, open-toed, hot pink shoes, school-girl outfits, and other things across the room. "Shit," she said. "I forgot my lotion at the other club!"

It was humorous the way she said "other" club, implying that this was also a club. But if that's what she needed to believe to keep going that was fine. She handed me a squirt bottle that looked something like a ketchup dispenser from a 1950s diner.

"Can you fill this up with half water and half lotion please? And hand it to me on my last song." She flipped her head upside down and sprayed it with hair spray; some of it burned my eye, as I stood in the corner holding her squirt bottle.

"Yeah, got it, sure," I said. I admittedly enjoyed being bossed around by a latex nurse.

I ran back to the store area, looking for something reminiscent of lotion. I could have sworn we had some, though I was having a hard time finding anything but lube and massage oil. In the small bachelorette party section of the shop, we did in fact have some kind of shaving cream that was called "Coochie Creme" that several women swore was a wonderful cream that left them with no razor burn in their bikini area. I guess that would have to do. The cream was rather expensive, close to $20 a bottle, but I justified the cost; 100+ people were, albeit illegally, paying to get into the store that would make up for the loss of any products we had to use. I took it into the bathroom, dumped it out into the squirt bottle, and mixed it with water. I had no idea what this science experiment would amount to and what it had to do with being a nurse but I was excited to find out. There was no time to waste! I ran back to the stripper room, pushed through the crowd, and headed straight to the corner. A sweatpants guy was guarding the speaker and the laptop. He had some kind of headset/earpiece on and he spoke into it: "Bring her out, we're ready," and he looked at me and nodded. I assumed this was the go ahead to play the music, so I plugged the laptop into the speaker and hit play.

The first song on her mix was titled "Bio Music," an in-your-face instrumental song. It filled the room like a fog, setting the stage for a sexy evening. I suddenly remembered that piece of paper with her credits she had called a bio. I had it stuffed in my pocket. I pulled it out, I looked at the screaming crowd stuffed into this room, and I looked at the sheet of paper and I listened to the guitar instrumental blasting through the speaker. Okay, maybe it wasn't exactly blasting because the speaker really wasn't powerful enough for this, but I could still hear it.

When I jumped up onto the platform where the stripper pole was, everyone quieted down.

"Hello everyone! Welcome to the—" I paused, "Joanna Angel special feature stripper show!"

Everyone cheered.

"She, um, she's an AVN Hall of Fame person. She is a porn star. She is the owner of BurningAngel Entertainment. She was the first tattooed centerfold of *Hustler* magazine. . ." I continued to go through the list of accolades and I read them off in my best impression of an announcer voice. I sounded ridiculous but the crowd was so restless and rowdy no one seemed to care. One of the sweatpants men looked at me and gave me a thumbs up.

I was just about finished with the list when Joanna entered the room. The room filled with cheers and applause. She was escorted in by the original sweatpants man who first came into the store; she jumped up on the platform with ease, shaking her ass to the loud metal music. I sincerely hoped my laptop wouldn't run out of batteries before the music ended because I didn't bring my charger to work.

She held onto the pole like it was the love of her

life, twirling around it, holding herself against it, doing anything she could to please it and earn its affection. People threw dollar bills at her. The sweatpants guy picked them up as they fell to the floor. She smiled at the men in the audience and seductively licked her teeth; this was for them, but also for herself. Her task was her ego, and it wasn't complete until every brain in that room lit up with desire for her and only her, until all of their dicks saluted her in ultimate devotion. She head-banged to the music, using the heavy beats as an excuse for exaggerated movement, but that alone wouldn't hold the attention she needed. Slowly she began to peel off the stretchy dress she had on, revealing her bare body inch by inch. The collective eyes below followed each pulled-back layer as it rolled down her breasts, her chests, her hips. Finally, she threw aside the dress like a shed skin, showing off a sparkly bikini top and matching thong. She had perky, natural breasts; you could see the smooth tops of them almost spilling out of the bikini top, luring people in, screaming *you there, yes you, I know you want to touch me*. She bounced them up and down to the beat of the music, which was impressive because the music had a ridiculously fast tempo. I had known several men in my life pretty intimately, and I never knew what they jerked off to—yet here were a bunch of strangers who practically admitted that she got them off. It was fascinating how much of themselves they would reveal in exchange for live boobs and naked skin. It was almost as if everyone in the room was stripping.

She undid the elastic in the back of her bikini top and she motioned for the crowd to yell louder if they wanted to see her top off. She wasn't saying anything but she conveyed that message pretty clearly. One of the sweat-pants men stepped up to the plate to be her interpreter.

"If you wanna see Joanna take her fucking tits out, make some noise!"

The crowd roared, almost drowning out the music. Joanna jumped around and motioned for people to get louder and louder. She aggressively threw her top off and it dropped to the ground, like it was a jailor who'd been keeping her breasts locked away from the rest of the world and she'd finally gotten their freedom and vengeance. I saw one of her fans try to run and grab the top, but I rushed over and intercepted him and saved the bikini top! Joanna looked directly at me and mouthed *thank you*. I smiled. I felt like I was uh, doing my job, whatever that was tonight.

The song switched, a more rock-type beat filling the room now. Joanna climbed to the top of the pole (her upper body strength must be incredible) and flipped upside down. She made a shocked, open-mouthed face, like she was saying, *Oh my, how did I get up here, and what will I do now?* But then she smiled, affirming her seductive control, and kicked her legs up even higher above her head. Using her feet and hips, she started to wiggle to the beat and grabbed the edge of her panties, slowly and deliberately sliding them off while suspended from the pole, flinging them off with a flourish. I instinctively knew to follow the panties' airborne path and I grabbed them before anyone else could. If her bra was almost stolen, I could only imagine what could happen to these panties (and from having a vague knowledge of shiny panties from my brief stint of working here, these were not cheap panties).

Joanna was still hanging out at the top of the pole

upside down, now completely naked. She took her one free hand and used it to rub her pussy. People cheered, as much for the act as it was for the release they felt at finally seeing her body. Hooray for upside-down masturbating here at Dreamz!

The rock song winded down, and the third and final song came on the speakers: a sensual metal ballad. Joanna shimmied down the pole, and she stuck her hand in her mouth and drooled all over her tits. She looked over at me and I remembered that I was supposed to hand her the lotion. I grabbed the bottle and handed it up to her, making slight contact with her hand. She winked at me, then turned and went to the middle of the stage. She reached her arms up, like a conductor signaling the big crescendo. Then she dropped to the ground, put her whole fist in her mouth, felt herself up and down aggressively, and then she grabbed the bottle of lotion and squirted it all over herself. I get it now. In the dark lighting it looked a lot like a bucket of cum was raining down on her, a collective finishing visual for the masses.

She let the lotion linger on her body, moving her torso so the light illuminated the cream. She rubbed it into her body, spreading lotion all over her tits, her stomach, her thighs, her ass. She rubbed it in, apparent ecstasy on her face, and she even let a few select members from the crowd help, showing them how to use their full hand to uniformly spread the substance. Eventually, she shooed the rubbers away, and slowly lowered herself off the stage. Then she walked around, showing off her shiny nakedness and demonstrated to the crowd the scientific fact that if you stuck a dollar bill to her greasy body, it would stick. People surrounded her and stuck dollar bills to her. She cheered and smiled, parading around and enticing more and more dollars to be put on her skin; she quickly became an animal, with cash for fur. Once her body was completely covered, she walked over to the security guy and shook the dollars off into the collection bag that he held open for her. But she wasn't done yet; there was still a bit of lotion in the bottle. She grabbed it, leaned forward against the stage, opened up her ass cheeks and squirted the remainder of the lotion directly into her asshole. A big fan—meaning, he was large in size and was also a very enthusiastic admirer of hers, it seemed—ran up and stuck a hundred-dollar bill right in there. She turned, a playful, shocked look on her face, then threw her arms around his neck and gave him a passionate, very wet kiss. The crowd went absolutely nuts, and it made sense—that was a whole lot of ass money!

The music faded out, leaving the room feeling a little empty, but the audience still cheered for Joanna. She took a large bow, droplets of lotion falling off her body, blew a kiss to everyone, and was rushed back to her makeshift dressing room by the heroic men in sweatpants.

I immediately took my laptop that literally had about one percent battery left in it and returned it to my backpack that was in the storage room of the store. My mind was still on the dancing; I can't believe we pulled that off; I can't believe *I* did! I couldn't wait to see how much we made off the show. I imagined handing a cool bag full of cash to Sandy, saying, "Yeah, we had a porn star dance in here while you were gone; it's no big deal, really." In my mind she was thrilled about it; I hope real life was as kind. As my thoughts raced, I checked my phone. I suddenly snapped back to reality.

On my screen was a text notification from Amanda.

Wow. I hadn't thought about her at all during the event chaos. Even though an event in the store was technically her idea, this one fell so suddenly into my lap that I didn't even realize I was doing what she had suggested. That is, until now. I opened the text, half-excited to hear from her, half-annoyed that I'd done exactly what she wanted me to do without her even being here. I opened her text:

"Holy shit, is Joanna Angel at your fucking store right now? I just saw something on her Facebook page."

"Yeah," I answered. "You told me to do an event and I did."

"I'm impressed! That was fast."

"Yeah, well, I didn't do it for you ;)" I answered. I saw a bunch of blue dots appear and disappear in the little circular bar at the bottom of my phone. That implied that she was trying to think of what to say but didn't know what to say. Holy shit! I couldn't believe it. The ball was currently in my court and I was going to leave it there by playing the same game she played with me and not responding. Or maybe I would, in just a little bit. At the moment, I had some expensive panties to return to its rightful owner.

To go back and see Taryn host a swingers party in the store, turn to page 154.

Continue with Taryn in this fantasy, turn to page 157.

I signed up for a login for the "Tampa Lifestyles" message board and several minutes later I was approved. I officially gave myself a promotion and made myself the events coordinator of Dreamz. Events (plural) was probably a bit presumptuous because technically, I was only planning one event, but no one else needed to know that.

I picked a date, a few weeks from today, and made an official thread on the message board. "Dreamz Come True—April 23" I posted as the title.

"Come and play at Dreamz! Lingerie, toys, lube, XXX movies, private rooms, and more. Meet new people and have some fun! Drinks and refreshments will be provided, no entry fee. 9:00 P.M. – midnight." With slight hesitation, I posted the note. I had no idea what the response would be. I could always delete the post if several days went by and no one replied; I could swipe this from the internet like it never existed with a click of a button.

Amanda are you proud of me? I did it! I did something. Now come and bend me over in my bed and put one of your various dildos inside me while you kiss my lips. Please? I did my homework. I think.

And just then, my phone buzzed. It was on the other side of my bed since I was legitimately engrossed in my own research instead of waiting for the phone to ring. My distraction led to an interaction. Did I successfully play hard to get by not texting? If so, great, but I couldn't keep it up any longer. I dove across the bed to retrieve my prize.

My phone blared its notification: 1 New Text Message, from Amanda. I opened it.

"Just saying hi. ;)"

My stomach turned, and my hands shook. I wanted to scream. What did this mean? I felt so giddy. I—I had to respond. I had to tell her how much I missed her, how I could still feel her body on mine, how she quickly became the driving forces of my ultimate fantasies. Wait. No.

I had to tell her about the event.

I took a screenshot of my posting, and sent it to her as my response. I eagerly awaited for a reply. I saw those little dots appear and reappear on my iPhone screen. Was she just as nervous as I was? She seemed to be thinking carefully about what to say. I eagerly awaited for the dots to turn into words.

"Damn! You did it!!!!!!" Along with several "clap your hands" emojis. She was proud of me!

"You didn't think I would?" I replied.

"Honestly? No. I didn't," along with the emoji that has its eyes staring up. You know, the one that looked like it just got away with murder.

"You said you would come help me! I don't know what the fuck I'm doing." I texted back.

"I know! I'll be there," with another happy face. But not an emoji. Like an old school manual with a semicolon and a parenthesis. Which doesn't show nearly as much emotion as the emoji.

"I miss you," I typed. My fingers moved faster than my brain.

The dots appeared and disappeared several times and there was no response. Ten minutes went by. Twenty minutes went by. Thirty minutes went by. Ugh. It was like a dagger in my gut. Maybe, her phone died. Maybe she was in a different time zone. Or maybe she didn't miss me at all.

To continue to the swinger party, turn to page 169.

Joanna was wiping herself off with a towel that I knew once lived inside the bathroom here. I wasn't entirely sure how clean it was or how it wound up here, but I wasn't going to ask. There was a bottle of vodka being passed around between her and some of the Fantasies people. They looked relieved; I felt a certain kinship with them. They seemed proud of my on-the-fly DJ skills. One of them handed me the vodka bottle and I took a swig of it. I handed Joanna her bra and panties.

"Here you go—you don't want to forget these!" I said.

"Thank you so much for all your help. Everything went great! I can't believe we all pulled this off!" she laughed. One of the Fantasies men was lounging on the couch, counting sticky dollar bills and putting them into piles.

"What was your name, again?" Joanna asked me.

"It's Taryn!"

"Well, Taryn, I have had professional DJs who have been doing this for years fuck up my music, and you got it perfectly. Thank you."

"It was good music! I think I'll keep it on my laptop and listen to it sometime. I mean, I could use a break from listening to Neutral Milk Hotel, all their songs start to sound the same after a while," I nervously laughed.

"I used to listen to them when I was in college," Joanna said. "They're still around?"

"You went to college?" I asked. Shit. Why did I say

that? I mean, I went to college, too, and here I was picking up panties from the floor.

"Yeah, I mean, where else would I learn that lotion mixed with water looks perfectly like jizz?" she laughed.

"You are totally right, I'm sorry," I answered.

She held up her hand in a forget-about-it manner. She was sitting on the couch completely naked, with her pussy and tits hanging out. I couldn't help but look at her. I felt privileged to be allowed in this green room, even though they were technically at my work, and I was the only one who had the key to the room we were in.

"How long have you been working here for?" Joanna asked.

"Just a couple weeks."

"Do you like it?"

"Ah, well, I like it when people randomly barge in here and turn it into a strip club!" I laughed. "But that doesn't happen often. Or, like, ever," I said.

"Do people really use these rooms to fuck in?"

"Yeah! They really do!"

"Well, that's pretty cool!" she said. "Did you ever get to fuck in here yourself?" she laughed and said, as she swigged another gulp of vodka (I really couldn't tell if she was an old-looking 25-year-old or a young-looking 45-year-old. I felt it was probably better not to ask). The men in sweatpants rolled their eyeballs; one of them started laughing.

"Here we go again," one of them said.

"Oh, shut up!" Joanna yelled.

"What?" I asked. "Am I missing something?"

"You wanna be in one of her movies?" one of the guys asked.

"What?!"

Joanna leaned in close to me; I could still smell the lotion on her skin. She looked directly into my eyes, fire flowing through her pupils. I wasn't sure if she was trying to seduce me or eat me.

"I have this 'on the road' series, where I film sex scenes with random people when I travel. If you wanna do it, I can give you $700 and it will only take about 20 minutes," Joanna said.

Seduce me, it is!

I had read articles about sleazy pornographers who tried to get innocent girls into the porn industry. But I never thought that sleazy pornographers could be so attractive and charming and female, and I also guess I was not all that innocent since I was in an adult video store at midnight, and planned on being here for the next six hours.

"So you get to, like, pick people you want to have sex with and pay them for their—time?"

"Yeah! Not a bad life, right? I basically bribe people into fucking me," she said with a large smile. "I mean, you're welcome to fuck me for fun, too. And I don't have to film it." She laughed. And then she grabbed me and started kissing me. She strongly smelled like scented lotion and money. All the men in sweatpants left the room. I hope they could watch over the store for me. I didn't know what the hell I was doing here, but I wanted to keep going.

I let myself think of Amanda for a split second, then pushed her to the back of my mind.

After a minute of making out, Joanna threw me down on the ground and lifted my little black dress up and over my head, throwing it across the room. She was aggressive, it seemed, and wasted no time at all getting what she wanted—my bra was next, not at all noticed by her swift hands except as a barrier between her hands and my breasts that she needed gone.

"Ohhhh, I love your little tits!" She looked from my boobs to me with these perfect fuck-me eyes. She arched her back and lifted her ass up in the air as she crawled up my legs. It was almost as though she was doing the same stripper moves she did out there, but on top of me, and I was ok at it. She was attractive but not in the classic or traditional sense. If you looked up pretty in the dictionary her picture wouldn't be there, but she truly became a completely different animal when anything sexual was going on. It's like she had a nympho button she could turn on and off, her fist could be in her mouth one minute and she could like, be reading the newspaper the next minute. I liked it.

She slapped my tits rather hard, leaving a giant red mark on them. It stung, the vibrations circling the bulk of my breasts until it faded into delightful tingly pleasure. I wanted her to do it again but I didn't know how to properly ask her to do that again.

"You like that?" she asked.

"Yeah, I do!" I answered quite honestly.

She slapped me harder, again and again, like a symphonic drum hitting my right and left boob, one after another. She squished my breasts together, leaned down, and licked them, lavishing them with soothing saliva; then suddenly, she bit me! Little nips perked up all over my breast, Joanna putting just the right amount of pressure and pain into her bites. This woman sure knew how to use her mouth! Then she sat up, grabbed the bottle of vodka and took a giant swig of it, laughing maniacally at me as she swallowed. What did I get myself into? I was petrified and excited for whatever came next.

She reached her hands down and slid them underneath my French-cut cotton panties. She briskly moved her fingers around, almost as if she lost her keys in her purse and was blindly looking for them. What was she doing? What was she searching for? Although, maybe it didn't matter, because her touch was incredible either way. Oh—yeah—that was it.

She found my clitoris—her eyes lit up like a jackpot sign—and rubbed it hard. I started to shake.

"There it is," she said. She continued to rub up and down and up and down, back and forth and back and forth. This was literally record time of anyone finding my clitoris—she found it faster than I could find it myself, sometimes!

She continued to kiss me, pulling away from my lips every so often to bite my neck and suck on it like a vampire (from her taste in music, I couldn't be sure she wasn't actually part vampire). She rubbed my clit harder and my legs began to tremble. She then got bored, I guess, of sucking on my neck because she suddenly pulled away, holding my chest to the ground, took her mouth and went down to my vagina. She replaced her fingers with her tongue, not wasting any time with kisses or teasing, licking faster and with more pressure than a lot of the things that vibrated here in the store. She licked and licked, she spit on my pussy and then continued to lick it. She sucked it hard, tonguing the inside of my lips and then finally my hole, fucking me like her tongue was a dick. It was so filthy and hot, and the more turned-on I got, the more she laughed.

She flipped me over, turning my body with ease like I was a sex pancake, browned on one side, raw on the other. She kept me pinned to the floor, my breasts squished against the hardwood. Not that I wanted to move anyway; I could feel her playing with my asscheeks, fondling them and spreading them apart. Then, an unexpected wetness was on my asshole—Joanna was licking it. So this is what an ass-licking felt like! Nerves I had no idea existed were suddenly highlighted to an extreme, sending an entire ocean of pleasure up my spine. She licked my asshole, she licked my clit from the back angle. She took her fingers and stuck them inside of me and continued to lick my completely unshaven asshole. I was so embarrassed thinking about it; the people she was with were probably completely hairless. But she didn't seem to care. She smacked my ass, and when I moaned loudly in reply, she smacked it harder.

"I'm going to make your ass match the color of my hair," she giggled and said. She should really use this line in a movie. It was a good one.

She went insane with the smacks on my ass, one strike after another. She put more fingers inside of me—how many could she fit in there? I was so wet, more than I'd ever been, it felt like. Admittedly, more wet than I was with Amanda. A third then a fourth finger went inside me, while she continued to suck on my clit. She curved her hand inside me. I don't know what the hell she did, but that was the spot. I found myself moaning uncontrollably.

"Are you cumming, you little bitch?" she asked. I softly moaned.

"I SAID, ARE YOU CUMMING?!"

I moaned louder.

She smacked me across the face, harder than any strike she'd given me this whole time, which was pretty fucking hard.

"SAY IT!" she commanded.

"Yes! I'm cumming!" I said. I screamed at the top of my lungs. I had never found myself screaming so loud during sex. This wasn't even sex, was it? This was just another event, a close up of intensive desire and beyond incredible pleasure. I should have let her film this.

I wondered if Amanda would have watched it.

I shook and trembled and I felt my pussy tense up on all her fingers. I was clenched so tight, I was worried I would snap her whole hand off.

"Good girl!" she said. "Good fucking girl! Keep cumming!"

Joanna shifted the position of her hand inside me and it felt like she found a whole new orgasm. My entire pussy loosened up, and she somehow found room to stick her thumb inside me; now all five of her fingers were inside my pussy. She went in and out and in and out incredibly fast. How were her long, acrylic nails not scratching my entire insides? I don't get it. She must have had some kind of magic vaginal protectant coating on them. I didn't get it. I suppose it was a special porn star secret I wasn't meant to know about. My body was tingling everywhere. There was a big rollercoaster inside of me and I was at the top about to come down. I had reached such an insane climax, I was shaking like crazy, and panting and moaning. Slowly the orgasm began to calm down, descending into a relaxing state. My pussy felt so swollen and amazing. She removed her hand from my vagina and it was covered in juices; they slightly resembled her lotion/water mixture. She put it in her mouth and licked it off her fingers.

"You taste so good," she said, and she continued to lick her hand until all the juices had been cleared into her mouth. Then she giggled and drank more vodka.

She grabbed a large dildo that was sitting on top of her suitcase. She turned a switch on the bottom of it and it started to glow, like an incredibly sexy light saber. What was she planning on doing with that? Was that for me? In the dark! She spit a large loogie of spit on it and then lay on the floor and spread her legs wide open. She stuck her hand in her mouth and gagged on it, then she stuck the dildo as far down her throat as she could and gagged on that as well. Her hand and dildo were sufficiently full of spit. Was I supposed to do anything here? I was still shaking from my giant orgasm. I felt limp. How could I take any more?

Joanna licked her hand again and rubbed the spit up and down the shaft of the dildo, a hand job with purpose. Then, without any other lubrication, she stuck the dildo in her ass. It went in with incredible ease. Very impressive! Though I noticed her pussy remained untouched. Did she really not want anything at all in there? Should I step in and assist? She had large, meaty lips, and a small but long landing strip.

"Come here and fuck my ass," she said. She seemed to be doing a pretty good job of that herself, the dildo moving in and out of her anus expertly, but I stepped in and did what I could. I didn't want to hurt her, though. I had never fucked anyone's ass before and I had zero experience with doing anything with glow-in-the-dark dildos, and didn't want to do it incorrectly. Like the former parts of our sex, she had no patience for hesitation.

"Harder!" she screamed. "Just destroy my fucking asshole, I don't care. Don't be a pussy!" Joanna yelled. Jeez! I was frightened, yet so turned-on.

I had to give this woman what she asked for, but for some extra safety precaution I grabbed a handful of lube that was conveniently placed on the table. She was a guest in my house, after all; I really didn't want her leaving with a torn asshole. I am guessing she has to use it quite regularly for her occupation. As the dildo came out, I hastily rubbed lube on the shaft. It became that much easier to fuck her with the glowing dildo. I mimicked what she did to me on my clit and tried to find hers. I rubbed her pussy with my fingers while I continued to fuck her ass with the glowing dick.

"Yes, yes, yes! Fuck me! Fuck me! YES!" she yelled, her legs spreading more and more open. The entire dildo was buried in her asshole. How did it all fit in there? She was so small! I couldn't get it any further than it was. I rubbed and rubbed and I just instinctively put my tongue on her pussy because I truly wanted to taste her. Her pussy tasted like peach lotion and dirty money. I would be lying if I said I didn't like it.

After several minutes of tasting, feeling, and deep dildo ass fucking, she made a very large vocal announcement to me that she was cumming. She trembled and kept repeating it over and over again. A final moan came from her lips, and then I felt everything relax. Did I really just make a porn star cum? That was so cool! I mean, the dildo did most of the work but I was still patting myself on the back.

"You're fun!" she said between deep breaths. This was the first time I saw her stop and sit for a moment, without doing anything else. We laid on the floor together, both in post-orgasm bliss. It didn't last too long; suddenly, as that's how she did most things, she was up, getting dressed, and packing up her stuff.

"So, you're a pretty amazing assistant. You cued up my music, you handed me my lotion at the right time, you saved my $70 thong, and you have a great-tasting pussy."

"Well, thank you!" I said. I truly was flattered. I had a lot of fun doing this. I could only imagine what this job would be like in a real strip club and not a room in the back of a porn store.

"I have to come back and dance in Orlando next weekend—just a few hours away. Wanna come help me?"

"Yeah!" I said, "I would love that!" I was sure I could work out the logistics with Sandy and work during the week instead of the weekend. I didn't want to pass this up.

Joanna quickly packed up her suitcase, putting all the garments of clothing on the floor into little Ziploc bags. She wiped herself off with some baby wipes, zipped up her large bag, and put on her leggings and T-shirt. She handed me a card.

"Text me—I'll give you all the details."

"All right!" I said.

"And hey—" I added, "maybe next weekend we can do that again, and, like, someone could film it. If you want."

"Fuck yes!" Joanna said. "Let's do it, girly! Wanna walk me out? I gotta get a cab to the airport," she said.

I threw my clothing back on, and Joanna and I walked out to the store with her giant suitcase. Several of her fans were there and I took photos of her and them. I called her a cab, kissed her good-bye, and watched my sex angel ride off into the sunset. Or sunrise, actually.

* * *

I went back into the store. The Fantasies guys did a really good job putting everything back in order; they even cleaned up the stage room for me! They must have left while Joanna and I were fucking, but there was an envelope with Sandy's name on it full of cash on the counter. I counted it out: $700! There was also a note in there, addressed to me:

> *Taryn,*
>
> *Great job with the talent tonight; Thank you.*
> *U RULE.*
>
> *—Tyler, Fantasies manager*

They also kindly left me a Fantasies T-shirt. It was definitely too big for me now, but if I followed in their footsteps I could eventually grow into it.

It was like a light went off inside me. Not because of the oversized pants, but because of the rush of the evening. I decided that I needed to spend my life mixing lotion and water together, and having sex with more strippers. I'm sorry. I meant: *features*.

I made a decision, if one could say that; it felt like I didn't have a choice. If I didn't go after this opportunity, I would miss my one true calling in life.

I was leaving Dreamz.

Sandy would be sad, no doubt, but she'd find another person to help her with the store. I'd tell her as soon as I could. For right now, I just wanted to celebrate.

I grabbed my phone to call Tyler and accept my new

path. I turned on the phone and saw that there were several missed calls from Amanda, and a text message that said "Hey—I'm gonna come see you next weekend!" with multiple happy faced emojis. Something I felt was so out of character for her. I couldn't believe a porn star coming into my store (and me cumming on her fingers, though she didn't know that) would reduce Amanda to use eighth grade flirting methods.

"I'm busy," I wrote back. "And I don't know when I'll be free next."

I watched the dots appear and disappear in the message box. I still missed her, but I wasn't going to obsess over her any longer. I'd been freed by an angel and I was going to strip club heaven filled with lotion/water cocktails, and shiny panties. I was moving on. On to the next town, the next strip club, the next bottle of cheap vodka. And if I ever look back, it's gonna be at my own ass, and maybe one day I'll even put something inside of it.

The End

To go back and see Taryn host a swinger party, turn to page 154.

To go back and find a different fantasy, turn to page 55.

Within a few days, my post on the swingers' message board had over twenty responses! People seemed excited. I checked my new and exciting inbox during work; there were several people asking me questions, responses to which I made up as I went along.

"Thanks for your posting! Question: Is this just a meet-up party or a play party?" wrote someone who went by the name of "FunTimeSheena."

With the use of a swingers' glossary I found online, I deduced that she was interested in knowing if she could actually have sex with people at the party, or just meet someone at the party and have sex elsewhere. I mean, isn't every party and bar and nightclub and even coffee shop kind of a "meet-up" party then? Anyone can meet anyone anywhere, then take them home and have sex with them. I suppose the title limited the people present to people who strictly went out with a sexual intent.

"Yes! This is a play party. It is an adult video store where anything is allowed! There are rooms available for people to do whatever they want!" I answered.

One person posted, "I had no idea that store was still around! I got my first porn there when I turned eighteen." He ended his post with a fast-moving GIF of himself (I think it was him) jerking off. He was a very well-endowed black man, and underneath the image it said "BULL." My swinger dictionary told me "bull" referred to a single guy with a big cock who was readily available to fuck

169

people's wives, or be in double penetrations and three-somes with husbands and wives. I wondered if he had to get crowned as a bull or if he was self-appointed. Was there a board that approved you based on your abilities? I had so many questions for the swingers; hopefully we'd have a full store for the event, unlike this fine Wednesday at 11:00 P.M., which was particularly empty. There was no one in the store but a man with a pizza-stained Disney World T-shirt looking to buy a blow-up doll. I rang him up with a smile, I asked him the doll's name, I asked what their plans were for the evening, and I offered him and his plastic lover a room, but he said he preferred their first intimate experience to be in the privacy of their own home. Understood.

There was still one thing I needed to do for the event—tell Sandy. If she said no, it wouldn't matter how much planning I put into this, it wouldn't happen. This is still her store.

I found her in the tiny stock room, dressed in pink heels and a strapless terrycloth dress. She was already half-drunk on apple-pie flavored moonshine, going through a bunch of receipts.

"Sandy, I want to have an event in the store," I told her.

"You do?" she replied.

"Actually—I am doing one. I already posted about it. I should have told you earlier!"

"Honey, I can't pay you any extra money," she said.

"No! It's fine! I just want to help bring some new people in here. It gets so boring in here when it's slow. Oh, I didn't mean this place is boring or anything! I just meant, there's so much more I can bring to my work!" I stammered.

"Heh. Yes, I can understand that. Gotta make the day more exciting. Well, the more the merrier!" she said, not even bothering to look up from the long slip of annotated paper from Thongs-R-Us. She was smiling though; I think I got my yes!

I kept obsessively loading the message board on my phone while I was at work. Replies steadily came in. An attractive blonde couple in their early thirties, whose profile photo featured the two of them on the beach with surfboards, posted that they would be coming and they were looking for a couple to do a "same room swap." An interracial couple, who could also be called an "inter-height" couple as he was fairly tall and she was pretty short, asked if anyone wanted to "bang the wife" while the husband watched. A good-looking Latino man responded with a thumbs-up emoji and said he'd be there. People were so particular and direct about their sexual arrangements; it was completely different than the college parties I went to where men and women stayed in their own respective corners, and only began speaking once they were appropriately buzzed. Very short, anti-climactic sex in a bathroom, closet, or a room where several people were actually sleeping would occur if you were lucky— which I rarely was.

Amanda never responded to my "I miss you" text; in fact, she hadn't talked to me at all since that night. It had been a few days, and I'd since sent her some questions about how I should be planning this event. Was I supposed to provide alcohol? Do I need decorations? Am I expected to have music going? I needed professional help for this professional party; besides the post on the forum, I really didn't know what I was doing. But there was only silence from Amanda for five days until she suddenly sent me a text asking how work was going.

I was boggled. Did she not see my texts? Or did she just not care? I thought she was supposed to help me! Contacting swingers in a suburb outside of Tampa was never something I saw myself doing in the name of love. Wait, I shouldn't have said love. Don't tell her I said that.

I was conflicted. I was happy that Sandy had given me permission to do what I had already been planning to do, and half sad that a person I'd fell head over heels for was apparently ignoring me. Around 1:00 A.M., a beautiful black woman in an elegant black dress, and a tall, white, business-looking man in a khaki sport coat, combed-back dark hair, and black suit pants came inside. Definitely not our usual customer base, especially at this hour.

"Hi! Can I help you guys?" I asked.

"Hello, we, um, read about this place on the lifestyles board?" the woman said.

Holy shit.

"Oh, hey! I'm Taryn, the event coordinator," I paused, "but the event isn't for another two weeks. It will look waaaaay more exciting by then. I promise." The man looked around, sizing up the store as if he was some kind of health inspector.

"Where does the play take place? We're in the middle of a store? I can't bring our pet here! Where would we engage? On top of a stash of magazines?"

"We, um, don't allow pets in the store. Unless they're service animals, of course."

The couple looked at me with disgust.

"Let's go honey, I had a feeling this was a scam." The man walked in the direction of the door.

"There's no scam here! I promise." Then I quickly realized they meant a pet human, who served them sexually, and not a yippy Chihuahua that this woman would carry around in an oversized purse. I needed to make myself some flashcards with all the terms from the swinger dictionary so I could memorize them. "I'm so sorry," I said. "It's my first event here! I'm in the process of putting away the magazines. They won't be in the way."

His wife wandered off to look at the shoes. We actually had a great shoe selection, most likely because Sandy really loves heels. She found a pair of stiletto heels on the rack, then bent down to look for a pair in her size. Finding one, she slipped off her little block wedges, and inserted her stocking-clad feet into the nine-inch, patent-leather Mary Janes.

"You like these, Chuck?" she asked. If he didn't say yes, he must be blind. She looked incredible, the height of the shoes elongating her already graceful, dark legs. Anyone would want those legs wrapped around them. The husband smiled and nodded in approval. His mood changed to a slightly calmer energy as he ogled his wife in the heels.

"So, we have these private rooms here, where you can do anything you want. And it's of course pet friendly." I smiled. "Do you want me to give you a tour?"

"Yeah, sure!" the woman said. The man grumbled and went along.

I guided them through the back of the store, and showed them all the ROOMZ and the special features of each. I showed them how to work the TV in the big room (even though it literally entailed pushing an "on" button on a remote), I showed them our selection of lubes, I did whatever I could in my power to make six dirty rooms with tissues and televisions in them as exotic as possible. I felt like a used car salesman. The couple looked pretty stoic and unimpressed. I desperately didn't want my event to fail before it even started. What if this couple went to the forums and told everyone how lame this place was? I couldn't stop thinking about how they could so easily dash my dreams; it was the only thing on my mind—well, except for the thoughts of Amanda that hadn't left my brain since we met, and my amazement at how this woman could walk in those heels. She still had them on, and she was rocking them all over the store.

"I love this place," the man said suddenly. I was completely caught off guard. "It has like a '70s vintage porn theater feel. It's awesome. I assume no photographs are allowed in here, correct?"

"Uh, yes." Note to self, put up a sign that says *No photography allowed* and then—it will be official. No photography will be allowed. I can make that happen.

"So, are the rooms always available? Or just during events?" the woman asked me. I like how she said "events" as if there were lots of them all the time.

"Ha! These rooms are literally open 24 hours a day, 7 days a week. I think they MIGHT be closed on Christmas—for, like, an hour." I laughed, and they laughed with me. I was glad my humor was able to bring us all on the same page.

The couple gave each other a sly smile.

"A year ago we had a child," the woman said.

"Congrats! That must be one beautiful child," I said. Was that inappropriate? Either way, it was definitely true.

"The baby sleeps in our room and it's been so hard to find time to . . ."

"To fuck?" I said.

"Yes!" they both answered.

"We have a sitter for the next two hours—our evening plans ended earlier than expected," the husband said.

"Oh! Sure, I'd be happy to set you guys up in a room. In fact, if you buy the shoes and any toy in the store I can let you use the room for free!" I took it upon myself to make a package deal. These could be great repeat customers, with extra money to spend, and a good sexual attitude.

"Honey, go pick out a toy," the woman said, although before she was even done with her sentence her husband was off to find one for them to use.

"So, what's your name?" I asked, after a few moments of awkward silence.

"Cherise," she said. "And yours?"

"I'm Taryn!"

"Taryn, are you a unicorn?"

Ha!

"Oh, ha, ha, no I'm not special or anything. I'm just, you know, doing my job. Unless, you were asking if I was literally a unicorn—but I don't think those actually exist."

Damn it, I was losing her! *I can't ruin this now, I've gotta think of something clever to say.*

But before I could utter another word, she leaned in and kissed me. Her big dark lips tasted like peaches, because of her lip-gloss. I was in shock. I could smell her perfume, it was a bubble-gum scent, but a sophisticated one. I could feel her soft skin, silky but almost plastic.

"You're new in this lifestyle aren't you?" She smirked at me.

"Yeah, kind of. I guess you can say that."

"Why don't you join us?" she said, and then she kissed

me again, more intensely this time. With her silky dress, giant breasts, and fake hair, it felt like kissing a Barbie doll. It was definitely nice fake hair, that moved like hair and looked like hair, but I could feel little pieces of tape in her head where the hairpiece attached.

Would Amanda be proud of me if I joined? I got more aroused by imagining this as some kind of sexual test I had to pass in order to get her to come back, a hurdle in an obstacle course of cock and pussy that I had to conquer to get the prize. I was up for the challenge.

I nodded a hopefully seductive "Yes" to answer her question.

Chuck returned with a toy in his hand; I'm so glad he picked that one, now that I was (hopefully) joining in. I'd always wanted to use one of those, but I never thought I'd have the chance. Chuck and Cherise scanned each other, Cherise tilting her head toward me, raising an eyebrow in an almost sinister look, as if asking "shall we bring a mouse for us cats to play with?" Chuck looked at me seriously for the first time that night, observing my body like a chef picking out his meat for the night's special. Finally, he nodded his approval; they came over, each grabbed one of my hands, and guided me into the room.

To read about Chuck grabbing a riding crop, turn to page 177.

To read about Chuck grabbing a strap-on, turn to page 184.

Chuck placed the riding crop, plus handcuffs and a convenient two-pack of blindfolds, on the small table in the room. That had always confused me on a practical level: Why sell them in packs of two? Two people obviously can't be blindfolded at the same time. The imagery of the thought always made me laugh. Was one there in case one had broken? In case one was lost? However, now being in a room with Cherise and her husband it all began to make sense. He smiled from ear to ear, and watched me kiss his wife.

I kissed Cherise again and she grabbed me closer to her. She sucked my lips with hers and jetted her tongue down my throat. She slipped her hands underneath my top and goosebumps appeared all over my chest and my nipples became rock hard.

Kissing her was magical and the thought of what we were about to do was so enticing, but my head was still part-way at the counter. What if a customer needed me? What if someone needed to buy lube? What would I do? Though at the same time, I supposed Cherise was a customer, and she did need me. So this was totally fine.

"Hello," I said bashfully, staring into Cherise's eyes as I pulled away from our kiss. Chuck came over and put a hand on Cherise's shoulder.

"Good job," he said, "you caught a unicorn."

I was completely aroused and excited to indulge in a rendezvous with people who were likely to have been prom king and queen, but I did not want to roleplay as a horse, not even as a magical one.

"Seriously, what is with you guys and unicorns?" I asked.

Cherise chuckled, "It's a term for sexy single females in the lifestyle."

"They're rare, and most people have never even seen one, but Cherise has been lucky enough to find a few," Chuck said.

"Ohhhhhh, I get it. Well, I'm not too surprised." I tried to think of a witty response that related to sex and majestic horses in some way, but I was gladly swallowed by Cherise's mouth before I had a moment to think of anything that would have been more likely to ruin our moment.

As much as I was loving kissing Cherise, the riding crop and blindfolds were looming large in my mind, exciting me to no end. Both items were 100 percent leather, high-end products that were coincidentally made by the company Amanda worked for, JT Stockroom. It's like she was here in spirit.

Chuck must have noticed my anticipation, because he went over and grabbed the riding crop. He got behind Cherise, and pulled her dress down exposing her large perfect breasts, with tan colored areolas. He smacked her nipples with the riding crop and it made a sharp, loud sound, leather cracking against the skin. "More," she whispered, and he hit her again, harder this time. "MORE!" she then shouted more aggressively and he hit her even harder. I could see her nipples getting red; she let out an elegant moan. Chuck put the whip down and then gently tickled her breasts, and blew on them with his mouth. It was so fascinating to see someone so aroused without anything happening below the waist, as if her nipples sent a signal over to the rest of her body.

In my recent week of sexual exploration, I learned that my nipples were rather sensitive as well, and I wanted to experience this pain and pleasure. I boldly unbuttoned my top and sat on my knees and waited patiently for my boob beating.

"Do you really think you deserve this?" Chuck asked me, standing over me with the crop in hand.

"Well, yeah. It's my room. I deserve to get what I want, right?" I smirked.

"She is feisty!" Cherise said, and suddenly a blindfold was placed on me, and my hands were cuffed behind my back. I closed my eyes underneath the mask because I truly didn't want to see anything; I wanted the full blind-fold experience. I could feel hands going up and down my body and I wasn't sure whose was whose. My leggings came down and my shoes came off. I felt very much like a rag doll; my body belonged to them as I laid there anxious of what would come.

My pussy lips were spread open and a tongue quickly found my clit. Another pair of hands grabbed my nipples, pinched them, pulled them, and the more they were pulled the more I pushed into the mysterious mouth. The riding crop whacked my breasts. It felt incredible, the pain almost too quickly fading into a sensation of sexy numb-ness. Again, it hit me, I moaned, the right nipple, then the left nipple, the right the left, back and forth. I moaned and moaned. I felt helpless, I loved the sting of the sharp leather against me.

My neck was grabbed, my legs were pushed apart, and

the tongue was still going all over my vagina. I was dripping wet, my body covered in so many different sensations from the top of my pussy to the bottom. My legs were weak, and my breasts were being beaten harder and harder. A finger penetrated my pussy, then two, then three. They slid right inside me without any lube at all; I was so worked up.

"Take me!" I started yelling uncontrollably. "Use me, please!" I had never thought I would say something so blunt to a lover, let alone two lovers who were strangers. My pelvis thrusted so hard into the mouth that was on me, my throat was grabbed, and then suddenly I felt an unexpected but incredibly erotic slap across my face; it unlocked sensory organs in my body I didn't know existed! Fingers were inside me hitting my G-spot, my body submitted to impact coming at it from two different sets of hands and—what was happening—ah!

Was I peeing all over them? I lost control over anything inside me and I felt liquid gush from out of me. I was helplessly crying and cumming and possibly peeing all over the place.

"Keep going, keep going!" Cherise encouraged me.

"A dirty fucking girl," Chuck said, he slapped me with his hands and then whacked me with the crop.

"I can't stop, I can't stop!" I said. I felt myself making a giant mess. I whimpered and moaned, and then suddenly there was a cock in my mouth, invading the last of my sexual senses and driving me wild.

"Suck his dick," Cherise said.

I tried to respond but since my mouth was full it was nothing but grumbles and gagging. I worked up as much spit as I could from the gagging in the back of my throat. I felt Cherise take my head and push it down his cock, and she kissed my ears and my neck and encouraged me.

"Show me how you suck that cock, baby, show me, pretty girl."

Since I was still blindfolded, I couldn't tell how big this cock was but it was certainly bigger than my mouth. I was then picked up and pushed to the corner of the room, tossed aside like a chewed up dog bone. I couldn't move my arms, I was covered in my own sweat and juices. I could hear slapping and thrusting and deep, heavy moaning.

"Fuck me, Daddy, fuck me!" Cherise shouted, and I could hear Chuck grunt, and I could smell the sex on their bodies from across the room. I wanted to watch them. I wanted to touch myself. I wanted to gag on his cock again but I was helpless and couldn't move.

"Take me," I said weakly, almost panicking in my lust.

"You gotta wait your turn, baby," Cherise answered in between panting.

Their sex sounded so musical. Two horny, professional adults ravaging each other; it was so carnal and so romantic. I could hear them both getting louder and louder, the thrusting became faster and faster, I could hear his testicles slapping against her body. Her deep breaths and moans turned into loud yells. I desperately wanted to lick her, I wanted to taste her sweat, I wanted to taste her juices off his cock. Yet I couldn't even touch myself. I tried breaking out of the cuffs and I couldn't. Tears ran down my face, I was hungry and desperate for their abuse. This was no way to treat a unicorn!

I hobbled over to their side of the room by following their physical sounds.

"Feed me," I said. I was getting really weird and acting

like the exotic animal I never thought I could be. Being inside of a blindfold made me feel like I was inside of a dream, where the words I said and the things I did were outside of myself. I felt Chuck's muscular hand grab the back of my head, and he shoved my face right inside of Cherise's pussy. I yelled "thank you," but I wasn't sure if they could make it out because my mouth was stuffed. I could taste her sweetness, I had never actually gone down on a woman before, and wanted to do to her what she did to me. I wanted to please her. I wanted to inject the smell of her amazing vagina inside myself. I still couldn't see, my mouth was all over the place tasting her inner thighs, her taint, her clit, and the sides of her lips. I was then pushed down and she sat on top of my face and I was covered in her juices. I was smothered, I could barely breathe but the small amount of air I gathered tasted like incredible vagina. I stuck my tongue out and searched for her hole, I wanted to be as deep in her as I possibly could. She grinded on my face. If I died of suffocation right now, I would die so happy.

I then felt Chuck's dick slide inside of me, still with Cherise on my face. He had a thick cock; it had been so long since a cock had been inside me, and this was not like getting fucked by a college boy. He felt manly and aggressive, I could barely move because I was restrained by Cherise and her amazingly large pussy lips, but he pounded away at my vagina that was now sore from squirting and cumming, but I still wanted more.

Cherise got off me and I breathed the actual air again, though it wasn't nearly as nice as my nose ingesting her bodily scent. Chuck's cock escaped me, I could hear him fucking her, then he went back to me, then her. He switched back and forth, having two dripping wet pussies at his disposal.

He ripped the blindfold off me. "Open your eyes," he said. I opened, I could see his scruffy face and his dark brown hair right on top of me. I looked down and loved the way my pussy looked being stretched and penetrated. Cherise had such an amazing curvy body that still smelled like bubble gum, even after I possibly sprayed her with my own piss.

"Cum for me, Daddy," Cherise begged. That sounded like a good plan. I followed her lead.

"Yes! Cum for me, Daddy!" I chimed in. We sounded like a musical acapella group of ladies begging for cum at different octaves simultaneously. He grabbed Cherise and flipped her over and fucked her doggy at what seemed like the speed of light. Cherise quivered and cried, "I'm cumming, I'm cumming, I'm cumming!" a beautiful, strong orgasm as the climax of all the other orgasms. Chuck pulled out, Cherise and I dropped to our knees, and he sprayed his sperm all over our faces. Most was on hers, and rightfully so, but I got a few drops for myself. I cherished them like a gift. My entire body relaxed in the most wonderful way. I felt so sexy, so beautiful, and so, so satisfied.

I could certainly get used to life as a unicorn.

To go back and have Chuck grab the strap-on, turn to page 184.

Continue with Taryn in this fantasy, turn to page 194.

I kissed Cherise again and she grabbed me closer to her. She sucked my lips with hers and jetted her tongue down my throat. She slipped her hands underneath my top and goosebumps appeared all over my chest and my nipples grew rock hard. What if a customer needed me? What would I do? I supposed she was a customer, and she did need me. So this was totally fine. Right?

"Hello," I said bashfully.

"Good job," Chuck said. "You caught a unicorn."

I was completely aroused and excited to indulge in a rendezvous with people who were likely to have been prom king and queen, but I did not want to roleplay as a horse, not even as a magical one.

"Seriously, what is with you guys and unicorns?" I asked.

Cherise chuckled. "It's a term for sexy single females in the lifestyle."

"They're rare, and most people have never even seen one, but Cherise has been lucky enough to find a few," Chuck said.

"Ohhhhhh, I get it. Well I'm not surprised." I tried to think of a witty response that related to sex and majestic horses in some way, but I was gladly swallowed by Cherise's mouth before I had a moment to think of anything that would have been more likely to ruin our moment.

Chuck held onto a strap-on, grinning wildly. Was Cherise going to fuck me with it? I felt like that kind of intimacy should be reserved for me and Amanda. I mean, I'm sure she was boning multiple women across the country, or the world, with strap-ons, but I didn't want any other woman to do that to me. Well, not right now. My thoughts were complicated. Complicated and sexy as fuck.

Cherise sat down on the leather couch, like a queen on a royal throne. She lifted her skirt up, and Chuck began kissing and licking her black patent-leather shoes, sucking on the heel, and kissing her feet. She pointed at her right foot and he kissed every possible inch of her right foot and toe, and then she pointed at her left foot and he caressed every inch of that one. I think I understood now who the strap-on was for, and it wasn't going to be inside of me.

"Sit down," Cherise demanded to me. She spoke with such poise and command. She kissed me as Chuck continued to worship her feet. Her lips were large and soft, her skin felt like butter. She pointed at my feet, and Chuck on his hands and knees moved over to me and he slowly unlaced my Converse sneakers, removed my socks, and kissed my feet. I was self-conscious because I had been on my feet all day; maybe my feet weren't exactly prepared to be in someone's mouth, but he massaged them, kissed them, and even got a whole lot of my foot in his mouth and didn't seem to mind. I was so thankful I had given myself a DIY home pedicure just a few days before. My toes were painted light pink and my toenails were filed down and cut short.

Chuck took my foot out of his mouth and looked at it intently. "You have such a nice arch," he said. He started to massage my foot, working the arch he so admired. It felt incredibly nice! Cherise grabbed a bottle of peppermint flavored lotion from her purse, and squirted it on my feet. It felt cold and it tingled, but in a very alluring way. Chuck rubbed the lotion in my feet and I could see a big beautiful bulge forming underneath his pants. I took notice and rubbed my greased-up foot against his boner on top of his pants; his cock became visibly harder.

"Good girl," Cherise said and she kissed me more passionately, reaching her hand inside my hair and grabbing it by the root. She pulled my hair and kissed me, and I could feel my nipples getting harder and my vagina getting wet. She had such an intense hold. I felt safe in her arms, and the combination of a cock on my feet and her lips on mine was unique but amazing. Being a unicorn definitely had perks!

Chuck unzipped his pants, and revealed a thick, long, and very hard cock. It was empowering to know that just my foot alone was able to make his cock rise to the extent it did. Cherise held my feet in place, in what almost looked like a yoga pose. She placed them together and the arches enabled a small window between them. Chuck grabbed some lube and squirted some on his cock and rubbed some around the arches of my feet, slowly inserting his cock into my created foothole. He slowly started thrusting back and forth as he closed his eyes and grunted. The sensation of watching a cockhead thrusting up at me while feeling his shaft on the soles of my feet was both somewhat alarming and incredibly arousing.

Cherise continued to kiss me while Chuck penetrated my feet. She reached her hands down my pants and touched the top of my plain cotton underwear. With all this recent new sexual activity in my life I really needed to get new and more exciting undergarments, but luckily

Cherise was such an erotic pro, I still felt sexy in them. She rubbed up and down, from the top to the bottom of my pussy, and the cotton grew more and more moist. She was slow and sensual but confidant in the way that she touched me. It was like she was previously given a map of my pussy and studied it and knew exactly where to go. She tickled my thighs, pinched my nipples, grabbed my breasts, and kissed my neck. She slid my shirt off, still teasing me on top of my unflattering underwear, while Chuck's cock continued to fuck my feet.

Cherise was definitely running the show here. She pushed Chuck down and sat in between us, touching my pussy with one hand and now stroking Chuck's cock with the other. The queen was pleasing her court jesters for a change. It was a medley of moans, mine and Chuck's, the two of us getting further entranced by her touch. She then shifted positions and crawled on all fours, and she looked back and commanded to Chuck, "Make me cum."

He inserted himself inside her, her eyes rolled to the back of her head as he penetrated her. She rocked back and forth on his cock, with the intent of getting her orgasm the exact way she wanted it. Her round, dark ass had a perfect bounce to it. Her hips gyrated, showing off her many different curves. I was beginning to feel like an adolescent boy sitting next to her, so turned-on, yet so helpless to do anything but stare blankly.

She bit her lip and closed her eyes, each breath of hers got louder and louder the more Chuck thrust inside her. I touched myself while I watched them, two perfect-looking, professional people aching to get as much plea-sure as possible before they returned to their everyday lives. I touched myself fiercely, and, my hand gravitated toward my own pussy, but this seemed to have offended the Queen! She aggressively pushed my hand away and pulled my panties to the side, then changed the arch in her back and got her ass higher in the air and she put her mouth on my pussy. She licked me up and down, she worked up saliva in her mouth and spit it on my vagina. It was already wet from being aroused and my own juices and her spit mixed to form a beautiful mesh of liquid. Her lips were so robust, she easily covered so much pussy surface area by barely opening her mouth. I smelled a mix of perfume, sweat, and sex, and her multitasking was just so impressive. She didn't miss a beat on his cock, her back stayed perfectly arched, and her mouth and tongue continued to work me. I pushed myself into her, I wanted my pussy so far into her mouth, I wanted to feel the sensation of her perfectly pink tongue from the top of my clit to the bottom of my taint.

Just last week was my first experience with a woman, and I very much felt like all I could do was lay there while she serviced me. The intensity of looking at breasts while kissing someone, and the feeling of such an extended amount of oral sex was so incredibly overwhelming I truly couldn't do much other than flop around like a fish. I lost control of all my sensory organs, and enjoyed the ride. This time I felt slightly more in control of my own orgasm. Like I knew where it was coming from, and I knew where it was going. It was a familiar friend knocking on my door, ready to come on in and make me feel awesome. The next time Amanda came back I would know what to do. I could make her proud, I could impress her. Though I probably shouldn't be thinking about Amanda while another beautiful woman is going down on me.

Cherise took her mouth off my vagina for a brief moment, she looked back at Chuck and said, "She's got some good pussy," and she spit into his mouth. He drank it and thanked her profusely, and she dove right back into me, and he fucked her more furiously. She moaned with her mouth full of pussy and it created a fun buzzing sensation, like she was her own giant human vibrator. She licked and sucked and swallowed all my wetness while she was getting fucked harder and faster.

"That's the spot, baby, that's the spot!" she yelled.

She inserted two fingers inside my dripping wet hole, and sucked on my clit. Her mouth was powerful, like a Dyson vacuum cleaner lifting up a bowling ball. Her firm lips and her fast fingers created the perfect sensation, I could feel the orgasm getting closer and closer, like it was crawling up through my toes and ready to explode out of me. I loved watching her get fucked, I loved the intent look on Chuck's face, so determined to please his wife. She definitely loved her cock and her pussy equally, enveloping my lower lips in her upper lips, moaning louder and louder. I could hear their bodies slapping against one another. His entire cock was swallowed by her arched ass, while my thighs were wrapped around her face. Cherise the royal queen, our bodies belong to you and we are here to be your toys.

She lifted her big brown eyes, perfectly painted with golden eyeshadow, up to mine and looked right at me with her mouth stuffed full of my pubic hair and pussy lips. She nodded and gave me this seal of approval that granted me permission to cum. I could hear her eyes speaking to me. I wrapped my legs tighter around her face, she moaned and squealed and I physically don't think Chuck could fuck her any harder than he was. The pitch of her moans changed and sounded deeper. The tension in my body released in her mouth, as she quivered on Chuck's cock. It was our own special ladies night, where the girls got to cum first!

Cherise got out of her doggy position and sat with her back against the couch, unable to stop smiling. However, I noticed that Chuck still had a massive hard-on.

"How were you able to fuck her that hard without cumming? I don't get it!" I asked Chuck.

"She hasn't given me permission yet," he replied. His cock glistened with Cherise's juices, and it looked so enticing, the first time a cock truly emulated sexiness for me. I crawled over and licked off the pussy liquid; he shivered as my tongue hit his shaft. I licked until I got every last drop off of him, I'm sure.

"Go on—suck his cock," Cherise instructed me. Now was my time to shine! I replayed Nina Hartley's instructional sex video in my head: I used my mouth and my hands, I licked every part of his balls and his shaft and both him, and Cherise seemed pleased with the execution. I felt confident, being able to suck a cock with such direction. Giving a blow job is so much more fun when you know what to do.

As I kept Chuck occupied like an obedient pet unicorn, Cherise then slipped on her new leather holster and attached a curved black colored dildo to the O-ring in the center. As soon as Chuck could see that she was fastened in properly, he immediately dropped to his hands and knees. Truly, I had never seen a man positioned like that and I was incredibly turned-on by it.

"Keep sucking his cock," Cherise said, which excited

me. That was a sure sign that she approved of how I serviced her husband. It took some geometric configuring: I slid underneath him and laid down, and he thrust inside my mouth, his penis hitting the back of my throat. I gagged on it, and worked up more spit to keep it as moist as possible and able to take his cock as far down my throat as I could. Meanwhile, Cherise got behind him, covered her dildo with lube, spread his ass cheeks, and proceeded to penetrate him. He was breathing hard, submitting to Cherise with such comfort. She was stern but gentle. She smacked his ass and the sound echoed throughout the room, and he looked incredibly happy. He grunted and groaned, and he clenched onto her ankles. I could see the communication they had between them, he tapped her and she went faster and when he dug his fingers into her she went slower.

"Good boy," she said. It doesn't matter how old or how young we are, or how rich or how poor we are—we all seem to like being treated like pets when we're having sex sometimes. It's like we all go back to the basics and want to be told we're good and given treats and petted and attended to. She thrust her pelvis in and out and in and out, at a very moderate pace. She was incredibly careful and as she went faster she slathered on more lube.

I wonder how this became part of their sexual repertoire. Did they always do it? Was this a new thing? I was curious. I had no idea what they actually did for a living, but I assumed it involved a very fancy office, and definitely a water cooler. I wonder if he stood around that water cooler and talked about receiving anal sex from his wife with his other handsome friends in expensive suits.

He flipped over, pushing me out of the way, and

Cherise changed her position and she was now fucking him from a missionary position. He definitely looked more vulnerable and even kind of adorable, with his legs up in the air. I wanted to be back in the action, so I got on top of him, grabbed his cock, and continued to stroke it and swallow it. His legs began to shake and quiver, she thrusted deeper into his ass, and the entire dildo disappeared inside him. She paused and he let out a big "Oh Yeah" as she stretched him open. I stroked his cock faster and faster into my mouth. She looked at me and smiled! I felt rewarded and justified as my place as the third partner in their sexual adventure.

Cherise then stopped holding back and she went at a faster pace. I continued to suck his cock, she went faster and faster. He got louder and louder and cried in a helpless way.

"Do I have permission to cum?"

"Yes baby, yes, cum for me!" Cherise said, and she proceeded to pound away at his asshole, while I took him out of my mouth and jerked him off with my hand. He winced, his eyes shut as he shook vigorously; a large fountain of white jizz came out of his cock and landed on his stomach. It was impressive!

"Thank you both. That was . . . incredible," I said.

"I like this spot. I'm certainly glad we stopped by," Cherise said.

"We will definitely be back," Chuck said, still panting heavily.

"Take your time cleaning up. I'll be out at the register—you know—working." I collected myself as much as I could and I exited the room.

I wiped myself down with baby wipes and hand

sanitizer, giving myself a very unsatisfying shower. I couldn't believe everything I just saw and felt. My underwear was soaked with my cum; I chose not to put them back on. I would treat myself to a new pair of wholesale lace panties as a reward for my new sexual accolades. I couldn't wait to tell Amanda what I'd done tonight.

To go back and have Chuck grab the riding crop, turn to page 177.

Continue with Taryn in this fantasy, turn to page 210.

I returned to the register incredibly disheveled, smelling like sex and sanitizer. A few customers meandered around the store.

"I'm sorry, I was on break!" I shouted, as a general announcement. One guy nodded. The others weren't fazed. I had sex while still on the clock and got away with it, which I think was pretty impressive! I shouldn't take that for granted. I definitely didn't have that luxury when I worked at JC Penny.

A guy approached the register holding a pornographic movie titled *Make Me Creamy*. He was wearing what looked like a hybrid of shorts and pants. They were definitely too long to be shorts and too short to be pants. He was big and stocky, with a Florida State University hat on, and a black sweatshirt. He slid the DVD over to me like it was some kind of contraband and wouldn't look me in the eye. "I'll take a room, please," he said.

"Did you need one with a DVD player in it?" I asked.

"Yeah."

"All right! Here you go," I said, with a big smile, handing him a key. "Have fun in there!" He cracked a smile. No one should feel guilty about going to jerk off.

Moments later Cherise and Chuck came out of the big room, looking completely put together. I don't know how they did it. Her makeup was re-applied with perfection, all of his buttons were buttoned and his shirt was tucked in. They looked like two people who just left a charity auction, and not a dark room with seventies decor where they fucked a complete stranger.

"See you in two weeks, I hope!" I said to the ravishing couple.

"Have a great evening," Cherise said, and they left the store.

I watched their asses as they left, remembering fondly their shape and feel. I almost got completely lost in my thoughts, but I shook my head; I had to work! To clear my brain, I took out my phone to check for new message board replies, but, whoa! To my surprise, there was an unexpected missed call from Amanda.

I couldn't believe it. No text, no voicemail. Just her name in bold red text telling me she'd called while I was having amazing sex. Was it a mistake? Did she mean to actually call me? My heart pounded, and I immediately attempted to call her back. It went straight to voicemail. It was probably for the best, I didn't know what to say! I decided to text her instead.

"I saw you called!" I wrote out.

No, the exclamation point was too eager.

"Hey, did you call me?"

No, no. That was a pointless text that wouldn't lead to anything sexy at all.

Meanwhile, on the store monitor, I saw the shorts/pants guy juggling an intricate jerk-off routine. He put on a particular scene on the DVD he purchased, then fast forwarded to the end of the scene where there was an up close shot of a whole bunch of semen spilled out of a girl's vagina. He began to jerk off, then he stopped and rewound the DVD back to the same part. He would get in about four seconds of jerking off, then he would stop and rewind again and again and again. Why wouldn't he just pause it? I wish there was some way I could help. It was so frustrating to watch his flaccid penis come in and out of his pants without any progression. Perhaps I could make some sort of loop for him of semen filled vaginas if I downloaded a few videos? That's technologically possible, right? I should look into that. Again and again and again, he rewound, stroked, rewound again, stroked, and his cock was not getting any harder. So strange that in the room next door to him not even twenty minutes ago three people managed to fuck the shit out of each other and he couldn't pull off fucking himself.

And then my phone rang. It was Amanda. I grabbed my phone and my shaking fingers made it slip from my hands and fall to the ground and landed face-down with a sickening *CRACK!* I picked it up and already the breaks were spidering all around my screen. Damn it! It still displayed Amanda's call though, and I managed to pick it up on what was certainly the last ring.

"Hello?" I answered, as cool and calm as I possibly could. I had slid my finger against the shattered case to answer the call and now it was bloody. I tried not to think about it—Amanda was on the line!

"Hey, you," she said.

"Hi!" I said. I froze. It is so impractical to agonize over someone calling you, and then have nothing to say when they actually do. Damn it, what is wrong with me!

"What are you doing? Are you at work?"

"Yeah! I am. It's been a really interesting night here."

"So, I'm actually stuck at the Orlando airport the next twelve hours—my flight to Charlotte had to do an emergency landing here because they were low on fuel."

"Who the fuck is Charlotte!" The words blurted out of me. Even though I shouldn't be getting jealous when I was the one who just engaged in unicorn activities.

"Oh—a really hot. . ." she paused and I could feel tears beginning to form in my eyes. My bloody finger dripped on my palm as I clenched my hand into a fist. ". . . City in North Carolina! You psycho." She couldn't stop laughing.

"I'm not psycho!" I said. "I just don't like North Carolina. It's a swing state and it always messes up elections, okay?" Up until about four days ago, I only thought of elections when anyone mentioned the word "swing," but now it has a whole other meaning.

"Are you working all night?" she asked.

"Yes."

"I'll come by and keep you company!" she said.

"Oh! Okay," I said. I wanted to jump up and down and scream FUCK YES but a very subdued *okay* made up for my schizoid Charlotte comment. They balanced each other out. I'd have to stop the bleeding before she got here though, or else my craziness would be inescapable.

"My phone is gonna die but I'll let you know when I'm on the road," she said, and hung up. How was she even getting here? Orlando was like two hours from the store. I couldn't believe this was happening. I pinched myself. I needed to take a more proper shower; I still smelled like a threesome.

I quickly went to the bathroom for a quick "kind-of" shower. I took bottles of Dasani and spilled them on myself, rubbing off as much sweat as I could. It worked to some degree, but I don't think it covered all of it. My breath was a whole other issue. I couldn't find any mints or candy in the store, but I did find out that Sandy keeps a toothbrush in the bathroom. I mean, she was sort of like a family member at this point, right? I could totally use her toothbrush.

I scrubbed as much of my body as I could, running out in between washes to check on the store. Every time the bell on the door rang, my heart felt like it dropped to the floor, much like my cell phone.

Each time I came out of the bathroom, I checked in on shorts/pants guy. After a grueling twenty minutes, he successfully achieved a boner. His problem was that he was too concerned with watching the actual DVD, which didn't give him what he needed. He was now watching the DVD menu, which had five boxes on it, and within each box was a mini version of each scene. So it was essentially a loop of moments of sex and moments of cum inside of vaginas. I was happy to see he found a solution. He was a grower and not a shower. He didn't take his shorts/pants off. His cock just peeked through the zipper. Magic. I was happy for him.

As I went into the bathroom for another clean, wondering why I still reeked of sex, I realized that my shirt was still heavily wafting smells of arousal all around me. Shit. I didn't have a change of clothes at the store; I guess I'd have to put on something from the shelves.

I looked through the selection of clothing in the store, and I decided to wear this purple corset that was on display. It wasn't too revealing, it looked more like some-thing people with adventurous lives would wear as a top. It zipped in the middle and it was laced in the back. I was able to slide it on comfortably, and it actually looked quite good with the leggings I had on, and my Converse were an interesting touch. My styling looked intentional, sort of like I was a cute, wacky next door neighbor character on a sitcom. When I worked retail, I was always required to wear clothing from the store to work because my bosses thought it would help sell the clothing. I don't see why that shouldn't apply here. That would be my cover story if Amanda didn't like my corset; I will blame it on the corporate policy of this obviously non-corporate store.

Once the shorts/pants guy got going he was done pretty quickly. I was beginning to enjoy the ever-growing visual Rolodex of people and their O faces inside my brain. Everyone had their own unique orgasm: some people were loud, some were quiet, some kept their eyes open, some kept them closed, some sat down, some stood up, some people ran out of the room as soon as they ejaculated, and some people sat around and decompressed for a moment. Some people wiped everything off immediately and some people tasted their own cum, some people used an excessive amount of lube and some used none. The cream-pie guy spit in his hand and masturbated swiftly; he stared at the TV screen and ejaculated a small load into his hands, wiped them off with tissue and exited the store immediately. I tried to say good-bye, but he speed-walked right past me, leaving his DVD behind. I suppose it was a one-time use. I was glad he was done, though; I didn't really want anything distracting me from what I hoped was a very sensual night.

About two hours later, Amanda walked through the door, in a black blazer, black jeans, black boots, and a soft, white T-shirt.

She was smokin' hot. I tried not to stare at her; I failed.

Meanwhile, I looked like a somewhat grown version of Punky Brewster in my multicolored half-lingerie half-laundry day leggings ensemble. But you know what? I was feeling it. We were an odd couple, a sexy, horny odd couple and that's okay.

"You look cute," she said, as she stood in the doorway. I ran over to her, threw my arms around her neck, and kissed her. I hope she realized how new and improved my kiss was; I expected compliments at some point.

"I can't believe you're here!" I said.

"Yeah—I randomly appear sometimes!" she answered. She kissed my neck, and put her hands in my back pocket and grabbed onto my ass. We were right in the doorway causing an adorable fire hazard—a very drunk guy practically knocked us over trying to get inside. We laughed, and I pulled her behind the counter and grabbed her a seat.

"So, you're stuck here?" I asked.

"Well, in Orlando, yeah. I guess so!"

"I can't say I'm not happy about that. Even though I know it kind of sucks for you," I said.

"Yeah, I know," she replied with a very smug smile. She vaguely knew the power she had over me. I couldn't yet figure out if she found it endearing or annoying.

The drunk guy stumbled around the store; I could smell the potent cologne and wafts of vodka from across the room. He squinted and looked at a handful of movies. He then attempted to put them back, but he dropped them all on the floor.

"Easy, there!" Amanda said, and she walked over to him and put movies he dropped back into their place.

"Can I help you?" she asked him. This woman took control over my brain and now she was taking control over my store. I don't know how she did it.

"Where's the bathroom?" he slurred.

"Over there," I pointed to it. He then walked toward the bathroom but halfway he just began urinating on the floor.

"Are you fucking kidding me?" Amanda yelled, and went over to him and smacked him upside the head, somehow stopping the pee coming out of him. She pushed a few buttons on her phone.

"I got a cab coming for you, all right buddy?" He tried to reach out and grab her breasts and she pushed him back. "No!" She pointed at him and yelled, like speaking to a bad dog. She pulled him outside the store while I went and cleaned up his piss with Clorox wipes.

She walked back inside and the two of us burst out laughing.

"Well, I'm glad you got to meet some of Tampa's finest!" I said.

"It happens everywhere. Every city has their own set of hidden gems."

"You're very good with drunks."

"Well it takes one to know one!" she replied.

"I don't see you as the type to pee in a store," I said.

"Hey, if you're into that I'd be happy to." She kissed me. And truly, I actually thought about it for a minute.

"I AM KIDDING!" she said. "Don't you know how to take a joke?" she asked while pulling the back of my hair in such an aggressively sexy way.

I was relieved. Kind of. But I would be lying if I said I didn't find it slightly erotic at all.

"So—I swear, I didn't do this for you—but I did actually put the word out to swinger couples to come hang out here and I'm planning an event specifically for them in two weeks."

"Really?"

"Yes, really."

"Where is the flier for it? I don't see one!" she said.

"I don't have a printed flier! They're so old-fashioned. And not in the budget," I said. "But it's all over this one message board! And a couple read it and came in earlier tonight to check the place out and, and, I . . . had sex with them!"

"You WHAT?!" she said, looking incredibly surprised. And I could tell she didn't believe me.

"I did! I was their unicorn!" I said.

"Oh look at you—quick with your swinger terminology. Is that why you're wearing bright purple?" she asked

"No! I'm wearing bright purple because my other shirt got too sweaty after I had sex with them, so I put on this purple thing to look nice for you." We paused and just blankly stared at each other. "Along with these panties!" I pulled my pants down and showed her the top of my black lace panties, with a little pink bow on top. I think she actually was starting to believe me. I felt guilt and pride at the same time.

"I am really shocked, little Taryn."

"I wasn't doing it for you, but I thought of you the whole time. Well, for a good portion of it anyway. And I feel like, your plane must have landed here for some cosmic reason so I could tell you in person. I wasn't sure how to tell you over the phone. Mostly because you rarely answer my texts," I said.

"I answer the ones I feel like answering," she smirked.

"Yeah, I can see that." I jumped in her chair and kissed her and kissed her, again and again. I felt so emotionally drained. I kind of wanted to scream. I wanted to bottle up this moment and drink it later when I would inevitably miss her again and she would inevitably not respond to me.

"What's this?" She picked up the copy of *Make Me Creamy* that the shorts/pants customer so abruptly left on the store counter.

"Oh, it's uh, a return. A guy came in and, well, he used it, and left it here. I guess he didn't want it!" I said.

"Well, let's watch it!" she said. "You've got a TV back there and nothing playing on it!"

I actually forgot that the thing on the wall in the back of the store was, in fact, a TV. It had never been used and I treated it like a decoration. Why didn't I ever put a movie on? So many boring hours could have been spent with my eyes focused on something else. Between the sporadic live sex in the store that I observed on a small monitor, I could have been watching pre-recorded sex on a large screen.

Amanda bent down and wiped the dust off the DVD player behind the counter, and successfully figured out how to insert the disk (*god, is there anything this woman can't insert?*). And there we were, me and Amanda, sitting at the cash register as it turned from dark to dusk outside watching a surgically enhanced blonde girl strip her fishnet bikini off in slow motion, in front of an Olympic-size swimming pool. She held my hand. We were on a date.

Our porn cuddles were sometimes interrupted by customers wanting to make a purchase. I rang up a few of them here and there with an incredible amount of enthusiasm. I could see that Amanda liked when I was a diligent worker, even if it meant ringing up blow-up dolls, fake vaginas, and herbal Viagra. She barely blinked an eye at the fact that I literally had sex with two people at the same time not even three hours earlier, but she did get incredibly offended by the fact that I almost sold someone silicone lube instead of water-based lube with their Fleshlight.

"You know that will basically ruin the product?" she barked at me. She was basically like an encyclopedia for things that gave people orgasms. She genuinely cared. It's like she had a PhD in sex toys.

"I had no idea," I said.

"It says 'USE WITH WATER-BASED LUBE' on the back of the box!" she exclaimed. "How do you not know?"

I didn't know what to say.

"How does she fuck standing up in those heels?!" Amanda said, pointing at the screen that displayed a woman in what seemed to be nine-inch heels, on a staircase, having sex with a muscular man with a large cock. I thought of Cherise who also successfully had sex in large heels just a few hours earlier, but she was on a couch most of the time and not standing on a staircase.

"Sometimes heels make some women feel sexy," I said. "It turns them into superwomen."

"Well, not me," she replied.

"Have you ever even worn high heels?" I asked.

"My mom made me when I was in a dance recital in the fifth grade! I fell flat on my face. And then just a few weeks later I came out of the closet."

Well, well, well. Finally, something I had more experience in than Amanda had. It was time for a lesson.

I grabbed a pair of red, patent-leather heels that we had in stock. I sat on the floor, slipped off my Converses, and put the heels on. My toes bunched up and stuck out of the open-toe shoe, daggers of sharp black hairs jutted out of the area around my ankle that I buckled the strap around. I should really shave more meticulously if my sex life was going to remain active like this. I now actually looked like a younger version of Sandy with giant red heels, a purple corset, and cotton leggings. I walked around the store like it was a catwalk, my ass and calves felt tighter, and my posture felt incredibly statuesque.

"How do I look?" I batted my eyes at her.

"A little ridiculous, and kinda hot!" she answered. She kissed me, in the middle of the empty store, and we did a middle school slow dance to the loop of generic keyboard sounds playing on the porn DVD behind us. I could see the Tampa morning sun peeking in through the crack under the door and knew that soon enough she would be going back to the airport.

"I don't want you to leave," I whispered into her ear as we danced.

"Well, I have something for you—to keep us together even when we're apart," she said. She went over to the counter, kneeled down, and reached inside of her backpack. What was happening? The rational part of my brain knew there was no way she could be proposing to me, but the rational part of my brain also visibly saw her kneeling on one knee, and reaching inside of a bag. What else was I supposed to think?

She pulled out a very sleek-looking box. I thought she might be giving me a new unreleased version of the iPhone (which would have come in handy since she was indirectly the reason why my screen was now broken) but it said "We-Vibe" on the front.

"What is that?" I said.

She opened the box and pulled out this purple, curved, mini U-shaped thing. It reminded me of a clip my mother used to use on bags of potato chips to make sure they wouldn't go stale.

"Put this on," she said.

"Uh, ok?" I stretched it apart and put it on like a bracelet.

"No, no—stick it IN you," she said with delight.

I was skeptical, but I complied, pulling my pants down around my ankles and moving the lace panties to one side. I felt like I was balancing on stilts, with the new shoes I was wearing and my pants limiting my movement. I channeled my inner porn star getting fucked by a staircase and held my balance.

"The skinnier side goes inside, the thicker one is for the outside."

Tentatively, I slid it inside me. It fit quite snug, like a magnet pressed against my pussy. She then pulled out her phone and pressed a few buttons, and, what the fuck! Out of nowhere, I felt a strong vibrating sensation against my clit. Amanda laughed maniacally.

"What did you just do?" I asked.

"This is the future of novelties. Welcome. I can control this from anywhere in the world, from my phone," she said.

"What?!"

"Seriously—look!"

She walked outside the door, into the Pasco County morning sun. There was nothing but silence in the store, I thought this was an evil trick to leave me without saying good-bye. But moments later, I felt it. A strong sensation, pulsating on my pussy. It went harder, and softer, then it turned off, then it jolted back on, to what I think was the highest decibel it could possibly go, and it made me fall straight to the floor in my wobbly heels. She walked back into the store, holding her phone with confidence, like it was a detonator to a nuclear bomb.

"See—I told you!" She came back and found me laying on the ground, embarrassed, bruised from my fall, and almost about to cum from the feeling of this neat little toy. I was her personal remote-controlled car, which wasn't far off from how things usually were but now a piece of sexual technology made that dynamic more official.

She kept pushing buttons on her phone like she was playing an instrument. The vibrations inside me got stronger, and softer, and pulsated at different speeds, like it was changing radio stations to find the perfect song to play inside my pussy.

"Amanda," I yelled. She held my hand standing up while I sat on the ground. I looked in her eyes, shining wickedly. It was like being on some kind of drug. She kneeled down and grabbed me by the throat. She stuck her fingers down my new panties that were now soaked in moisture (ironic, since these panties were purchased for the sole purpose of replacing my other cum-soaked panties).

She tickled my pussy lips anywhere around the vibe she possibly had room, and kissed me as she held onto my throat. I waved my arms and grabbed onto her tits, her pussy, her face, anything I could latch onto while I bounced up and down and looked deep into her brown eyes.

"Are you gonna cum?" she asked. I nodded slowly. This was incredible. And then, right then and there, she shut her phone off.

"Oh my god! Turn it back on, you monster!" I gasped.

She threw me up against the register and pulled my pants completely off. She licked my thighs, she licked my asshole, she licked everywhere around my vagina that wasn't being smothered with a vibrator. The curved purple toy stayed snug inside me. She pushed a few buttons on her phone and it vibrated once again, at a strong steady pace inside me while she sucked on my clit and playfully slapped my thighs. I came so hard inside her mouth.

I felt at peace. Like this is everywhere my body has ever wanted to be, up against a cash register, looking at Amanda between my thighs in her sexy suit. I felt juices gushing out of me. I kept yelling her name. I quivered and fell to the ground. We both lied down on the cold, dirty concrete floor; I held her closely. My pussy was still swollen from her sucking. It belonged to her and her mouth.

"Well, that was amazing," I said, breathing deeply to reclaim the blood that had flown to my crotch.

"I want you to keep it. Charge it and leave it in you at all times and you'll never know when I decide to play. It might be in the morning, it might be in the evening— you'll never know! But I'll be with you all the time."

"Am I ever going to physically see you again?" I asked, almost afraid of the answer.

"You will!" she said. "But you know my work takes me all over. I'll come back when I can."

"I suppose I won't know when that will happen, either!" This must be what it felt like to come down off a drug: The downward spiral of reality setting in, making you crave another hit. My shift was almost over, and I didn't know when I would ever feel her again.

"Are you even coming to the event I put together? I will have no clue what I'm doing, and it was all your idea!" I said.

"I can't promise to come, but I can promise to try," she responded. "I want to. I do. But—work comes first."

A heavy silence hung between us, even as we held each other. I could tell she meant what she said, but that didn't make it hurt any less.

"I should head back to the airport. I gotta go through security all over again and shit," she added, after several moments of complete silence, other than the sound of a girl getting fucked really hard and repeating, "Ohhh, *Make Me Creamy*, baby." (I must say I truly respected the way the actresses had so much passion for the title of the movie.)

Amanda stood up, straightened herself, put her blazer back on, kissed me, and walked out the door. I was alone in the store, the place that in recent memory had held my greatest joys and my greatest heartaches. It was a little after 8:00 A.M. One more hour to go.

I spent the last part of my shift in a half-post-orgasm glow, half-mopey sadness. Only once did a customer come in; he purchased a Fleshlight and I directed him to the appropriate water-based lube to go with it. No vagina in a can will go ruined on my watch ever again.

And just as I was in the register gathering him the appropriate change, the vibrator inside me went off. I squirmed and giggled and jumped around. It was the perfect last good-bye kiss for the night I desperately needed. Oh, wait. She just set it off one more time. Let's see if I can successfully sweep the floor while I continue to vibrate.

Continue with Taryn in this fantasy, turn to the next page.

O ver the next two weeks my post on the swingers' message board gained over a hundred new replies, and I had about eighty official RSVPs. Cherise and Chuck wrote a very favorable review of Dreamz as one of the responses to the post. They said it was comfortable and laid back, with a good selection of products and private, very affordable ROOMZ, and they politely mentioned the incredibly accommodating staff without getting into any details.

I kept my We Vibe charged up and left inside me as much as I possibly could. In true Amanda fashion, she set it off with no routine schedule at all. I never knew when it was coming (or, more accurately, when I would be cumming). She had power over my vagina at any time of the day. Her cell phone was like an erogenous Voodoo doll, but causing pleasure instead of pain.

One evening before I went to work, we Skyped with each other and she essentially jerked me off from the other side of the country. She knew exactly what setting to put it on to make me go insane. It's like she had figured out an exact algorithm to make my pussy climax. She laughed when I orgasmed. She was truly sadistic with her love for toying with my emotions and body, and I was truly masochistic for enjoying it. The other day it went off while my landlord was over trying to show me how to reset the hot water heater. I immediately had to excuse myself, and as a result, he never finished explaining it to me. My shower has unfortunately remained cold.

Amanda never gave me a definite answer on whether she was coming to my event or not. I had no idea how someone could be wishy washy about plans when they are happening in a different state.

On the day of the event, I eagerly awaited a text or call from her saying, *I'm on my way*, or *I'll be there soon*, or *Taryn, I love you so much I can't wait to fuck you in front of a whole bunch of people tonight*. But the hours passed by, and my eagerness turned to frustration as I wallowed in the radio silence from my lover. By 5:00 P.M., I decided that enough was enough and I texted her.

"Are you at the airport?" I stared at the message, willing a response to show. Please let a response show soon!

Five minutes later, she replied.

"Yeah, but I'm always at the airport ;)"

She was so frustrating. Every time I felt like I was close to sending some kind of dramatic text with an ultimatum on our relationship and her behavior, she would make a remote orgasm happen and I would forget why I was ever angry in the first place. But not this time, damn it! This was my night, and I wasn't going to let my anger at Amanda ruin it, and I wouldn't forgive her for missing it. I was still hopeful she'd show, but if she didn't, well, I wouldn't be having any more technologically transmitted orgasms, that's for sure.

I continued getting ready for the event. Sandy made her signature "punch," with apple-pie flavored moonshine and some kind of cranberry drink. I researched what foods were the best aphrodisiacs and the internet kept telling me oysters, but there was no way I was going to bring raw fish into Dreamz. Semen is one thing, but raw fish sitting out for a long time had to be against our health code. I settled for a giant bag of heart shaped chocolates I found at CVS, and Sandy brought a giant tub of imitation Cheetos (the generic brand that is just called "cheese puffs") that she loves so much. I'm not entirely sure what is in Sandy's diet other than moonshine and cheese puffs.

I put up signs all over the store, hand printed signs I made with markers and scrap paper, posting sales and package deals on toys, lingerie, and ROOMZ. I put *Make Me Creamy* on the TV. I had actually played it almost every night; I had every last sex position memorized by this point. It reminded me of Amanda and I felt a warm nostalgic comfort when cum spilled out of those vaginas.

I wore a little pastel pink dress; it was tight up top and flowy on the bottom, shaped like a bell. Underneath I wore a pair of black high-cut lace panties. Since I last saw Amanda, I had developed a small collection of bras and panties that served some fashion and not purely just a function. Most importantly, my direct telecommunicator to Amanda was fully charged and sat comfortably inside me, clipped on my inside and outside like a paper clip.

I wasn't sure what would happen tonight. I didn't have an itinerary, just free snacks and half-priced dildos, but from the little I'd learned about this culture of sexually advanced couples I think that should suffice. Sandy was putting her fire-engine red lipstick on. About sixty percent of it was on her actual lips.

"So, who is coming in here tonight?" Sandy asked me.

"Oh! Well, hopefully, a bunch of couples who wanna have threesomes and trade partners and stuff," I said.

"They're called swingers," Sandy said. I don't know why I assumed Sandy didn't know the proper terminology.

"Yeah, I uh, I just learned that recently!" I said.

"My ex-husband and I used to be in the lifestyle! And when we first opened we had a lot of parties here."

"Oh really? I had no idea!" I did wonder sometimes what the old Dreamz was like. Knowing this information made me feel slightly less guilty about having sex while on the clock. Even though I didn't actually feel that guilty in the first place.

"What happened? Why did you stop?" I asked.

"Well, I got divorced. And things got a little compli-cated, and now my friends from that scene are just too old. You don't want them coming in here and having sex!" She laughed. I didn't think about couples who got divorced in the lifestyle. Can you get promoted (or demoted?) from a swinger to a unicorn? Watching your husband have sex with your friends could be fun—watching your ex-husband have sex with your friends would be a different story. But I didn't need to think about these things right now. Tonight was going to be filled with lots of sex, fun, cheese puffs, and possibly Amanda.

A few hours later, the store began to fill up. I watched as couple after couple came into the store, some beau-tiful, some really not, some that looked so mismatched I couldn't picture them having sex if I tried! Then, of course, there were the couples who were like gods on earth: so incredibly hot, each bone perfectly placed, skin gleaming, eyes sparkling in a way that said *I'll be the best fuck you've ever had.*

I couldn't believe all of these people were here because of me! In my head, I quickly gave myself a congratulatory pat on the back, then went to mingle and sell things.

It was interesting to overhear the conversations that went on. Different types of couples meandered around the store, scoping each other out, making professional arrangements as to who should have sex with whom, and what their limitations were. Some couples insisted on their "swap" being in the same room. Other preferred to be separated. Some were simply looking for another couple to have oral sex with, without any "below the belt" penetration. One couple asked me if they could have sex somewhere in the store, because they wanted everyone to just watch but they didn't want anyone else interacting with them; I told them that they could make an announcement and let people watch them on the ROOMZ monitor. They happily agreed and purchased one of the ROOMZ. One couple eagerly awaited for a single man they had prior arrangements with to double penetrate his wife, but he was nowhere to be found. The wife wasn't pleased. I tried to sell them an extra-large dildo to solve the problem and they seemed moderately insulted. It was their loss, I knew first-hand that it was a truly good dildo.

There was one unfortunate disgruntled couple who came in—everything about their synergy was just off. The man clearly didn't want to be there; he huffed and puffed the whole time. He was short and scrawny, with dark hair that looked like a Brillo pad on top of his head, swimming inside his jeans and his oversized flannel. His wife was a very tall, blonde woman with large, broad shoulders that made her look like a linebacker.

"My husband can't give me orgasms anymore. What

the fuck do we do about this?" the woman abruptly came up to the counter and asked me.

"Oh! I am so sorry. My name is Taryn! Maybe I can recommend some toys to help you guys out?"

"Hi, I'm Jen," she shouted. She was a little rough around the edges, and struck me as someone who might have a slight case of Asperger's. Her husband looked petrified and didn't speak.

I picked out a few things from around the store that I thought would help. I mean, they still wouldn't be orgasms her husband was giving her but he could hold the toy while it did the job for her. A Hitachi wand, a vibrating egg, and a rather expensive eight-inch curved metal wand with circles on it that were supposed to hit your G-spot. It was a product that I thought was a little too advanced for the Dreamz customer base but Amanda swore by it and made me order it wholesale. I felt like this big angry woman needed a big solid toy to make her cum. They purchased a room together without attempting to invite anyone else in.

"Good luck!" I shouted to them.

Sandy mingled with everyone—casually grabbing guys' cocks, and kissing girls on the lips (leaving their faces stained red). She served her punch in plastic cups, and carefully arranged the snacks on paper plates as if it was some kind of charcuterie board (I learned what that was at the "gastropub" I went to with Amanda).

The couples were all starting to split off, some making out in dark corners, some purchasing time in ROOMZ, or buying toys and leaving to partake in sexual excursions elsewhere. There were plenty of people here, even some single men who had come to provide additional services. I did not see any single girls there to be a third party to the couples. I guess unicorns really are rare.

As I was pondering whether my own unicorn standing was a one-time thing or not, my vibrator went off. She kept it at a slow, steady pace where I felt moderately aroused but still in control of my senses. She must have known I was working and didn't want to distract me *too* much. Was this a sign that she was coming? As I walked around the party with my pussy buzzing, I felt like I was on a cool kind of drug, one that made you tingly but kept you functional.

Speaking of drugs, Sandy brought out a cardboard box full of little brown bottles with little white caps and placed it on the table. She took one out, unscrewed the cap, and inhaled it.

"If anyone wants one—let me know! Just twenty dollars!" Sandy held up the tiny glass bottle and put it on display like it was some kind of expensive champagne. Then she whiffed about three more.

"What is that?" I said.

"If anyone asks—it's VCR cleaner." She winked at me.

"But *I'm* asking," I said.

A few of the couples bought these little bottles from her. Was I supposed to ring them up? Was I supposed to give them receipts? Did all these people actually clean their VCRs? Did people actually *have* VCRs anymore? There was definitely something I was missing here, but I was happily enjoying the vibration in my panties sporadically surprising my G-spot with glee, so I didn't care that much.

I was leaning against the counter, surveying the party kingdom when Chuck and Cherise came in. They arrived fashionably late and made a grand entrance, like the king and queen of the ball, only this ball was inside of a strip-mall with overhead fluorescent lights. Cherise was in a low-cut, black, tight, shiny catsuit, with large boots. Her hair was delicately wavy and pushed to one side. I could see every single curve on her body, and even though I'd already seen them uncovered, I felt so privileged to witness them again in any circumstance. Chuck wore dark denim and a navy blue polo shirt, like a suave playboy about to sweep all the ladies off their collective feet. Cherise handed him her purse and coat and he held onto them obediently as she strutted around the store, saying hello to everyone. I went over to him.

"Hey there!" I was happy to see him. He was handsome and his love for his wife made him more attractive to me, and it oddly made me want to have sex with him. I never thought I would want to fuck a married man in general, let alone someone whose wife I liked, admired, and had sex with as well. This was a new world I had entered.

"Hello there, my little slut," he smiled and said to me, and he kissed me on the cheek. Normally my feminist instincts would tell me to punch someone who spoke to me in this manner, but with his tone, the look in his eyes, and the dynamic of our relationship, it came across as incredibly polite.

"I can take the Queen's coat for you!" I said, and I took the coat and purse from him. We didn't exactly have a coat check but I was going to create one.

"Thank you," he said. He patted me on the head like I was a little bunny rabbit. It was subtle and sexy and I liked it.

217

Sandy turned some music on, but the porn DVD was also still on, so it sounded like a re-mix of radio hits with sexy moans and manly grunts behind it. It actually worked really well and people cheered for the impromptu sexy songs. Meanwhile, several more couples purchased ROOMZ along with handfuls of bottles of what everyone kept calling "VCR cleaner." I'd come to guess that it was some sort of "sex upper" that maybe wasn't quite legal in the country. Everyone did seem to really be enjoying it though, so who was I to judge?

The monitor behind the register was now divided into six different screens, from all the different people purchasing ROOMZ. This was something I had never seen before because I had never actually seen more than one room purchased at a time. I was on a penis and vagina sensory overload; I didn't even know where to look.

In one section of the screen, I saw a big, hairy man with gold chains, slicked back hair, and a penis that was small in comparison with the rest of his body giving some incredibly determined oral sex to two different women. Back and forth he went, being smothered in between two pairs of legs. On the occasion that he came up for air, his face dripped in sweat and pussy juices. A tall, very skinny man with glasses jerked off in the corner. I wonder why he wasn't part of the action. The big man servicing the women was not very well endowed and he was incredibly hairy but his thirst for eating pussy was fucking hot. I would choose him over the skinny guy on any day. Maybe he was banished to the corner because he was bad at eating pussy? Holy shit. One of the women in the room, I just realized, was the hygienist at the dentist's office I went to as a kid. I stared at her when she first came in the store, trying to figure out where I knew her from; something about the face she was making while she was getting her clit licked made it all click—that was the very same face she made when she asked me what flavor of fluoride I wanted. (For the record, I always chose bubblegum.)

In another square on the screen were two younger-looking couples, who appeared to be in their early thirties. They had a timer stationed in the middle of the room, something similar to the one my mother used when she used to bake pies. I saw them each stick to their own corners of the room and then the timer would reach a certain point and the girls would switch. Then they switched again, like clockwork, every seven minutes. The two women gazed at each other from across the room as they both got fucked on all fours. Their orgasms were simultaneous. The two men in the room both fucked at the exact same pace and the couples mimicked the same positions. This was a very well-choreographed dance; I wonder how many times they rehearsed it. They were like synchronized swimmers, with penetration.

Unfortunately, in one square was Jen, the large blonde lady and her timid husband, relentlessly trying every toy without success. His penis was limp, and she looked like she was about to cry. I felt like a failure. I bet Amanda would have been able to help them. Where the hell was she?

I had to look away from the sad scene. Luckily, the next section was much hotter: on the monitor, an entrancing game was taking place. I found this corner of debauchery more entertaining than the others. A woman sat in the center of the room with a blindfold on, with four other men and three other females. The woman in the center had her mouth open and her hands tied behind her back.

The group decided amongst each other which cock should go in the woman's mouth. After a few minutes of her licking and sucking a chosen person's cock, balls, and even taint (on some of them), she had to guess whose cock it was. If she guessed it correctly she received a prize—and that was several minutes of continuous pussy licking from the person of her choice in the group. All three of the women played the game, one after another after another, happily sucking all the mystery cocks, and receiving their oral sex when they deserved it. A score was tallied in the end, and the woman with the most correct amount of cock guesses was rewarded with sex from everyone in the room, including all the men and women, and the women wore strap-ons when the winner's sex finale ensued.

The winner was a redhead, with short, curly hair, pale skin, lots of freckles, small breasts, and pierced nipples. A merry go round of men and women with cocks strapped to them with hot pink holsters (that were recommended and sold to them by me!), took turns penetrating her. Cocks were in her mouth, cocks were in her pussy, and one man went in her ass. He happened to be the man that she came in with, who I assumed to be her husband/ boyfriend/partner. It makes sense that he got the butt! I loved the way she sucked on the dildos with just as much passion as she did with the real cocks, and I found it so provocative the way the women took turns fucking her in the same exact way the men did. She was literally having sex with more people at one time than I had in my entire life. It was remarkable. Everyone in the room focused on fucking her brains out; she squirted multiple times, I couldn't hear her but I could see the expressions on her face and the way her body became more and more limp with every earth-shattering orgasm until she could hardly sit up. After her circle of fucking, she laid there, in the middle of the room, covered in sweat and sperm. It was so depraved and filthy, part of me wished I was her and I could just for a moment feel what she was feeling. The other part of me was petrified.

"Oh, nice! A gang bang!" Sandy walked by the monitor and said, while speaking very loudly and not entirely standing up straight. Ah. So that's what a gang bang was. I had heard the term before. An entire gang, "banging" one person. It made very literal sense.

Sandy stumbled past me, mumbling, "I'll be right back," and passed out in our back room, on top of a stack of magazines, boxes of DVDs, and piles of unopened mail. I would have been concerned, but she looked quite comfortable sleeping back there. I grabbed her large gaudy faux fur leopard print coat and put it on top of her.

When I came back, I noticed my favorite couple being subtly frisky in between the store shelves. Cherise sat on a plastic folding chair in the corner of the store, while Chuck was on his knees, putting different pairs of heels on her and massaging her feet. In reality this was a folding chair that was collecting dust in the storage cabinet until tonight, but the poise and presence that Cherise had made it look like a majestic throne. She put on our tallest pair of stilettos, nine inches, black patent leather, and he licked her toes. Chuck created a tall tower of shoeboxes, of all the pairs of heels that Cherise liked. He snapped my attention away from the monitor of moving bodies, and focused it on him.

"I'll take all of these," he said.

"Of course!" I answered, as he continued to worship Cherise's feet.

I began ringing up the various pairs of high heels. Clear ones, pink ones, sparkly red ones, open-toe and close-toe ones, and some were thigh-high boots. I imagined their house having a giant walk-in closet with multiple levels, like the ones seen on the TV show *Million Dollar Listing*, with a secret speakeasy-style wall that swung around and revealed all her various shoes and dildos and anything else scandalous from the part of her life that I get to see and not everyone else does.

Couples came and went as I rang things up. Someone with a ski mask walked in the door, alone. That was pretty kinky. I liked all the different types of people this event was bringing in. Perhaps he was the guy who was supposed to double penetrate the couple? His mask was made of cotton—perhaps I could get him to swap that out for something leather; I did have some new nifty leather masks in stock.

And then—he pulled out a gun.

"Freeze! Nobody move! Everyone put your hands up!"

I'd never had a gun pointed at me before. I just learned what a gang bang was not even thirty minutes ago. I had so much life left to live. I really didn't want to die. Did this store have an alarm? Was Sandy going to wake up?! What the hell was I supposed to do?!

I looked at Chuck and Cherise who were rightfully panicking in the corner of the store. I felt horrible. I brought them here. If they died this would be all my fault.

"If I see anyone touch their phone, I'll blow their fucking head off."

He locked the door. I held my hands up, trembling.

"Open the register," he said. *Fuck*. I was so disappointed in myself. This had to have been the highest grossing night of sales in the entire time I've worked here and the money is going to be completely gone. Sandy would be at a loss for all the expensive products that were used. I felt horrible. Oh yeah, I was also afraid to die. For someone who read so much Sylvia Plath and Edgar Alan Poe in college and romanticized death so much, it was a truly sobering feeling now being faced with actual death. There was nothing beautiful or poetic about this; it was humiliating. I wanted to throw up, and I felt like an asshole taking for granted all that time I spent in life being miserable. There were so many beautiful things to live for. Like Amanda. I really didn't want to die.

I started taking money out of the register and I looked to the right of me where the shopping bags usually were and noticed they were gone.

"I . . . I don't have anything to put it in, um, did you bring a bag, do you want me to just hand this to you? I don't know how this works."

"What do you mean? You don't have any bags?!"

"We ran out! This was a busy night! We don't usually use this many bags but tonight we used a lot of bags!" I was crying.

"Take this!! Take this!" Cherise panicked, holding up her Givenchy bag that was probably worth more than what I make in a year.

"You can take my wallet, my credit cards, and anything in there! Take it! Please—whatever you want," she cried.

I couldn't stop crying. I knew they had a child. They even came ahead of time to make sure this place was legit, and now they're being held up at gunpoint. I noticed, in the monitor, Jen and her disgruntled husband had given up on trying to have an orgasm and they were walking out. *Fuck! No—I wish they would just stay in there. Can I signal to them somehow?* Everyone in the gang bang room was hanging out naked, smoking cigarettes, which technically wasn't allowed in there but now was not the time to bring that up.

They walked out of view of the monitor, with all their toys that failed them, and walked into the main room of the store. The robber noticed them and quickly shifted his stance and pointed his gun at them.

"Where the fuck did you come from? Put your hands up!" The husband had a very high-pitched girly scream, and Jen's was deep and husky. They dropped their stash of toys, their various vibrating wands and dildos fell to the ground, and they put their hands up.

The robber grabbed Cherise's purse and began looking through it. He threw out all her credit cards and took several hundred dollars in cash. He took out a small bottle of perfume and threw it on the ground. It smashed on the floor and now there was a strong scent of her beautiful grass aroma throughout the store. If we all died, at least it would smell amazing in here. He took her cell phone out of the bag and threw it on the ground. Damn. That was definitely the brand new iPhone, and there was no way AppleCare was going to cover that.

My own cell was sitting right next to the register on silent (usually it sits in my pocket but my fancy dress this evening had none) and I could see an incoming call from Amanda. Fuck! Should I risk my whole life and pick up the phone?

She called several times. This was so infuriating;

Amanda finally calls me and I can't pick up the phone, because it will induce me getting my head blown off.

The robber was still rifling through Cherise's bag. There was a lot in there and I'm not sure what he was looking for. I think he just enjoyed going through all her precious belongings and destroying them. A very rude payback for her, when she just so graciously offered her own bag for him to put his fucking stolen money into.

I scanned the room. The poor customers were so afraid, but I actually noticed that Jen was literally smiling from ear to ear, and she had such a large head, so this was an incredibly large smile. And then she let out an incredibly out of character girly giggle. The robber pointed the gun directly at her, and literally put it up to her head. Everyone else screamed.

"What the fuck is so funny?!" he screamed. And she let out an incredibly loud, sexy moan.

"Oh my god this is so fucking hot! This is so hot! I'm so wet right now."

The robber looked incredibly confused, which is an odd adjective to use to describe someone holding a gun.

"Take me, take me!" she screamed. And she pulled her pants down, and bent over, holding on to a shelf full of dildos, and her husband, also apparently aroused by danger, pulled a hard cock out of his pants and started fucking her! Right there in the middle of everything. I could tell she was incredibly wet; he slid right in her, I could hear the moisture. She was moaning, "Fuck me, fuck me, fuck me, Daddy, fuck me," while the gun was pressed against her head. The robber legitimately looked so uncomfortable. Definitely because of the obvious, but also because a six-foot-tall woman was calling a five-foot-tall man "Daddy."

He started to back away and Jen yelled, "Please put that gun back up to my head!"

"Fucking freak!" he said. However, he did what she asked, pointing the gun back to her head.

"Just finish getting that fucking money together. Come on. I wanna get out of here. I want all of it, and I'm gonna check when you're done."

I thought a metal wand with balls at the end that hit your G-spot could fix Jen's orgasm problems. Clearly, in addition to selling drugs, porn dildos and vibrators, I guess we should look into selling guns because apparently they get some people off. Her husband fucked her so hard, he smacked her ass, he pulled her hair, and the robber was trying to look away but also kindly kept the gun to her head.

"She has a hard time having orgasms—thank you, kind sir, this means a lot!" I said.

"Just shut up and get the money," he said.

I saw my phone ring again, and then a text message flashed on the screen "I'm outside—why is the door locked?" A fit of rage came over me that this man was getting between me and Amanda! I had to do something. I couldn't just die without trying to see her, at least one more time. I tried to think of a plan, of anything I could do. Jen was now yelling louder and louder, her husband was calling her a dirty bitch and saying, "Yeah, give me your fucking cunt."

"Yes, Daddy, yes, yes!" she screamed.

And just then the gang bang room members entered, literally all of them naked, the women still wearing their strap-ons. They saw the sex, and they saw the robber. The curly haired redhead that was covered in dried semen chimed in.

"Fuck yeah, this night is just getting started!" And she grabbed a bottle of VCR cleaner from the snack table and inhaled it right away. The robber pointed the gun at her.

"PUT YOUR FUCKING HANDS UP!"

"All right, all right. I'll play along, this is hot!"

And then, a moment of power came over me. The thought of Amanda sitting outside trying to find me and unable to get in, the excitement I had from a woman finally having good sex with her husband who couldn't do that prior to coming in here, my concern for Cherise and Chuck and not wanting them to get hurt all channeled into a giant fit of rage, happiness, power, and adrenaline.

I quickly swooped up the metal G-spot stimulator that wasn't able to make Jen cum from the ground. It was really dense and heavy, and I threw it at the robber's head, making direct contact with his skull. I froze.

Everyone instinctively followed me. All the girls quickly removed their strap-on pink penises and threw them at him. Cherise grabbed a nine-inch pair of heels and threw it at him. And the robber went down, collapsing on the ground, his gun flying out of his hand and landing across the room. Cherise quickly picked it up.

I could see him breathing. Thank goodness. He's an ass, but I didn't want to kill him. Not tonight. I planned on learning a lot of new things tonight, but murder wasn't one of them.

"Someone call the cops," I yelled, "quickly, before he wakes up!"

I ran to the door and unlocked it. Amanda stood in the doorway with her cell phone, looking pissed.

"Amanda!" I let her in, hugged her tightly, and kissed her. "Thank god you're safe; we're being held up!"

"What?!"

She barged into the store and saw the weird scene before her: Jen, with cum all over her face looking incredibly happy, Cherise holding the gun, naked sweaty men next to naked girls with holsters on, and a mound of hot-pink dildos on the ground next to a guy who was unconscious.

Seeing Cherise with the gun, Amanda must have assumed she was the assailant because she charged right at her, fists clenched, looking like she was going to really hurt her.

"NO!" I shouted at her. "That's not the robber—this guy on the floor is. I threw the metal dildo at him and it hit him in the head and he fell down. I swear! I did! This is Cherise and she's amazing and I had sex with her and her husband!"

They both waved and smiled and somehow went back to looking incredibly proper.

"Really?! Are you lying?"

"About which part?!" I said. "I mean, I'm not lying about any of it."

"Let's please get this monster out of the store! Before he wakes up! Please!" Cherise said, soft tears welling in her eyes. She held onto the gun like it was some kind of tea cup. She had no idea what to do with it.

Chuck was talking to the police, giving them all the information.

"Wait, that was actually all real?!" Amanda stared at all of us, not quite knowing where to look. "Are you serious? That wasn't just a good old-fashioned harpaxophelia role-playing game?"

"What does that mean? Do you not think I'm cool

enough to throw a dildo at a guy with a gun and knock him out?"

"It's a fetish for being burglarized," Amanda said, "And no, I still don't believe you at all." Amanda couldn't stop laughing.

Cherise was getting really angry and she inadvertently pointed the gun directly at Amanda.

"Please! Get him out of here. Now!"

Amanda shook her head, but grabbed one of the robber's hands. Big Jen stepped in and grabbed the other and the two of them dragged him across the store out of the door. Amanda locked it.

Finally, Cherise snapped out of her trance of terror.

"Oh, sweet Jesus, did I just point a gun at your girl-friend?" she asked. "I'm so sorry!"

"It's ok, Cherise, she totally deserved it." My heart was racing.

"Let's all just stay in this room until the cops get here. Is everyone ok?" Amanda asked.

Everyone in the store started cheering. Half the people in the store were naked.

"Amanda! I love you!" I yelled. I was frantic. "I'm not afraid to say that. I could have just died, and it would have sucked to die and not tell you that I love you." I was crying. Everyone in the store hugged their significant others, then the other partners they had sex with. Relief and love spread across the room. I looked at Amanda. She looked back at me, right into my eyes.

Amidst the hugging and cries of joy, Sandy appeared, stumbling out of the back room.

"So, sorry honey—I passed out! How long was I asleep for?" Sandy said.

"Sandy—we were robbed!"

"What? Shit. Are you serious? Did you push the alarm? I have good friends at the station who know to come right away when that happens!"

"We have an alarm?" I asked.

"Oh yes, of course we do," Sandy said. "It's right here!" She pointed at a small button right next to the register.

"You never fucking told me about the alarm!"

"I could have sworn I did!"

"No. You didn't," I said. I could feel a cloud of anger building inside me. I was so woefully unprepared for this situation; all this time I could have solved it with the press of a button?!

"Oh well. I'm sorry, hon'. Now you know for next time! Is everyone ok? Did you have to give him all the money?"

"No Sandy, I hit him with a dildo and he's unconscious outside. All your money is here, though." I picked up the bag and tossed it to her. She caught it, but stumbled back a bit against its weight. "Sorry, there's a lot in there."

"Oh, dear," Sandy said. She put the bag on the floor and walked over to me, embracing me in a tight hug.

"I knew there was something very special about you when I first hired you," Sandy said.

Ugh. How could I stay mad at her? She's trying her best.

"You sure about that?" I laughed. "I think you were just happy I was available and willing to work under the table."

"No, Taryn. I knew. Old ladies like me have good intuition."

"More punch, anyone?!" she shouted to everyone in

the store, and from behind the counter she lifted up a mason jar filled with her magical, clear liquid and held it in the air. She went over to the table and mixed it with fruit punch. Everyone rejoiced and drank punch. Chuck actually passed on the punch and drank the moonshine straight out of the jar.

I picked up the heavy, metal, G-spot stimulator from the ground and saw there was blood on it.

"Does this make you believe me?" I showed it to Amanda. I felt like a real bad-ass. Seriously.

"No! I still don't believe you. But I'm glad you're alive."

We kissed and kissed and kissed, we couldn't stop kissing. And this kiss was different than our previous kisses. I didn't feel vulnerable and helpless like I usually do. I felt like an equal. I had courage, and confidence that I never had before.

"I'm going to call you my girlfriend," I said to her.

"Oh really?" she replied.

"Yes. And you're going to call me your girlfriend.

"OH? Am I?" she replied.

"I know you live a very exciting life, and you probably know a lot of attractive, smart people with good jobs, but no one loves you as much as I do. And I know I make you laugh, and I know you must like me a little bit, because, you know what? I looked it up. I scoured the internet and I looked everywhere on the American Airlines website. I know that's the only airline you fly and there were no flights that had emergency landings in Orlando the night you came to see me two weeks ago."

"You are so psycho. You're perfect for me," she said. "Why don't you come on the road with me? You can visit some stores with me; you can come to my workshops, and

I'll teach you more about this industry. You just saved the store while your boss was passed out in the back. I think you're entitled to a paid vacation," Amanda said.

"I would like that!" I said.

We kissed and sat behind the register and watched Tampa's horniest inhabitants get drunk. Sandy turned the music up and everyone started dancing. Amanda and I held hands, and watched the remainder of our favorite movie *Make Me Creamy*, as it played on the TV on the wall. My heart was full, my pussy was vibrating, and the sweet sounds of orgasms were blaring behind me. It was the classic American love story, at least, it was for me.

The End

Go back and discover a different fantasy, turn to page 28.

Everything looked different to me the next time I came into work. The florescent lighting didn't seem so dim, and the dust on the floor didn't seem dirty; it was just part of the store's charm. I was alone in the store, with several hours to go on my shift, and I wasn't playing Solitaire on my phone to pass the time. I couldn't stop smiling, which is quite unlike me.

My brief encounter with Billy was on my mind. I actually had a dream about him the night before. We were both dancing in a birch forest wearing flannel shirts, sheer tights, and panties. He chopped down a tree with his big, manly axe, and built a cozy cabin out of the wood. We started kissing and then . . . my roommate woke me up to ask me to move my car because it was blocking him in the driveway.

I wanted to know more about Billy. I was intrigued by his duality, and I wanted to know so much more about him. He left fairly early on Saturday (early in this store meant about 1:00 A.M.) because he actually worked a night shift as well, driving throughout the night to make produce deliveries to supermarkets throughout the county. I knew he would be back at some point—who else would help him pick out perfect panties?—but that didn't make it any easier to say goodbye. Before he left, he asked me if he could keep his lingerie here in the store, saying he wasn't sure where else he could comfortably wear it. Oh yeah, he'd be back. I put it in a paper bag with his name on it and kept it on a shelf, much like the way they keep your clothing stored away if you were checked into a prison. He pecked my cheek and thanked me for a wonderful time as he headed out the door. I watched from the door as he clambered into his truck and sped away into the night.

I was already daydreaming about his return, to both me and his bag-o'-delicates. Perhaps I could find some kind of locker I could leave behind the register that he could have access to at any time. Would that be more beneficial to him as he explored this new part of himself? Actually, I liked the fact that I had to be here for him to access the clothing. We were in this together.

The thought of his next visit also inspired me to organize the lingerie. It certainly needed to be done; it was a mess! There were literally ripped cardboard boxes with things like SIZE XS – THONG scribbled in magic marker on them. I had seen more glamor in the displays at the Salvation Army.

So Sunday night found me dumping out hundreds of skimpy pieces of negligée onto the floor in front of me, waiting to be organized in some fashion. It was fine work for a weekend shift. Plus, the night had turned cold and rainy, as Florida nights randomly do sometimes. I wasn't anticipating too many customers, so I decided to make my time alone useful.

There was a good selection here. Bras, panties, garters, G-strings, corsets, thigh-highs, full, high-waist stockings, and even some bikinis. There were "roleplaying" costumes like French maid, cop, schoolgirl, and the generic brightly colored spandex thing with a cape—a mashup of all the comic book characters that ever existed—that was simply called "superhero." Some of it looked like it belonged on your bedroom floor at the end of the night on Valentine's Day, some looked like it belonged on a go-go dancer, and some looked like it was taken from a Party City store.

I separated everything into different piles: all the lacey stuff went into a pile together, along with anything that seemed frilly enough to be lace (I couldn't always tell). The items with shiny patterns and the ones with fur, whether fake or real, went into distinct piles of their own. It seemed like it made sense. From the little amount of time I'd spent here, to realize that there was a very different demographic for each of these genres of skimpy clothing, so they shouldn't be mixed together. I found empty display cases and plastic drawers in the back room, along with a few mannequins. I pulled everything out and blocked the aisles with a giant mess of shelving and headless bodies.

There was something very exciting about the neon spandex panties with extra-long ties on the end. I actually think they were way too bright for me to *wear* per se (my complexion didn't really support clothes that make one look like a highlighter), but I found them to be sexually thrilling, like they weren't underwear, and I couldn't see them worn underneath anything, so these were for people who wore underwear as a substitute for pants. Jimmy's friends would definitely wear these, and they would certainly accentuate any small butt. This style of "panty," if they could even be called that, only came in one size, a mysterious and generic size on the tag that was just O/S— whatever that meant—and they only came in neon colors so I assumed they were only meant for people of a certain generic small size who spent lots of time in dark rooms with black lights. I slipped a pair of pink ones onto the mannequin bottom that I had found. I thought a pop of color in the store would make things more exciting in here. I had some more digging to do before I found a matching top, so for the time being, this pair would remain on a topless torso, molded into a sexy "come hither" pose on a folding chair.

I put all the neon stuff on hangers—it stuck out easily, and drew the eye to that section. If Jimmy's entourage ever came in here for a unicorn-fairy-orgy at the crack of dawn again, they would now have a much easier time finding what they wanted. If only we had a mailing list, I would let them know, but we didn't, so we would just have to hope that if I built it, they would come.

The lacey pile was next. All of the items there felt a lot more intimate. I loved the way it was kind of see through, but not really; they were truly panties of mystery. The patterns were soft and textured at the same time, and the garters were such a timeless accessory that so many generations identified as something sexy. I could see some grand duchess eagerly awaiting her lover in the soft red stockings I held in my hand, held up by black, scandalous garters. I couldn't understand the logic behind why I found something so sexy about something whose sole purpose in life was to hold up a long sock, but what I was starting to learn from my experiences here was that my life needed a lot less logic in it and I should get more in tune with my own instincts. Getting rid of all logic was actually the most logical thing to do, at least when you spend your life interacting with more dildos than you do people.

The lacey lingerie thankfully actually had sizes, though the garments were too dainty to be hung up on hangers. I folded and separated all the panties and garters, and began placing them in the plastic storage drawers. In my mind this was a giant step up from the cardboard boxes; the drawers themselves elicited a kind of sexy vibe: *come, open these drawers and see what's inside.* I found a somewhat isolated corner in the store for the drawer to go, so people could look through the selection feeling like they are in their own private boudoir, only . . . made of plastic.

As I rifled through everything, I kept an eye out for pairs of XXXL lacey panties, stockings, and garters. Anytime I found one, I put it in the bottom drawer with Billy in mind. I smiled and folded everything carefully, I even found myself giggling a tiny bit which was usually something I scorned. I was certainly never a fucking giggler. That was an act reserved for an entirely different breed of female than me—or, it was. Turns out helping Billy get in touch with his feminine side was also helping me get in touch with mine.

This tiny revelation of femininity got me thinking: the closest I ever got to wearing lingerie in my life was occasionally wearing a matching bra and underwear. I had always been so self-conscious about putting anything dainty on my body. Dainty wasn't for feminists with an education degree. But Billy wore them with such ease, and you could see the heightened confidence surrounding him. Maybe I should also give them a try.

I pulled out a pair of purple lace panties. The small size looked right for me. They were shaped like a V in the back, they were a little bit stretchy, and there was a little bow in the front. It was still pouring rain outside, and there were various flood warnings throughout the area so naturally the store was completely dead. I had never put a garter on myself before, and since it didn't come with any instruction manual, there was a chance it could take a while.

I got creative, and mixed and matched. I pulled out the purple lace panties, a black lace bra that was not part of the same set as the purple lace panties, and a black garter. I contemplated between the nude stockings and the black stockings: what would look better? Which were more fashionably appropriate to wear to walk around an empty store and possibly take a few photos on my phone that I don't think I will ever post anywhere? It was an important decision to make.

I grabbed my mix-matched set and went into the bathroom. I slipped off my Converse sneakers and dark denim jeggings. One of my legs was smooth and one was covered in dark, prickly black hairs. I have this terrible habit of stepping into the shower, only shaving one leg, and then stepping out. I don't even realize that I forgot the other leg until much later. I need to hang up some kind of waterproof checklist to remind myself what to do. Fortunately, the stockings could cover up my mishap. My hairy solo leg wouldn't get in the way of this victorious moment I was trying to have with myself.

I slipped the lace panties on; this was the easy part. I turned my head as far back as it could go and looked in the mirror. I loved the way that V shape back made my butt look. It gave it this apple shape that I never quite saw it have. I shook my butt back and forth. I felt ridiculous. I attempted to do that twerk thing everyone seems to love doing: my ass went up and down, I bent my knees. *I think that's what you're supposed to do. Okay, if I'm doing this I'm gonna go all out and do this.* I got my phone and put on a hip hop station on Pandora, and I twerked my tiny

Jewish, white ass around the bathroom. I smiled, I shook my ass to the music, I leaned against the sink and used it to push my ass out more as I attempted to go a bit faster. I felt kind of sexy. I mean, I wasn't going to audition to be in a Lil Wayne music video anytime soon, but maybe next time I actually go to a party I might get up and dance instead of silently judge all the people having fun from the corner of the room.

Next, it was time to put on the bra. All the bras I owned were sports bras or these wireless things you slip on that I believe were called "bralettes." Both these things came in sizes XS to XL; they didn't have the typical letters and numbers bra sizes were supposed to have. Several years ago, my mother took me to Victoria's Secret to get my bra size measured, and they told me I was a 34 B. That was quite some time ago; when my freshman 15 turned into a sophomore 20, and later a senior 30, that added some diameter to my breasts. The size 34 C looked more appropriate to me, one size bigger. And I was right: I fastened it on and it fit perfectly. My breasts were cupped into a perfect shape, and looked incredibly grabbable in the mirror; I wanted nothing more than to hold them in my hands, massage them. I was used to my boobs being smooshed together into one tube-like formation with my unflattering bras. The bra cups were made of a translucent black material, and embroidered with tiny flowers. The lace overlapped on top of the cup of the bra and went onto my skin, like a gate guarding forbidden treasure. The smooth, shiny straps on the side highlighted my shoulders. I never thought of my shoulders as anything sexy, but something about the cleavage and the lace and the way my breasts fell into the cups and looked like two perfect buoyant circles also gave my shoulders some new kind of sex appeal I had never seen before.

My brown hair usually lived tied up into a messy ponytail, but this look demanded a free-flowing frame. I took the hair band out of my hair and let it fall down around my neck and shoulders. It was wavy and damp from the rain outside, but it actually kind of looked like I had intentionally styled it this way. I usually part my hair in the middle but this new skimpy outfit called for a new hair part. I used my fingers and pushed more hair over to one side, so some hair covered the corner of my eye, a seductive look.

I put the 1950s version of "Santa Baby" by Eartha Kitt on my phone. It was April, but that didn't matter. This outfit celebrated sexy retro and it seemed appropriate. I sat on the cold porcelain toilet, and slid on the nude nylons. Their sheer magical material covered all the imperfections in my legs; it was like I slipped into a second skin. I had never put on a pair of thigh-highs, only thick tights that covered up my entire crotch area, and I only wore them when it was cold. I stood up and they fell down. Shit. I pulled them back up again, then I stood up and they fell down again, like in a '50s sitcom comedic scene. A live studio audience would crack up laughing any second now.

I put the garter around my stomach and moved the back part to the front to fasten it. It seemed more practical than trying to fasten it in the back. I do remember when I first got a bra I would put them on that same way, moving the back to the front, then putting it back into place. Then came the biggest challenge of this entire ensemble, which was figuring out how to attach the garter to the stockings with these black little clasp things. I was so nervous

I would rip the stockings by attaching the garter clip to them. I had to push this black plastic button dangling off the bottom of the garter against the metal clasp, then that had to be slid together with such a thin small piece of stocking in between it. I tried slipping it through multiple times but I either had too much stocking bunched up to make it work or not quite enough. This was truly impractical. How did Billy manage to do this with his big, manly hands? Was there some kind of gadget on Amazon Prime that would do this for me? Should I do the front one first or the back one first? Did it matter at all?

I tried multiple times and finally got my entire left stocking all strapped together. It took at least fifteen minutes, and almost all my brain power. Passing my existential philosophy exam was easier for me than putting on a translucent sock. But I did it, and now my ass looked even nicer. It poked out even more. The garter pulling on the stocking to make it tighter gave my ass some extra oomph. Maybe I should start twerking again. Was it about that time? No, no, not yet—I had to get the right side on before I treated myself to a celebratory twerk.

Sadly, my thoughts of ass dances were suddenly interrupted.

"Is anyone here?" I heard a voice yelling. Shit. I quickly slipped my Converse sneakers back on, lacing up only the absolute necessary laces. I walked out of the bathroom in a bra, panties, and a garter only attached to one stocking on my left leg, the stocking on my right leg bunched down to my ankles. Since they were nude stockings it vaguely looked like it was my skin and not a stocking, like I had a minor case of elephantiasis. Coincidentally it happened to be the same leg I didn't shave. The left side of my body was in pretty bad shape right now, as if I needed some kind of *Phantom of the Opera* mask but, for my legs.

"Hi! So sorry about that," I said, attempting to act completely casual.

"Yeah! Nice! This is why I love this place!" He had a very flamboyant voice, and he was incredibly well dressed in a nice, striped sweater and tight blue jeans with stylish and intentional rips in the knees. His outfit was completely drenched from the rain but he didn't seem at all upset about it. He smiled and then gave me a high five. He must have thought I was having sex in the bathroom! Unfortunately I was just trying to figure out how to put on a stocking, but I wasn't going to tell my customer that. Let him dream.

He was holding a set of multi-colored cock-rings.

"I just need these and I'll be out of your hair and you can get back to your fun," he said. I smiled and rang him up, and he went back into the pouring rain outside without any umbrella, but with rings of various sizes and colors to help maintain his erection longer. I had a real respect and admiration for the customers who came in here and knew exactly what they wanted. And for anyone who ignores a flood warning for the sake of a better erection!

I didn't see the point in going back to the bathroom. I was already out in the open in lingerie. I just had to get this stocking up and over my one hairy leg. I fussed with the metal clasp and the black silicone ball thing, trying to find just the right amount of slack to put in the middle. I adjusted the straps on the garter. I don't know why this one was so much more difficult; I thought the second leg would be so much easier! I fastened it together but it didn't feel secure at all. I was going to have to undo this and start over eventually, but I would see how long it lasted.

And then, I heard the door open. The store was suddenly filled with the sound of heavy rain; a bolt of lightning illuminated the sky. And there, in the metal door frame, stood Billy, dripping wet, but smiling like an idiot.

My heart skipped a beat. My vagina beat twice.

"Hey, you!" I said. I ran from behind the register and went to give him a hug. As soon as I did, though, my stubborn right stocking completely fell down. Billy did a double take and then laughed when he noticed the wardrobe malfunction happening on me.

"What's going on? You're wearing a lot less clothes tonight!"

"I always wear this in the rain." I smiled and he laughed again. I could feel myself blushing. I hoped the red of my cheeks stood out against the black of my wonderful new bra.

"Do you need help over there?" He pointed to my fallen down nude thigh-high.

"Actually, I do! I tried. I'm three quarters of the way there."

"Sit down. I'll help you!" he said in his soothing voice. His flannel was dripping wet, creating a small pool of water at his feet.

"Lemme hang this up for you first, so it can dry!" I said. I took his shirt and hung it up in the bathroom. When I came back, Billy was in a white T-shirt, blue jeans, and cowboy boots. A classic all-American man, who could change your oil, fix your plumbing, and fasten your garter belt to your stocking, perfectly.

I grabbed a folding chair and placed it near the

register. I sat down, I stretched out my leg on top of him. He caressed my leg, he slowly made his way up to my thigh, and he snapped together my stocking and garter in a matter of milliseconds.

"Thank you," I said. I was embarrassed. This was my lingerie section, this was my store, and he knew his way around the hardware better than me.

"Is this too fancy for me?" I asked. "Do I look like a little girl playing dress-up?"

"You look like a beautiful WOMAN dressed up!"

The red on my face became deeper.

"Come here, I've got something to show you!" I said, and I took his hand and pulled him over to my new and improved lingerie section. Billy's eyes widened in astonishment.

"I upgraded from paper to plastic," I shrugged and said, referring to my organized plastic drawers as a vast improvement over the cardboard boxes. I know one was better for the environment but I think even the environment would forgive me for this. Those cardboard boxes had to go.

"Now you can find everything way easier! And so can everyone else." I displayed my new section like I was Vanna White, but in lingerie, and Converse sneakers.

He smiled and looked at the variety of stockings, a delicious grin spreading over his face. He opened up various drawers and he seemed unsure of what to do with all of the new-found options. He held pairs of lace panties in one hand, stockings of every color in the other, like a child clutching his birthday toys. Suddenly, I had an idea. I opened the bottom drawer with the XL and XXXL lingerie. And thanks to my Dewy Decimal System à la plastic, I easily and conveniently found the same exact bra, panties, and garter that I had on right now. I grabbed them and handed them to him.

"Put this on," I said. The idea of us both wearing the same set of undergarments excited me. We could explore our femininity together—with his full beard and my one hairy leg, hand in hand—we could exist feeling beautiful underneath the fluorescent lighting.

"Really?" he asked.

"Yeah! Put it on! It will be fun. I think these colors would look nice on you." The material was a bit stretchy, I was sure it could fit on him. It might take some scissors and safety pins but it could definitely work.

He took the set from me. He massaged the material, admiring the delicate embroidered patterns. Together we picked out a new pair of stockings to go with it. Since his pair in the back had a small run in them we figured it was best to start over with a fresh pair.

"Go ahead, put them on!" I said. He unzipped his jeans and revealed to me he was already wearing his own pair of turquoise lace panties. "But those don't match mine." I pouted.

"I don't know," he nervously fumbled.

"Come on!" I said. We heard another blast of thunder. The outside world felt incredibly apocalyptic. It gave me a rush.

He took the panty set and began heading toward the bathroom. I stopped him.

"Just change right here! I'll help you. There's no one in here . . . and there's nothing to be ashamed of, really."

The store was empty, and I figured anyone who would suffer through extreme weather conditions to come into an adult store would also be tolerant of a man changing into lingerie in the middle of the store. The bathroom was a terrible fitting room, anyway.

"It'll be fine! If anyone comes in you can hide behind the DVDs," I said with a wink.

He still seemed unsure. I batted my eyelashes and did my newly learned incredibly amateur twerk to entice him. He laughed, a hearty belly laugh, but I noticed that he didn't look away. I truly was learning how to become a proper female. I had never used my ass or my eyelashes for any kind of persuasive act before.

"Okay, okay, I'll change out here."

He unbuckled his pants and let them fall to the floor around his ankles. His long T-shirt went halfway down his thighs. He slid off his jeans and his boots. He made sure his crotch area was covered with his T-shirt. It was endearing that even while surrounded by blow-up dolls and dildos he was still nervous about showing off his own sexual package. He slipped his turquois panties off, and he rolled them up and put them in the pocket of his blue jeans. He took the purple lace panties and slid them up his hairy legs. The juxtaposition of masculinity and femininity mixed in one was arousing to me. He turned around and faced away from me and adjusted his cock so it would tuck in and fit appropriately inside his new bottoms.

"How do they fit?" I asked.

"They're great!" he said. I lifted up his shirt and he looked incredibly vulnerable and nervous, but I rubbed his belly and it seemed to soothe his demons. I took the garter and put it around his waist, I stretched it as far as it could go, and it successfully fit on the very last fastening ring in the back. We both cheered.

"Yay, it fits!" I cheered. I never cheer. What the hell has come over me?!

"Take your socks off," I said. I slid a chair over to him, and he sat down while I took out his new pair of nude thigh-highs. He took one sock off and revealed an unexpected very subtle pastel pink pedicure. His toe nails were short and filed down, and the skin on his feet looked incredibly smooth. I carefully tried putting the stocking over his toes while they were pointed up like an L shape, and then he changed positions and pointed his toes down and arched his feet like a ballerina. I didn't want to rip them, I remembered how sensitive he got about that last time.

"I read somewhere they would go on more easily like this," he said. He was indeed correct—the stockings rolled onto his feet and up his legs smoothly with just the slight change of direction. I could see the bottom of his balls sticking out from underneath his purple panties from where I was sitting. I never would have expected the combination of lace and testicles to turn me on, but it did. I slid the stockings up his thighs, as I sat with my knees on the dusty concrete floor, listening to the thunder and rain outside. I wasn't so sure about the structural integrity of this building; the roof could have blown off at any moment, and we would be flooded. Billy and I would be underwater, swimming down the street in our matching lingerie. The thought of that actually didn't frighten me.

He stood up, with his long T-shirt still on and the black garter straps dangling down his thighs. His big thigh muscles seemed to have temporarily held up the stockings, since they weren't falling down like mine did. However, this was no excuse to avoid the task of attaching the thigh-highs to the garter. Like Isaac Newton says, whatever goes up, must come down, unless it's fastened by a garter.

"Maybe I'll have an easier time getting these on you," I said.

He laughed. "I can do it if you want!"

"No, I got it!" I said. I wanted to wear the pants and the panties in whatever kind of fleeting relationship this was. I made the nylons my bitch, shoving them against the tiny clasp that so gracefully fell on his hairy leg, and I didn't let that little plastic ball escape from me. I felt like there had to be a more efficient way for these to have been made. Could they have been replaced with some kind of button? I guess that wouldn't work. It would tear the stocking. A buckle? No that wouldn't work either. An invisible zipper? Maybe? I was surprised that in the entire season marathon of *Shark Tank* that I watched on Sunday, not one housewife/entrepreneur had any solution to make this any easier.

I concentrated and successfully got the front of the right leg done. I was down on my knees, and looking up at him he seemed to be 100 feet tall. Like he was the giant and I was Jack, and the magic beans led to an adult store inside of a strip mall in the sky.

He reached down to help me and our hands met in the middle of his thigh. I missed out on that pre-pubescent romance everyone else had in middle school, where couples "accidentally" held hands inside their big buckets of popcorn on awkward dates at the movie theater. This was what it must have felt like. He gripped onto mine, strongly, our eyes locked, and I felt a rush throughout my entire body.

I moved to the back garter, and his furry, but firm, toned ass was right in my face. The garter tightly rested against it as I latched onto the stocking and locked it into place. This was going smoothly. Thank goodness. Moments later all six garters were done, three on each side. I stood up and hugged him, our bottoms matching in purple lace panties, black garter, and nude stockings. We held each other and listened to the loud rain, and the jazz instrumental track of what I believed was a Nickelback song, and then suddenly, the lights went out (and so did the song, but that was actually more of a relief than a stress).

It was now pitch black in the store, and cracking the door to peek outside I could see nothing but a charcoal sky. The street lights were off as was the glow in the nondescript marquis outside that never changed, reading "VIDEO, DVD, XXX." I had goosebumps all over me; the temperature must have dropped at least eight degrees in the past thirty seconds. Billy held me closer. He and I didn't know much about each other. I didn't even know his last name, but something about our chemistry just meshed. I literally, and figuratively, felt warm in his big, burly arms.

I boldly placed my hand on top of his panties. I went up and down his thighs and felt the garter I so brilliantly put together. It was on there so snugly. I felt the top of his thigh-highs, I slid my fingers up and down and felt where the stocking ended and his thigh began.

I slid his T-shirt above his head. I played with his chest hair, and my fingers ran through his beard.

"I don't know if I'm supposed to kiss you, but I'd like to." He put a finger on my lips to shush me. We remained in complete silence in the dark with only the hard noise of the rain. Our lips were close. I could feel his breath, minty from an Altoid. The boys in college never freshened their breath for me. They also never wore matching panties with me.

He put his hands on my shoulders, keeping me in place while he moved behind me. He kissed my neck, rather aggressively, moving my hair to one side. He slid his hands underneath the lace cups of the bra and played with my nipples and awoke so many different senses inside me that I didn't know my nipples were connected to. How did I manage to feel that in my toes? In my fingers? And everywhere else? He continued to kiss my neck, he put a few of his fingers in my mouth, and then he went back to my breasts, but now with moistened fingers, and my nipples grew incredibly more sensitive. They were warm and cold from the saliva and the severe drop in temperature in the store. I'm not sure why he didn't want to kiss my lips but he wanted to caress my body and kiss my neck. Is this what real men did? I wasn't so sure, but I liked it.

I could feel myself getting wet and I found myself wondering whether my panties could hold the moisture. He continued to touch my breasts and I started to squirm. I found my pelvis dry humping the air, like it was just trying to grab onto something. It was bizarre—my body wasn't sure what to do—it had never been touched like this before.

His fingers went over the garter and underneath my panties. I could feel a hard cock pressing through his matching lace panties behind me against my right butt cheek. I was soaking wet; his fingers were strong and thick, and they circled around the area between my legs with ease. I was beginning to shake. He kissed my neck harder and his fingers began going faster. The panties were getting looser on my body. He found my clit, and I started to breathe heavily as he moved his finger up and down and up and down on it. We had several hundred vibrators and dildos at our disposal but I wanted nothing but his fingers. His large bodily mass enveloped me, his beard scratched against my ear, and his stockings and cock were pressed up against my ass while he catered to my clit so powerfully. He then took his other hand, reached down my ass, went underneath me, and stuck a finger inside my vagina. There was so much wetness he quickly stuck in two, and I slid myself up and down on his fingers while he continued to put pressure on my clit. "More," I yelled. I wanted more. I wanted more fingers, toes, arms, whatever—I wanted more of him inside me. He put another finger inside me and I loved the way my vagina felt challenged. His four fingers were thicker than an average cock, and they moved inside of me further and further. I moaned and moaned; he held onto my neck and lightly choked me.

He turned me around and pushed me down into the folding chair. I'm not sure how I landed so gracefully on there in the dark, but I did. He got down on his knees and spread my legs far apart, he pushed my lace panties to the side. I wasn't sure what his plan was, but I quickly felt a jolt of steam hit my labia; his hot breath. He licked his tongue up and down my vagina, teasing me, showing off all he could do with his mouth. I could feel so many foreign juices of mine seep into his mouth. I wanted him to taste every bit of me. His tongue was just as powerful as his fingers, but he spoiled me by stabbing his four fingers back inside me, going deeper and deeper while keeping his mouth on my clit. He curled his fingers inside me. He went really hard while licking and licking furiously. I felt out of control. I was shaking vigorously and uncontrollably. It was dark in here—did he swipe a dildo off the shelf that I couldn't see that he was sticking inside me? He was hitting a new spot somewhere inside me with his powerful fingers. I felt myself open up, my legs were spreading further and further open. They felt like Jell-O, and I thought they might just detach from my body and walk away.

He sucked and licked, with my pubic hairs in his mouth and his fingers jackhammering my pussy. I didn't feel like I had a vagina anymore—it was now officially a pussy. This body part feeling this sensation right now didn't warrant a biological/anatomical name that would be used in a science class. It deserved a slutty name that could be found in the urban dictionary. It was now a coochie or a cunt. Something you would never say around your parents. He must have paved his own secret passageway inside my body, because nothing and no one who had ever been inside me had made me feel this way. I lost control and liquid gushed out of me everywhere. I screamed. He kept going with his fingers, and he opened his mouth and drank all the juices coming out of me. He stuck his thumb inside me, my hole was so open for him; I was panting and begging him for more as liquid streamed out of me like a garden hose watering his beard.

His whole hand was in me and he made a fist, inside of me. Holy shit. Was there really a fist inside me? I believe there was. I could see a hint of a glow from the roman numerals on his watch resting against the opening of my vagina.

He rubbed and rubbed my clit, I felt stuffed and tight and loose at the same time. I was screaming and practically crying. I couldn't stop cumming. I hadn't had an orgasm in so long and this one made up for lost time. This had to be like ten orgasms in one. My legs were up in the air. I clenched up and reached some kind of climax of a climax, which pushed his hand out of me. He stuck his hand in my face, and I licked my own juices off of him. As I sucked off my own body from his fingers, he began moaning louder. I saw his other hand moving up and down. He was jerking off, and I wanted to help. What should I do? He was clearly more experienced than I was. The fabric from the panties was still on his cock, and he moved his hand swiftly up and down. I wasn't sure what I should do, I felt drunk from my multiple orgasms.

He let out a big loud grunt. He had such a sexy deep voice that just got deeper as he was climaxing. It was hard to tell what was going on in the dark. He put his thigh up to my mouth, I could feel warm stickiness on top of his nylon. I licked it off, I licked everywhere in the entire surface area of his large thigh to make sure to get every last drop of cum that might be there. There was a cocktail of bodily fluids in my mouth and I didn't want the taste to ever wash away. It was like I bit into an apple full of sex.

"Let's get out of here," he said.

He threw his T-shirt on me, grabbed his jeans and his jacket, and I locked up the store. Outside in what I was sure was becoming a hurricane, while we were drenched in orgasms and hard rain, he finally gave me a kiss. I had felt his tongue on my pussy and neck but not on the lips on my face until now. Perhaps we could continue this defiance of the order of typical dating operations and next we will get dinner, and then, maybe after, learn each other's last names.

We headed toward his eighteen-wheeler semi truck. It looked so sexy and powerful next to my puny Honda Civic. Where we were headed, I wasn't so sure, but I was excited to see what would happen next.

Continue with Taryn in this fantasy, turn to the next page.

I had a beautiful night's sleep in the back of Billy's truck, in a tiny loft space he built on top of the seats. It was called a "sleeper," rather appropriately, with a small mattress that we fit on together snugly. His sheets were red and silky, his pillows were black and fluffy, and there were multiple bumpy foam egg crates between the sheet and the mattress, which gave it that extra *oomph* of comfort.

We slept parked underneath an overpass so the rain wouldn't hit the windows quite as hard. We woke up sometime in the afternoon, and watched downloaded episodes of *Twin Peaks* on his laptop. We heated up organic microwave burritos (I had no idea organic ones existed—microwave meals have come a long way) and Billy tried on different pieces of lingerie that he recently purchased from Walmart. The items weren't nearly as flattering as the ones from Dreamz. They looked cheap, and the lace didn't have quite the same feel, and the stockings ripped as soon as they came out of the package.

After the sixth pair of panties that would be too ugly for most women to even wear on laundry day, I asked, "Why did you get these? You have better taste than this!"

"I just needed to work up the courage to buy panties, in public," he answered. "It was important."

"You think anyone really looks at what anyone is buying in a Walmart?" I laughed. He wasn't laughing with me. I suppose it actually wasn't really a joke, just a statement about the ambivalence of the people at Walmart.

"There's nothing to be embarrassed about. Really!"

"I was in a panic the entire time—I felt like everyone was staring at me," he said.

"If anyone asked, you could have said it was for your girlfriend. But no one was going to ask, anyway!"

"I tried to say that once at Victoria's Secret and they kicked me out. I felt like a criminal. They must have just known," he said.

"Well, their stuff is way over priced and the people who work there are REALLY annoying. They practically kicked ME out of the store for not agreeing to get their credit card after purchasing one damn bra."

Then he actually laughed.

"Do you want to see what else I got?" he asked.

"Of course!" I answered.

"It's a secret," he said.

"I mean, you did put your fist inside me while I was technically on the clock. Your secret is definitely safe with me!"

He pulled out a big shoe box stored underneath his passenger seat. It was a large pair of pointy ankle boots. They sure were a "Secret"—strong enough for a man, but made for a woman.

"Did you try them on?" I asked.

"Not in the store, but yes. I did. And they fit perfectly!" He smiled.

"Is this your first pair of . . ." I stopped myself midsentence. I was going to say "women's shoes" but would that be offensive for me to imply these were shoes made for a woman and not a man? And if I said, "Is this your first pair of shoes?" then that would make him sound like a child, or a hobo, who didn't own any shoes. I was stuck inside of the ocean of a sentence and I wasn't sure how to move forward and I was too deep to go back.

"Yes, they are my first," he answered. He knew what I was trying to say. He squeezed his feet into the shoes and put them on. He smiled and held my hand.

"Thank you," he said.

"Thanks for what? Watching you put on a pair of shoes?"

"Yes, I suppose you're the first one to see me do this."

"You're talking about it like I'm watching you do heroin!" I said. "You need to relax!"

I hated when people told me to relax, and I was almost never relaxed. I felt hypocritical saying the words out loud.

"You can talk to me, Billy. But if you don't want to talk that's okay, too. I'm here and I love your shoes, and your panties—well, I like the panties you got from my store, not those other ones!" I kissed him, and he firmly held my hand. He squeezed it tightly.

"So I'm from Boca Raton," he said.

"Ha! Really? It's . . . incredibly fancy there," I answered.

"I was engaged to a woman I thought I was going to spend the rest of my life with. We were high school sweethearts, we dated through our early twenties. We went to college together, then she went on to med school, studying to be a surgeon. I was working with my father. He owned a construction business and he was training me to take it over from him so he could retire early."

"Okay. . ."

"Well, I had this strong urge to dress up ever since I was young. To feel the flowy fabrics against my skin.

To feel . . . pretty. I never got to explore it. I thought the urge would go away, but it didn't. It kept me up at night. Finally, I got myself just one pair of panties and a pair of stockings. I actually drove to a Rite Aid in a different county to get them. I hid them in the crawl space above my fiancée's and my bedroom that she never went into. I would put them on every Tuesday evening, when she had night class. I walked around the house, I would walk around on my tiptoes and pretend I was wearing high heels. I wasn't sure what I was doing. I just knew it was something I had to do." He paused.

"One Tuesday night, I wound up getting a little tipsy while I dressed up. I had accumulated panties, stockings, and a camisole I found at the Good Will. The outfit was a complete disaster but I was enjoying myself. I lost track of time, and my girlfriend came home. I quickly got everything off and shoved it under the bed. Thinking about it now, maybe I just wanted to get caught. I don't know. But she found them, and she brought them into my work the next day at the construction site, where I was with my father. She stormed right in and looked like she had been crying."

"Okay," I said, while he held me closer and teared up a bit as he continued to talk.

"She said, 'WHOSE ARE THESE?' She thought I was cheating on her. I thought an honest answer would be a sigh of relief, so I said they were mine. But I sure was wrong. My father punched me in the face and called me a faggot and had security remove me from the site. I haven't heard from either of them, or even my mother, ever since. They wouldn't answer my calls, they wouldn't even let me come get my stuff. So I got a job delivering produce. I stay in my truck and motel rooms and I just keep moving."

"When did that happen?" I asked.

"About two years ago," he said. "I was confused by this feeling and I still am. I mean, I'm not gay. I tried that when I first got on the road a few times and it—well it didn't really work, if you know what I mean. I never masturbated and thought of having sex with men. I'm not ashamed of my cock. I like my cock, but I don't want to see it when I put my panties on. I've tried fitting in with different groups of people in the past two years, and I don't really fit in anywhere. But I know that this part of me is important and I need to explore it more and I'm just sick of being embarrassed or ashamed."

I held him. I understood. Maybe not to the exact degree, but I was never quite weird enough for the weirdos and I was never normal enough for the normies. There were bits and pieces of me scattered all over the place and I wasn't quite sure how they all fit together. My iTunes never knew how to make a proper "genius" mix for me because my two favorite music artists at that moment were Ariana Grande and Depeche Mode. Seriously.

And yeah, the fact that there's no perfect Pandora station for me doesn't hold a candle to being punched in the face by your father, but I knew that I always had a hard time being comfortable with just about anyone I had ever met, anyone ever, except . . . Billy. Whose last name I still didn't know. That was a minor detail.

"Well, what should we do next?" I asked. "I have a day off, and I am up for anything."

"How about we start with taking a shower?"

"Right! Where exactly do you shower by the way?" I

asked. I looked under the bed as if there might be some kind of miniature, compact, folding bathroom underneath there. It wasn't completely outlandish to think that. There was, after all, a miniature microwave, a micro miniature fridge that made the usual college mini fridges look giant.

"Get ready, girl, for your first truck-stop shower!" he said. I know my apartment was a mere eight miles away and I fully just did pay for my portion of the water bill, but I felt like Billy and I were existing in some kind of dream bubble; going back to any semblance of my "real" life would make this bubble pop and the dream would end. And I wasn't ready for it to end.

Continue with Taryn in this fantasy, turn to the next page.

We still smelled like sex, but not the good leftover smell of sex. That smell had fermented into something more akin to mold on our bodies and we needed to wash it off, to make way for new and fresher sex smells. Billy slipped on a pair of sweatpants and sneakers, while I borrowed one of his flannels that went down to my knees and my Converse sneakers. We hopped into the truck's front seats and set off down the highway.

Not too long after, we pulled into some kind of parking lot with a whole bunch of different sized trucks filling the spaces. In the middle of the lot was a decent sized building. We parked at the back of the lot—those spots get more shade, Billy said—and parked the truck. As we walked through the lot, I saw several men sleeping at the wheel, though plenty more were partaking in outside activities: some were stretching and doing various pull-ups on bars suctioned to the outside of their trucks, some were reading outside on the back ledges of the truck, and some were talking on their cell phones. They nodded at us as we walked by. I was sure they thought I was some kind of stray hitchhiker he gave a ride to, and it actually wasn't completely far off from the truth. I was waiting at Dreamz for someone or something to take me to wherever my next step in life was, and that step seemed to be a truck filled with lots of pairs of panties.

We arrived at the building. It was plain-looking with gray paint on all sides, no windows, and only a door with a coin-operated lock. Billy pulled a few quarters out of his pocket, put them in the door, and turned the latch and it locked behind us.

"These are, like, the Mercedes of truck-stop showers. Only the finest for you!" he said with a grin. He opened the door with a flourish.

Inside, it was incredibly clean, with various soaps and shampoos and conditioners lined up on the wall for anyone's use. I never expected that a shower on an off-ramp on a highway could be so glamorous. It was a big open room with no shower curtain, and light and dark brown checkered tile. We quickly undressed, giddy at the thought of warm water rushing over us. He turned the shower on and it was the absolute perfect pressure, unlike the shower in my house which felt much like a very dehydrated person was peeing on me. The nozzle was large, like a flying saucer that rained down enough water to cover the both of us.

We let the water soothe our bodies, grabbing soap to scrub away the gross things on our skin, letting the suds of soap fizz up on us. We kissed in the stream of warm water—between this and the make-out session in the monsoon yesterday, we appeared to be quite good at kissing underwater. Something about the wetness pouring on our heads and our saliva mixing with one another's brought a beautiful energy between us. I grabbed a new body puff out of the package and soaped up his body. I cleaned his elbows and his knees, and his armpits. He scrubbed my breasts and my stomach—the smell of the soap was so pure and clean— and then he massaged shampoo into my hair, slowly, the way someone at a professional hair salon would do.

Eventually, I went down his body and soaped up his

crotch. I finally got a good look at his penis. It wasn't erect but it still looked thick, and his testicles were perfectly round and soft. I was giddy thinking about all the fun I could have with it. I rinsed the soap off, and put the conditioner in my hair. I had frizzy, uncooperative hair, and conditioner had to remain in it for at least eight to twelve minutes for it to be at all effective. I looked at Billy's cock and thought of a perfect way to pass the time. I knew the way his mouth tasted, I knew the way his cum tasted, and I knew the way his organic microwave burritos tasted, but I actually didn't know the way his cock tasted and I wanted that to change.

I knelt down on the tile floor with half a bottle of conditioner penetrating my hair and I began stroking Billy's cock. He looked down at me in anticipation, watching to see what move I would make next. It had been over a year since I had anyone's penis in my mouth—I was like some kind of born-again blow-job virgin. I really, really wanted to make him feel good. I had never experienced this feeling when confronted with a cock in my face. I will shamefully admit that with all the blow jobs in my life prior to this moment, I was just going through the motions, sucking dutifully until the cock was hard enough to stick inside of me. What a difference it was to have a cock in front of me attached to someone I truly wanted to please! I had some new visuals in my brain from the snippets of pornography I saw on the monitors in the ROOMZ at work. With a little inspiration from those, along with just following my own instincts, I would give a new and improved blow job.

I stroked his cock into my mouth. He let out a moan as my tongue hit his small head. I stroked it with one hand, and once it was erect it was large enough for both of my hands to fit around it. I used lots of spit—a tip I learned from the videos. Something about spitting large amounts of my saliva on a cock made me feel so incredibly powerful.

I loved looking at the way his eyes rolled back into his head; he looked so vulnerable. I paid attention to the way his expressions changed when I switched the positions of my hands. He scrunched his nose when I went harder and he moaned louder when I went softer. I jerked him off at the base of his cock while stuffing the rest of it in my mouth, using my tongue to swirl around his skin and work up as much spit as I possibly could. I moved a hand and put them on his balls. Quite honestly I wasn't even sure what to do with his balls, but I just wanted to make sure all parts of his genitalia were being accounted for.

I stroked and sucked, he started losing his balance and he leaned up against the wall. The water was left on but we weren't using it to wash ourselves. It was merely a sexy background at this point, like I was sucking his cock in front of a waterfall. Billy paid $2.25 to use this shower and part of that fee was having no regard for their water bill at all. I didn't feel at all guilty.

I was able to get my mouth further down his cock with him back up against the tile. It felt so good to have more of him in a part of me. I loved the way he tasted, I loved how his face lit up with pleasure when I licked up and down his shaft, I loved seeing what just my tongue and mouth and hands could do to someone. I wished I could go back in time and give a refund to all six of the people I had performed oral sex on. Those blow jobs weren't really blow jobs. This was my new standard of blow job and whatever dick would come into my mouth from here on out would be given this level of hospitality. I was really enjoying myself. My pussy was getting wet, and not just because we were in a shower. Actually enjoying a blow job is so satisfying.

"Put your hands behind your back," he demanded. I obeyed.

I opened my mouth wider and he thrust his cock in and out of me. So much saliva was coming out of my mouth, it was a waterfall of spit in front of our waterfall of truck-stop shower. I could feel him in the back of my throat and I could feel myself getting wetter and wetter as the tip of his cock hit my tonsils. He continued to thrust, and I swallowed as much of him as I possibly could. He went faster, then he slowed down. I could feel him throbbing. I sucked and licked and did whatever the hell I could possibly do with my mouth. He moaned loudly and I tasted an amazing gulp of warm cum seep directly down my throat. I felt his dick go from hard to flaccid in my mouth. I slurped up any last drop of semen that came out of him. No one would have to worry about getting any jizz on the floor of this pristine, pretty shower.

"That was incredible," he said between heavy breaths.

"I know," I said.

"Oh, do you?" he laughed.

I stood up and he immediately knew to wash the conditioner out of my hair. It was time. He massaged my head and a strong scent of coconut ran down my body.

"I want you to get all dressed up for me tonight. You know, in feminine clothes," I said. "And I want us to go out, like in public." I kissed him.

He looked nervous and excited.

"I've never done that," he said.

"I know. I think it's time," I said.

"I actually do have a dress in the truck. It's nothing amazing—I actually bought it at a maternity store. I said it was for my pregnant wife," he laughed.

"I'll look through everything you have and we can put it all together," I said.

I could see him tremble.

"In that case—I should really shave my beard," he said. He shut the water off and walked over to the porcelain bathroom sink, taking a small scissors and a razor out of his personal toiletry bag. He snipped away his lumber-jack beard until it was as short as it could possibly be. I lathered his face in some of this fine truck stop's complimentary shaving cream, and with his high-end disposable razors (the ones that had a sea foam green moisturizing strip on them) he shaved his face, revealing the velvety soft skin underneath his beard. I touched his face, now smooth as a river stone.

"I don't know how long we have before your five-o'clock shadow starts creeping in, so we better take advantage of this." He quivered, and I pulled him into my embrace. "I got you—everything will be okay."

We went back to the truck. Billy pulled out all the little fragments of femininity that he had. A half-empty bottle of foundation his ex-girlfriend threw in the trash when she got a sun-tan and her complexion changed. He pulled out a white ramekin that looked like it was used for a side of salad dressing at Applebee's, but it was filled with some kind of red, sticky goo that was apparently a lipstick that he made from scratch from a mix of bottles of lotion he had from motels, food coloring, and honey. It went on surprisingly smoothly and I put some on myself as well. He had some loose shimmer powder he created from a mix of spices, his panties and stockings from Dreamz, and various accessories he picked up at truck stops over the years. The dress went down to his knees, and the garter peeked through when he walked. It was subtle and incredibly classy with this vintage burlesque feel. The final touch was a wig that he had ordered online and picked up at a mail center somewhere during his travels. It was still in the packaging and had never been opened. It was long, wavy, and a shade of brown that perfectly matched his natural hair color. We took it out of the box, pinned it to his hair, snipped it, styled it, and we were ready to go. In the DIY crafty mood, I took one of his black V-neck shirts, pinned it in the back, and put a silk scarf thing that lived in the bottom of my purse around my waist and matched it with my Converse sneakers. I kind of looked like a modern version Punky Brewster, and he looked like a modern version of Aubrey Hepburn, and together we were ready to conquer the night and run to our destiny, with heels on. Or, ankle boots with short wedges, to be exact.

"So, where should we go?" I asked.

"There's a bar not too far from here that makes some great cocktails. Or, I heard there's a country fair in town; we could go ride some rides," Billy replied.

Both options sounded good, but which was the better ace to debut Billy's new look: a bar or a fair?

To go to the fair, turn to page 268.

To go to the fair, turn to page 268.

To go to a bar, turn to page 277.

Billy and I waited in line to buy our entrance tickets to the fair. The air smelled like corn dogs and hay. The ground was moist from the storm the night before. Last time I was here was when I was in the eighth grade with my friend Charlotte. I wasn't very cool in school, and she was my equally uncool friend, and we clung together for the sake of not being alone. We awkwardly ate funnel cake while the more socially adept teens who never gave us the time of day smoked cigarettes, drank vodka, and made out with each other underneath the bleachers. Twelve years later, I am still just as much of an outsider in this town, but I have proudly upgraded from a co-pilot with a back brace and acne to a beautiful man in a dress.

"Should I still call you Billy?" I asked.

"It's Bonnie," she said, as she kissed me and held my hand. I could feel her trembling, but she walked with confidence and poise.

"Shit. Now there's lipstick on your cheek!" She wiped it off my face. "That's a new thing I'll have to look out for," Bonnie said.

"Let's go on the Ferris wheel!" I said. I felt like having a destination would ease her nerves, and we could be alone in our own little rotating pod while still technically being out in public. We walked from one side of the park to the other. A few people did double-takes when looking at us, and some mothers made their children look away from us, like we were a walking, breathing R-rated movie that they weren't supposed to watch. I rolled my eyes, and considered flipping them off, but managed to stop myself. Whatever.

We stopped at a stand to get some junk food. Our afternoon microwaved burrito was organic after all, we deserved to let loose.

"I'll get one small cotton candy," I said to a man with very large and very few teeth, long hair, and pin-striped overalls. He nodded and began circulating the paper cone around the caramelized sugar, and a magical poof of edible, hot-pink cotton began to form.

"Anything for you ma'am?" he looked at Bonnie and said.

She paused. "No, thank you," she replied.

We walked away and there were tears in her eyes. "He called me ma'am! Did you hear that?"

"Yes! I did!" We skipped and cheered and got high off sugar. We felt victorious. The carnie with four teeth and an obvious, unpleasant stench had more manners than some of the people in the park. While I didn't fully understand how Bonnie felt, I could see the thrill in her eyes and her happiness was contagious.

"Let's go in here!" I said as we passed a House of Mirrors. Bonnie barely got the chance to look at herself as a woman, so I thought it would be exciting to see herself in hundreds of different mirrors, from multiple angles, in multiple heights and weights.

"Sure!" she said.

There was no line and we walked straight inside. The room was dark, and the music was creepy. Every few steps a high-pitched voice laughed maniacally from a hidden speaker in the wall. In the first group of mirrors, our heads were incredibly large and stretched out like chewed bubble gum, and then further down the hallway we got progressively shorter and fatter. We laughed at ourselves. Even though the result of going in these types of places is extremely predictable, it doesn't stop the joke from being funny. No matter how un-politically correct it sounds, seeing yourself as some kind of disfigured midget, is funny—and somehow oddly romantic for a date.

Bonnie slyly looked around the room, and then swiftly pulled my top down and exposed my breasts. It wasn't entirely difficult to do since I was wearing one of her T-shirts that was way too big on me, and I didn't have on a bra.

"Bonnie!" I giggled, and attempted to pull the shirt back up and she pulled it back down, further this time. The pre-recorded laughter got louder and louder, the organ polka music got more and more distorted, and I remained shirtless in a room full of mirrors. Something about the smell of hot dogs and the slow, distorted music alleviated all stress out of the evening and we were able to just relax and goof around and have fun.

"Let's see how many different sizes your boobs can be," Bonnie said. It was like the license plate game I used to play on long car rides, but with tits.

We walked down the hall and my breasts went through every imaginable bra size, from a 32 A to a 38 GG. In one particular mirror, they multiplied exponentially. Bonnie put her hands on all sixteen of my breasts.

"How does that feel?" she asked.

It was a turn-on to see her feel me up in so many different ways. I wished I could actually grow fourteen more pairs of boobs so she could molest all of them. She pinched my nipple, and watching the freak-show of myself turned me on fourteen times more than normal for a pinched nipple. I felt myself getting wet. Then I heard the sound of screaming children somewhere in the vicinity and I pulled my shirt up instantly. The thrill of getting caught scared me and aroused me, so naturally I pulled my tits out again. Just moments later, the shrill of the children's voices went away.

After we had exhausted all optical possibilities in the little house of mirrors, we exited and continued to walk toward the Ferris wheel. I was aroused and giddy from the brief stint of public nipple play mixed with the sugars circulating inside my body.

"You're walking flawlessly in those heels," I said. "And it's muddy out. That's impressive!"

"I am so scared of falling on my ass. It's all I can think about! I feel like I'm walking a tightrope in the circus," she replied.

"You're not gonna fall! I won't let you. That's just not an option."

As the night got later, the park became more crowded, and the more people there, the more people scowled and hissed at our existence. As we proceeded to walk through the carnival, people escaped our presence and parted like the red sea. We paved our own path and walked through it proudly. Or at least, I was proud. I could tell Bonnie was nervous, but she walked with determination, poise, and confidence.

We waited in the line for the Ferris wheel. I could feel everyone whispering, I could see everyone pointing. Boys who couldn't have been older than sixteen were holding open containers of alcohol, but this didn't seem to concern anyone as much as we did.

"Maybe we should just go," Bonnie suggested.

"No way!" I answered. "Really, ever since I was in middle school I've always wanted someone to kiss on the Ferris wheel."

"Oh come on, I'm sure you've kissed plenty of people on the Ferris wheel!"

"No, I haven't. Honestly," I said. "The only person to kiss me in high school was someone who got stuck with me on a game of spin the bottle. And he tried to get out of it!" I laughed. "Literally he tried blowing the bottle so he could kiss my friend Jill instead of me."

She laughed.

"What was high school like for you?" I asked, trying to make conversation to distract Bonnie's attention away from the people staring, though I was also genuinely interested.

"Well, I played football," she said.

"Oh, jeez. Well, I'm sure you had no problem finding any willing partners to make out with you!"

"That's true. But I was more interested in trying the girls' clothing on than I was in getting their clothing off!"

"Well, you could have done both with me. Although I doubt you would have wanted to wear my thrift-store Dickies and my argyle sweaters."

Our place in line advanced to the front and we were let into our own carriage. The way they did it was just so impractical. It was like jumping into a moving vehicle. Why was it impossible for it to come to a complete stop before people went on? But Bonnie grabbed my hand and pulled me in. We jumped on without skipping a beat; she was a more seasoned Ferris wheel rider than I was. I followed her lead and together we were ready to get slowly lifted in the air, go around in a circle, and gaze at the view of Pasco County, which is mostly motels, strip malls, and chain restaurants. Still, everything looks better from above.

The ride slowly started and stopped. I never paid attention to how rickety these things felt when I was younger. Did I develop a small case of vertigo in my twenties? I felt slightly uneasy, but I didn't want to mess up the romantic moment I insisted on creating. After what felt like a bit too much starting and stopping, we were at a full stop at the top of the wheel. The temperature was humid and I could smell wafts of grease from deep fried everything in the air, which I will admit I actually liked.

"It's time for my very first carnival kiss!" I said. I handed her a tissue. "Blot your lipstick first, though."

"What on earth does that mean?" she asked.

"Oh! You basically just give this Kleenex a kiss," I said. "Just put it between your lips, and slightly less of it will wind up on my face."

I held the tissue up and she opened her mouth as if I was feeding it to her. She clamped down on it, I moved the tissue around and she blotted herself on all the corners of the tissue. She enjoyed indulging in this feminine activity. I took for granted the little pieces of seemingly mundane activity that went into being a woman. I never had to blot my lips much, because I rarely wore lipstick and rarely kissed people, until now.

She leaned over after the blotting activity was complete. I stuffed the tissue back into my purse—I wanted to save it for some kind of Billy/Bonnie scrapbook, or maybe if I never wound up seeing her again, I could pull this out and taste her lips on this tissue. Was that creepy? I should be savoring the moment. I don't know why I was stressing about our possibly doomed ending when we had barely reached our beginning. The fair was bringing back some déjà vu of the loneliness and isolation I felt growing up and I just didn't want this moment to end.

Bonnie leaned over and kissed me. I grabbed onto her, I put my hands up her skirt and felt up and down her stockings and her garter. The feeling of a cock underneath a dress with panty hose was such a thrill. Her kiss was so intense and beautiful, I felt it inside my entire body. We wrapped our tongues around each other, and I ran my fingers through her long, wavy hair. Unfortunately, I got a bit too aggressive with my heavy petting, and accidentally knocked the wig off her head. It was caught by a strong wind and blew off, away into the air. Shit.

Bonnie followed it with her eyes, her face suddenly white. It was as if I ripped off a piece of her body and threw it in the trash.

"Oh god, I'm so sorry," I said.

"I must look ridiculous," she frowned.

"No you don't! There's plenty of sexy women with shaved heads!" I said. "You look like a badass!" I exclaimed. I wasn't sure if I was making anything better at all.

"I just want to bury my head in the sand," she said.

"I . . . don't have any sand. What about here?" I don't know what came over me: I took her head and I pushed it down to my pussy. Our carriage rocked back and forth, I must have been high on cotton candy to have gained this burst of slight confidence, mixed with simply feeling invincible. Apparently when I was 500 feet in the air, I became kind of dominant. Plus I wanted to do anything to distract her.

She pulled my panties to the side and quickly played with my clit. She licked the sides of my labia. It felt so good to have her back between my legs. I was already super moist, so she plunged three fingers inside me and bit my thigh. She came back up and kissed my neck; I didn't care if it wound up being covered in lipstick. I could feel her thick fingers stuffing me, immediately hitting my G-spot, and I began to tremble. I wanted to shout *I'm cumming!* from the top of the wheel, but I knew that would be inappropriate. She knew the inside of my pussy so well, she knew exactly where to go. She could make me cum so easily, it was like she just had to turn on a switch. She must have ridden the Ferris wheel so many times in high school with her football in one hand and a cheer-leader's pussy in the other, and that's how she just knew exactly what to do. She took her fingers from out of me and stuck them in my mouth. They tasted so powerful. I could taste the aroused state of my vagina right off of her. I was learning how juicy my pussy got when it was touched the right way. I had never felt this much moisture out of me from anyone who touched me in the past.

She had to have loved the power she had over my pussy. I can only imagine what it must feel like to be able to make someone lose control over their own body so quickly. She seemed more relaxed. I was drunk from cumming and she was drunk from her own fingering mastery. The Ferris wheel began to go down slowly, people were getting off (not in the same way I had, and I felt bad for those people). I could tell that Bonnie's insecurities were coming back; I didn't want people to laugh at her as we exited the park. I took my silk scarf from around my waist and I put it on her head. Bonnie began to laugh.

"What on earth?"

"I was the understudy for Tzeitel in my middle school's *Fiddler on the Roof* play. I got really good at putting on a scarf!"

We walked off the Ferris wheel, hand in hand, and we exited the park, while remnants of my orgasm ran down my leg, and Bonnie looking like a sexy Russian babushka. It was time to retreat back to her truck. I wasn't sure if I would be lying in a mini sleeper under a bridge with Bonnie or Billy that night, but either way, it was the only place I wanted to be.

To go back and go with Billy to a bar instead, turn to page 277.

To see how the fantasy ends, turn to page 292.

I called a cab to come pick us both up at the truck stop (I didn't think the clubs would have parking spaces big enough for a commercial truck) and got a text saying one was on the way. I will admit I was nervous about picking the right bar. Going out in general was not my area of expertise, and choosing a place that would allow Billy to be comfortable in drag for the first time in public was a daunting responsibility. After going through the not-too-extensive list of options around us (TGI Fridays was about the most hip place in the vicinity), I decided that we should drive to an area of downtown Tampa filled with bars and nightclubs.

"All right, let's go!" I said. Billy trembled, and didn't seem to want to leave.

"Come on!" I tried pulling him and he froze. I kissed him, and his red homemade lipstick transferred from his lips to mine. I put my hands up his skirt and rubbed his thigh, basking in the unique feeling of a garter against a hairy thigh. As I stroked him, he seemed calmer, but I could still see the nervousness on his face.

We walked out of the truck and the other drivers sitting outside their vehicles definitely did a double take. The looks were inquisitive, but not hateful. I definitely saw one man in particular checking him out.

"Should I call you something different?" I asked. Billy thought about this for a moment.

"Yeah! Call me Bonnie," she said.

"All right, I can do that!" I replied. We walked hand in hand through the parking lot toward the cab. Even though we had spent the past twenty-four hours together, I was now being reintroduced to someone completely new. It reminded me of my roommate in college who successfully juggled two relationships at the same time. I don't know how she did it. I could barely get a text back from someone I had sex with and she had scheduled times of when to text who and what. Her cheating involved flowcharts and lots of strategy. Okay, maybe what was going on with me right now wasn't exactly like that, but the thrill of dating one person by day and a different one at night was intoxicating.

As we crammed into the cab's back seat, the driver definitely glanced at us through the rearview mirror a few times, but he shrugged and set off on our path. I snuck my hand up Bonnie's skirt in the back of the cab and I could feel the beginning of a boner through her panties.

"The good thing about this bell-shaped maternity dress as opposed to your tight jeans is that you can get a boner out in public and no one will know!"

She laughed. I kissed her neck. I put my fingers through her wig, getting turned-on by the softness of the fibers. I had always been curious about being with a woman, but never found one that I really clicked with. Being with a woman who also had a cock was the best of all worlds. I was lucky.

We had arrived and the cab fare of $37 lit up on his meter. Bonnie handed the driver a fifty and said, "Keep the change, hon'." She whispered it in a very Marilyn Monroe way. I think she was doing her best to try to figure out what her voice should be, and a whisper was better than a manly voice, or an obvious, exaggerated falsetto.

"Thanks, ma'am, have a good night!"

I don't think she heard the driver because she was so nervous and distracted and was in the middle of opening the door when he responded. Once we were out of the car, I jumped up and down like a little girl who had just been offered extra ice cream.

"What's going on? You just happy to be out somewhere that isn't work?" she laughed.

"Did you hear the cab driver?"

"No, I handed him his money—did I miss something?"

"He called you 'Ma'am!' Don't you think that's exciting?"

Bonnie stopped dead in her path and tears welled up in her eyes.

"You know, I wasn't even paying attention!" she said, "Thank you."

"Thank YOU for letting me be a part of this. I am honored!" And I really was. Between the fisting and the homemade lipstick, this had been a rollercoaster of incredible emotions.

We walked down Bayshore Boulevard. I didn't exactly have a destination in mind—it was a five-mile road along the water, with a handful of bars. Truly I had no idea which place was best to go, but the sidewalk was nicely paved and it seemed like a comfortable place for Bonnie to practice walking in her short wedges, and the reflection of the giant Bank of America blue and red lights bouncing off the water paired quite well with her yellow dress.

We walked past a 1920s prohibition themed bar, complete with a man out front in a brown plaid suit that looked like it had at least eight different pieces to it. He had a Sherlock Holmes style monocle on his face. He appeared to be the door guy.

"Wanna go in here?" I asked.

"All right," she replied. Her long, wavy hair was lightly blowing in the wind. We pinned that fucker on quite perfectly. I was proud.

"Good evening," the doorman said.

"Hello!"

"How many people are in your party?"

"Just two of us!"

"Fabulous!" He had a mini iPad in his hands, with something that looked like a floor plan on it. He pushed in two little circles on the plan with an electronic pen. For someone who dressed like they existed before television was invented, I found it odd that their way of seating tables was so futuristic.

"May I see your IDs?"

"Sure!" I reached inside my bag and pulled out my wallet, I opened it instinctually and pulled out my ID. Bonnie trembled. Shit. I didn't think about identification. She looked at me, she fumbled around, and I felt like I was going to panic, too. I didn't want our night ruined before we even got in the door. She could show her ID and the door man could probably just do a double take and let her go by. That would be the best scenario. But he could also say, "This isn't your fucking ID," and then Bonnie would have to prove she is legally Billy and that would definitely be a buzz kill to say the least. If the man was as old-fashioned as his suit, he could be incredibly closed minded, and have us tarred and feathered in the town square. If he was as modern as his iPad, then he would understand the situation and let Bonnie enjoy her night. Last time I really went out was on my graduation night, to a farewell party at the only LGBT friendly fraternity on campus. I certainly couldn't predict the behavior of a door guy at an upscale bar.

"Shit, Bonnie, did you forget your ID again?" I asked. I thought this would be a good save.

"I'm an old lady, I can't even remember the last time someone asked me for it!" She laughed at her own joke as enthusiastically as possible, and I jumped in and laughed too.

"You might be old Aunt Bonnie, but you sure are young at heart!" The turn of the century door guy was incredibly confused. While we weren't kissing or making out, the nature of Bonnie and my hand holding was a little too provocative for an aunt and a niece. I don't know why I even said that. I just thought the back story of a girl out on the town with her aunt and she innocently forgot her ID was believable.

"Please let us in, we drove an hour to get here—she's definitely of age." I gave him a sad look, trying to connect with him, hoping he might pick up on it and either have sympathy for the fact that I desperately wanted a night out with my aunt, or I desperately needed to get my new lover identifying with a different gender this evening. Not sure which was more relatable.

"I was born in 1978, when Jimmy Carter was president. Does that help? Would a twenty-year-old even know who Jimmy Carter was?" She laughed again and the *Boardwalk Empire* reincarnated door man actually cracked a smile, too. Bonnie was quite a charmer as a lady!

The door guy looked around, and surrendered. "All right, go in. Just bring your ID next time, and tip your bartender, please!"

"Thank you!" I said. I almost went to hug him but I

stopped myself because I realized that would be kind of strange.

We walked in like we were Bonnie and Clyde, all confident and cool. Or actually, more like Bonnie and Taryn.

On entering the bar we found the old-fashioned flapper theme was kept to the utmost extent. There was a lot of exposed brick and dark wood, multiple kinds of syrups, bitters, and herbs, and brands of liquors I hadn't ever heard of. This was nothing like a frat party.

On the opposite side of the bar, toward the wall, there were velvet couches and tables and they were enclosed with dark curtains that could remain open or closed, like little pool cabanas.

"Where do you want to sit?" I asked.

"Let's get one of these private tables," she answered.

A sexy flapper hostess came up to us, with a fringed dress, short hair, a shiny sequin headband around her head, and a feather in her hair.

"How can I help you ladies this evening?" she asked.

"We'll take one of those tables if that's okay," Bonnie said.

"It's a three-hundred-dollar food and drink minimum, as long as that's fine—I can get you set up right away," said the hostess.

That was the amount of money I usually budgeted for groceries the entire month! If I'm not mistaken, I thought Coca-Cola cost a nickel in the 1920s. This bar definitely picked and chose what vintage elements to keep and which to ignore.

"Yeah, that's fine," Bonnie said. She handed her credit card to the hostess. While it goes against some of my feminist ideals, I will guiltily admit that I have always dreamed of being properly wined and dined by someone and I was aroused by the fact that it was someone in a dress and pretty lace panties, and not a suit and tie.

We sat down. The seats were plush and incredibly comfortable. The lighting was seductive and dark, with just enough candlelight to read the menus and each other's lips.

"Would you like to start off with a shot of absinthe?" the pretty flapper asked.

Was that the poisonous beverage that Edgar Allan Poe drank? I wasn't really into poisoning myself (more than your average cocktail would), but if Bonnie wanted shots, we'd do shots. I nodded at her, indicating it was her decision.

"Yes, we would," Bonnie said, "and what's your name?"

"I'm Janine! And what's yours?"

"Bonnie."

"And I'm Taryn!" I said.

"Nice to meet you, ladies! I will be right back with your aperitif!" Janine said.

I assumed this was the street name for absinthe, or something along those lines. I was incredibly confused but so excited; I just took it all in and did my best to blend in here, in a long V-neck T-shirt and Converse sneakers.

She returned with two long, skinny glasses filled with light green liquid. It looked like something out of a science lab.

"Cheers!" Janine said. Bonnie and I clinked our glasses together and chugged the liquid in the shot glass. It tasted like fresh-cut grass and licorice. It was cool and crisp in my mouth, then burned when it got down to my stomach. I wasn't hallucinating (at least not yet) but I did feel pleasantly buzzed.

"So how are you feeling?" I asked Bonnie.

"I feel really powerful and beautiful. I can't believe this is finally happening," she said.

"I'm glad!"

I didn't completely understand how Bonnie felt on the inside, but I felt like we were both figuring out how to be ourselves in different ways. I could openly buy heels, dresses, and lipstick anytime I wanted and I chose not to. I suppose I took it for granted. For Bonnie, putting on a dress and being out in public made her feel powerful. For me, well, learning that I could squirt liquid out of my vagina while a fist was inside there is what did it for me. I wondered if she would fuck more daintily as a woman. Would she want me to gag on her cock? Or would she be more soft and passionate? Would she always want to be Bonnie? Or would she go back to being Billy tomorrow? *I shouldn't ask. I should just indulge in the moment we currently exist in and let the future reveal itself as it happens.*

Janine came back with three more drinks. She dropped two on the table.

"What are these?" Bonnie asked.

"Bartender's special! Try it!" she smiled and answered.

It was a short glass with a large ice cube in the middle, a lemon peel and some fizzy liquid inside of it. It tasted like an Orange Crush, but with a lot of alcohol in it. Oddly enough, the first time I ever got drunk was in a park with a few friends, who poured vodka into a half-filled bottle of warm Orange Crush. Apparently all we were missing was a lemon peel and some oversized ice.

But the drink did taste quite good. I drank it quickly and I liked the way the large ice felt on my lips.

"Easy there!" Bonnie said. She barely had a sip to drink.

"Oh—I wasn't supposed to chug this?"

"No, silly, you're supposed to savor the taste!" Janine said.

"Like a cup of coffee!" I answered.

Bonnie laughed. "Yes exactly, like a cup of coffee," she said as she daintily sipped from her glass.

"So, what are you ladies up to tonight?" Janine said. Was it part of her job to make me feel like she had some kind of a crush on one of us or both of us? Or was that the orange fizz and the light green liquid getting to my brain? She had bright white teeth and matte red lipstick on. I felt like she had a twinkle in her smile, like someone out of an old-fashioned toothpaste commercial. She had on satin gloves, and she too had on a garter and stockings. I didn't even have panties on. I didn't know that when I got dressed for work forty-eight hours ago that I would be going to a speakeasy on a date with a cross-dresser. Perhaps I should always be prepared for this type of surprise to come up.

"Come over here!" Bonnie motioned for me to come to the same side of the table with her. Two people sitting side by side at a table when no one was on the other side is definitely romantic. No one does that unless they just can't keep their hands off one another. I obliged and made my way over there and jumped right into her large arms.

"You two are so cute!" Janine said. "Would you like some privacy?" She didn't wait for our response and she drew the curtains so they covered the table and we were now enclosed in our own little candle-lit fort.

"Have fun!" she said, and she did her smile-twinkle thing again. I wondered what kind of toothpaste she used.

And then Bonnie and I were alone in public, at a table lit by an electric candle. I kissed Bonnie on the neck. It was sexy in a vampire-like way, and it was also practical since it was intimate and didn't mess up her lipstick. She put her hands up my, um, well I guess we can call it a dress for all intents and purposes. I had goosebumps. I also had no panties on. Being felt up at a fancy bar, and being felt up by a fancy woman was something entirely different than what I was used to; however these days I wasn't really sure what I was used to anymore. Every hour of the past seventy-two hours had been completely different than the next. It was a pretty drastic shift from my life being exactly the same for about the past eighteen years.

Her hands were delicate, but large and firm. They were the same hands that touched me earlier, only now they were attached to a torso that smelled like perfume. She continued to slide her hand up my thigh, and I slid my hand up hers. Her ruffled garter tickled the back side of my hand. This one had tiny white bows that fastened the thigh-high and the garter together. They remained fastened tightly even as I rubbed up and down. I couldn't quite put my finger on why I loved this feeling of lace, nylon, and man all mixed into one, but I did.

I could feel her cock getting hard underneath her dress and panties. Were we safe inside this enclosed space? Did the $300 minimum include a pass for exposed boners? I couldn't help myself. I was just so attracted to her; I was so swept away by the absurdity of how we came into each other's lives and then into each other's mouths.

She pushed me under the table and I sat with my knees on the floor and I put her cock in my mouth, moving her panties to the side. She sat at the table like a classy lady and drank cocktails while I shoved her thick cock as far as I could down my throat. I rubbed the lace material up against the skin of her shaft and I could feel her getting harder and harder. She pushed her legs together and squished my head in between her knees. I felt like I was in some kind of awesome sexy headlock, and I will admit that I liked the feeling of the hair on her thighs against my cheek.

She moved her legs open again, and I felt around her balls. I licked the stockings and garter; I liked the texture of the lingerie against my tongue. I saw the light get slightly brighter from my view underneath the table, and saw a pair of black Mary Janes along with nude stockings at my eye level. It was Janine. I was now getting acquainted with the bottom half of her body.

"I've got some more drinks for you!" I heard her say. It felt like when I used to watch *The Muppets* on Saturday morning and I only saw the mother's legs and heard her muffled voice.

"Thank you!" Bonnie said. Bonnie put her hand behind my head and pushed me further down on her cock. I obeyed her command and accepted my duty to be the blowjob giver underneath the table. I did it with as much spit and tongue as possible while trying to remain quiet.

"Where's your lady friend?" The waitress asked.

"She had to make a phone call. She," Bonnie paused, "will be," she paused again, "right back."

I liked this power that made her struggle with her words as she searched for the proper syllables to utter. I saw closed-toe short heels get closer to me. I inched away as to not let my knee touch her, because she was getting awfully close.

"But I didn't even see her leave the booth, how is that possible?" she asked slowly. I could taste a small amount of pre-cum at the tip of Bonnie's cock. I slurped it up immediately.

She then kneeled down underneath the table and I was looking her right in the face with a cock in my mouth. I would have apologized for my unruly behavior but . . . my mouth was full.

"What's going on down here?" she exclaimed. She didn't look upset at all. She reminded me very much of the mistress of a film noir detective. Or, perhaps she was the detective since she did such a good job of finding the hidden cock-sucker underneath the table. I took Bonnie's cock out of my mouth and looked shamefully downward.

"I was just . . . celebrating our private table in my own special way," I said.

"I hope a lady like you has some manners and knows to share," she uttered, with her perfect matte lipstick. I stuttered. Should I inconveniently lift my head up and get back to the top of the table and discuss with Bonnie as to whether I should share her cock or not? Should she get a say in this?

She drew the curtains again and crawled right next to me. She grabbed Bonnie's cock and put it right in her mouth, somehow without smudging any of her lipstick. Her face was so creamy and white, I could see a layer of thick powder on her face as she got closer to me. She was like a live Barbie from the 1940s; she was just too pretty to be sucking cock on the floor. This was more of a job for the young, frumpy girl in a T-shirt.

I continued to watch her stroke and suck Bonnie's cock. I wonder if she even knew up there that that was

Janine and not me? I was fine with her not knowing and I would happily take credit for this blow job. Janine was clearly more skilled in this department than I was. She took the cock out of her mouth and she grabbed my head and fed it into my mouth. She jerked Bonnie off right into me. I moved my head up and down and attempted to use as much of my tongue as possible as she worked her hands in a twisty-like motion on the base of Bonnie's cock. This entire evening this lovely lady has done a wonderful job of feeding a continuing stream of fine tasting things into my mouth, from green liquid, to big ice cubes, to cock.

My freshman year of college, I once walked in on my roommate fucking her boyfriend. I apologized and quickly started to head out the door and her boyfriend shouted, "It's totally cool, why don't you join in?" I had been a bit tipsy from a pot brownie I ate, and thought *hmmm, why not? This could be fun.* But then my roommate slapped her boyfriend and called him a jerk. I hadn't seen him since. This kind of ménage à trois experience being initiated by a woman, and with another woman, but still involving a cock was much better. I'm glad karma was giving me the proper threesome experience I was meant to have.

Janine and I giggled and fought over the cock and swapped it back and forth between one another. I really wanted to see the expression on Bonnie's face as this was all happening but I couldn't. I could just picture her eyes rolling back into her head and her laying there in ecstasy on her special night out. Was she smiling?

Janine took my hand and ran it up her thighs. I felt her garter and stocking with one hand and Bonnie's garter and stocking in another. I rubbed them both at once; Janine's nude stockings were quite thick, and her garter was made of some kind of nylon. It looked very retro—after we were done with this I thought I should ask her what brand these were because we certainly did not carry them at Dreamz.

We continued to switch off sucking. She got in a different position that looked like it involved some serious practice with yoga, and she leaned her head back upside down, and pushed Bonnie's cock downward into her mouth. Bonnie squatted on her face and thrust her cock directly in and out of Janine's mouth. This was impressive, a very well-choreographed upside-down blow job. Her skill in this department made up for that cheesy electric candle.

Bonnie continued to thrust into Janine's mouth. Her headband and feather still hadn't budged. I moved in and reached my tongue out and got in wherever I could. I got a small piece of the shaft as it was on its way down to her mouth. She was hungry for cock. She still kept a smile on her face while being aggressively pummeled. She truly loved it.

She released herself from her *Kama Sutra* contortionist stance and we went back to good old-fashioned cock sucking. I stroked, she sucked. She sucked, I stroked. I licked, she gagged, I cupped balls while she worked on the shaft. I saw Bonnie's knees begin to tremble, and we both sucked with more intensity, we sucked and stroked like our lives depended on it.

"Come on," Janine whispered, and she gave Bonnie one last big gulp and I noticed her feet shaking, and her hands clenching onto the table. That wasn't very nice! We so delightfully shared a cock, she should have rightfully shared the cum, too.

She kept her mouth closed and pulled me up back to civilization at the upside of the table. Bonnie was sitting there in relaxed ecstasy, not really looking at either of us, but up at the ceiling. I imagined she was seeing stars right then. I giggled.

Janine grabbed a cup off the table with half a cocktail left in it (something Bonnie was sipping on while she got her cock sucked) and she spit the cum into the cup. She stirred it around with a metal straw (seriously, they had metal straws) and she handed me the drink. With her lips still perfectly red and her powder completely still in place she handed me the glass and said, "Enjoy!"

It tasted like fresh, warm cum and herbs. There was a sprig of rosemary in it. Something I had once only seen inside of a Thanksgiving turkey was now flavoring semen and alcohol.

She exited our private area without saying anything. I gave Bonnie a kiss as I continued to drink her jizz. I took my time with it. After all, I was told the proper thing to do was to savor the taste, like a coffee, with a very special creamer.

To go back and go with Billy to the fair instead, turn to page 268.

To see how the Fantasy ends, turn to the next page.

The taxi cab dropped us off at the truck stop. Hand in hand, we walked through the lot lined with rows of various trucks. Many of the ones I'd seen earlier were gone, and new ones were pulling in. I was getting anxious, like my summer camp romance was ending. I would eventually have to go back to my apartment, back to work, and back to life. Or maybe I could just live on the open road with Billy and/or Bonnie and we could go from one sexual adventure to the next in each town.

We got back into the tuck, exhausted and satisfied. Bonnie started to get undressed, shedding her femininity. She got the dress off, but she was struggling with taking off her makeup. She kept scrubbing her face with soap and it wasn't budging.

"Should we go get some actual makeup remover?" Bonnie asked me, with a face full of suds, patches of foundation, and smeared lipstick on. Earlier this evening she resembled Marilyn Monroe but now she resembled Marilyn Manson. Either way, I was into it.

"No! That's a waste of money, here, use this!" I took a small bottle of olive oil he had on his very limited rack of spices and condiments. Next to it sat a salt and pepper shaker, little bottles of Tabasco, mustard, and ketchup.

"You want me to put that on my face? It's meant to go on my salad," she laughed.

"Yeah! It works, seriously. And it will keep your skin nice and smooth. All makeup remover really is, is a

bunch of different oils that break up the makeup parti-
cles."

She hesitantly but willingly took the olive oil out of
my hands, and wiped it across her face with a tissue. As I
suspected the makeup cleaned off impeccably well.

"So, what should I call you now?"

"I'm back to Billy," he said.

"All right!" I said.

"I know. Look, I'm new at this. Bonnie is an important
part of me. I've been waiting for her to walk around freely
for so many years! And this is really exciting. But I'm also
not ashamed of Billy. I am happy in my own skin, but I
need to express my feminine side sometimes. I guess the
best thing I can relate it to is how you would feel when
you put on high heels and a designer outfit. Doesn't it just
make you feel powerful and kind of like you're a different
person that evening?" he asked.

"I have literally never worn a designer outfit in my
life. Unless you consider American Apparel a designer. I
once spent $42 on a long-sleeve shirt from there and I
don't know if I felt powerful but I sure felt comfortable!"
I laughed.

After a pause I said, "Look, I'm fine with whoever you
want to be, whenever you want to be. I'm just happy to
be here!"

I kissed him, as Billy again. His cheeks were so silky
from the olive oil. An "extra virgin" skin remedy after a
night of public sexual escapades.

"So, where do you have to go next?' I asked. "And
when?" I wanted to begin to mentally prepare for my
abandonment. Eventually the magic that existed inside this
eighteen-wheeler would have to come to an end. I think.

"Actually, I'm not so sure right now," he said.

"What do you mean? Don't you have to, like, drive somewhere? Isn't that what truckers do?" I laughed.

"Well, this winter was abnormally cold," Billy said.

"Oh yeah, it was! I had to wear a real coat. AND boots. It was nuts!" I replied.

"Yeah, well when it gets that cold, the strawberries can't grow properly, and that's the primary fruit that I deliver. The farm I work for laid me off temporarily, until the next grow season."

"Oh! I'm so sorry," I said.

"Don't be! It's part of this business. I'm not sure what I will do. I have enough money saved to last me a while. That's what happens when you have basically no bills to pay! The trucking job was just for something to do. I'll just stick around here until I figure something out!"

"Well, I can't say I'm happy that you got laid off but I am happy that you don't have to leave."

He grabbed two more organic frozen burritos from the tiny ice box of shelf space in his mini fridge. We listened to the whooshing sounds of the microwave, and continued to make out until it beeped.

Going back to work was surreal. It felt like it had been days since I had been there and in those few days I had had seen a man transform into a woman, then back to a man, and have sexual interactions with both him and her in various public places. My car was still here. It felt like a dream.

On the other hand, the store was a complete disaster. The floor was damaged from the rainwater and vaguely smelled like mold. Hundreds of magazines were completely destroyed and several electrical cords were frayed that plugged in the neon lights that spelled out "VIDEO DVD XXX." At this point, I was pretty sure just being inside the store violated several safety codes.

I had no idea what to do. No one was at the store when I got there. I unlocked it at 6:30 P.M. Had anyone been here at all? Did Sandy know what was going on? Was I still on the clock right now even though nothing here really worked? Because I did desperately need my untaxed eleven bucks an hour.

The bell on the door rang (it was good to know that did still kind of work) and Sandy came in. She was wearing bright yellow galoshes, a bright orange skirt, and a silver puffy jacket, and of course, she had hot pink lipstick on her lips.

"Hello, honey!" She kissed me on the cheek and left a huge lip mark on me, which was fine because I had now become quite used to having a face stained with makeup. Instead of trying to wipe it off I just blended it into my face like a type of rouge.

"Hey, Sandy," I said.

"Would you like some punch? I can mix some for you!" she said.

"No, Sandy! I think, uh, I think we should probably figure out what the hell to do here before we start drinking punch, right?" I said.

She paused. "Well, drinking punch usually helps me figure out what to do!" She started laughing.

"All right. Let's drink some punch and maybe we'll get inspired."

Sandy pulled out a mason jar full of mystery pink liquid from her silver puffy jacket. She grabbed two plastic cups that she kept by the register, that had some sticky leftover pink residue in the bottom, and filled them up. We clinked our Solo cups together.

"Cheers!" she said. It was a small moment of joy in this half-run-down porn store.

"So what do we do?" I gave the punch a few minutes to circulate inside our bodies and seep into our brains. "I mean, don't you have insurance, or anything of the sort?"

"Well, I came in the morning after the storm with an insurance adjuster," she said.

"Oh, really?" I know it sounds incredibly insulting; it was just surprising to hear Sandy say the words "insurance adjuster." The store has been open for over twenty years; sometimes I don't give her enough credit.

"So what happened? Do they send someone to fix it?"

"Well, they couldn't find anyone to fix anything because there's too much damage everywhere in the town, and you know, we're not exactly the priority around here. They would be happy if we shut down! They did give me a check, though, and told me to take care of it myself."

"I mean, I'm sure you know plenty of repair people we could call, right?" I said.

"Honey, unfortunately the check they wrote me was for about one quarter of what it will cost to fix this place up. It was barely anything. A little less than four thousand dollars. My ex-husband was an electrician, and he owned a construction business. I know what these things cost—we will need at least fifteen thousand to fix this!" She continued to drink the punch. There were tears in her eyes.

"Sandy, why didn't you call me?! I would have come in here and talked to them for you." They completely took advantage of her. "Did you talk to Emma and Bradley next door? What happened to them?" I asked. There was a business right next to us run by an older couple that did vacuum cleaner and sewing machine repairs, and Sandy was friendly with them. They stayed open for about four hours a day, if that.

"Yes, they are getting full coverage. Hell, they'll probably just retire and use their money to buy a new house! They're getting a little over forty thousand dollars," she sighed.

"That's ridiculous! Their store is one-eighth the size of ours! Can't you get a lawyer? This can't be legal. I wish you wouldn't have signed off on this so quickly."

Shouldn't the local authorities know that masturbating is far more important than fixing a vacuum cleaner? Don't people actually just go and buy new ones when they break?

And then I remembered. After the fisting and before the public debauchery, Billy told me he used to work construction. He also told me he basically had nothing to do and a good amount of money in his bank account. Was this just meant to be? What were the chances that someone who drove up and down throughout the entire 500-mile stretch of the entire state of Florida would just happen to stumble upon this store? The fact that I worked here was completely random; I was supposed to be a substitute teacher somewhere in Pasco County, while attempting to get upgraded to an actual teacher somewhere in Hillsborough County. But that didn't happen. The fact that Billy wound up here was equally as random. He was supposed to be a married man by now, with a child, owning his father's construction business, living in a Boca Raton mansion, but instead, he was living in a truck.

People used to always tell me that everything happened for a reason. But nothing ever happened to me, so there were no reasons for anything. It truly felt like everything that happened in my life happened in the way that it did just so this moment would happen the way it was right now. From the power outage, to the frozen strawberries, the path of bizarre mishaps have led us to a broken porn store with no one to fix it. I pulled out my phone and called Billy.

"Hey!" I said, "It's me!"

"Hello! How's it going? I miss you, pretty."

I blushed.

"Well, the store is totally fucked up. I'm here with Sandy. Remember Sandy?"

"Hello love!" Sandy yelled loudly behind me.

"Yes, of course. The lady with the lipstick all over her face who made the punch."

"Yes. That's her!" I said. "So, I remember you said you worked construction. The insurance company came in here and totally ripped her off and gave her less than half of what she will need to get this place back up and running. Would you want to help?"

Silence came from his end. Shit. I don't know why I was expecting him to just suddenly say yes. Maybe this was a mistake.

"You can, like, think about it and call me back if you want," I said.

Sandy was now chugging her punch straight from the jar. She wasn't bothering to pour it into a cup any longer.

"I can do that—I'll come by and figure it out," he said.

"Really?" I said.

"Well yes, but I have a better idea. I can put some of

298

my savings back into fixing it, we can tear down the whole place and rebuild it, and make it amazing."

"I mean, that's not really my call. I make minimum wage here," I laughed.

"Sandy can still get her share. I'll just be another partner. I know a lot about running businesses. I would love to help," he said.

"Well, why don't you come over here? We have a lot to talk about!" I said.

"I'll be right over."

I hung up the phone. "Don't worry, Sandy, everything will be okay!" I turned to her and said.

"Are you sure?" she said.

"Yes. I am sure."

"Well, all right, lead the way!" she said. And she turned up the music in the store to the highest volume possible. Which wasn't very high at all because the speaker barely worked anymore. But through the crackles and the static and feedback of the now mono (that was once stereo) speaker system, she danced to an instrumental pop song.

Billy came by later and talked everything over with Sandy. They had a lot of complicated details to work out, but she seemed very excited. She hugged him and kissed him, and he brought from his truck a giant box of tools taller than me, and began making a plan on how to fix the store. We made a promise to each other that as soon as he removed all the ruined flooded carpets from the ROOMZ, we would christen it by having sex for the first time with each other in there—something we hadn't actually done yet. Our seventy-two-hour relationship had been limited to fisting, cum swallowing, and panty wearing, but no penis to vagina penetration. Not yet. Did I set my vagina up for something too strenuous? I wanted to fuck him, and I didn't want to wait too long to do it. Perhaps I should Google the details of how long it takes to reupholster damaged carpet so I had a timeframe.

He decided to do a quick fix on the speaker. Sandy didn't want to turn the music down, and the sad sounds of the burned-out speaker was painful to our ears. He got up on a stool and pulled out some wire cutters and began pulling out colored cords and fixing them up accordingly. His pants sunk down a bit, and on top of his sliver of adorable plumber's crack, he revealed that beneath his manly jeans he wore the original plain black garter he got here, tied in the back with safety pins and some twine. My heart melted. And I felt a drop of moisture in my own new pair of lace panties. I smiled to myself as I realized, there is nothing in this world he can't fix.

The End

Go back at find a different fantasy, turn to page 28.

Acknowledgements

Thank you to all for your input, support, and inspiration in this novel.

Aaron Thompson
Chris Nieratko
Juanito Blanco
Josie Jacobs
Anna de Ville
Dnothing
Kara Pond
Mitch Fontaine
Jiz Lee
Nikki Hearts
Peter Warren
Buck Angel
Jason Ellis
Hipster Dan
Michael Tully
Asa Akira
Angela White
Abella Danger
Jessica Drake
Mike Quasar
RVCC
Hustler Hollywood

Fantasyland Adult Supercenter
Tristan Taormino
Nina Hartley
Stephanie Lippit
JT Stockroom
We-Vibe
Vera Wylde
Mx Nillin
Betty Dodson and Carlin Ross
All performers who have ever worked for BurningAngel

My parents
Rebecca and Sarah

About the Author

JOANNA ANGEL is an adult film star, director, producer, author, and owner of the BurningAngel Empire, the company known for the emergence and prevalence of tattooed women in the adult film industry. Angel started her business in a college dorm room in 2002, and today the company has a network of websites, hundreds of DVDs to its credit, and over 50 adult industry awards, including Best Pornstar Website, Best Comedy, and many more. In 2016, Angel was the host of the AVN Awards and was inducted into AVN and XRCO's hall of fame. Angel has appeared in every major adult magazine (*Adult Video News, Club, Hustler, Picture Magazine*, and *Penthouse* to name a few), and she was the first tattooed centerfold of *Hustler* magazine. She has stormed mainstream TV and radio outlets, featured on Fox News, Playboy TV, Fuse TV, G4 TV, KROQ Radio, SIRIUS Radio, TLC's *LA Ink*, Vice TV, had a speaking role on Adult Swim's *Children's Hospital*, and starred in the indie drama *Scrapper*. Angel has appeared in the *New York Times, Newsweek, The Village Voice*, the *New York Press, Esquire UK, Details*, and is a regular columnist for AskMen.com. *Heeb Magazine* featured Joanna as their cover girl, naming her one of the "Top 100 Up-and-Coming Jews." *The New York Post* featured her as one of the "Top 25 Sexiest New Yorkers," and she has made CNBC's yearly "dirty dozen" (a list of the twelve biggest adult film stars) several times. Angel also made her mark in the sex toy world, becoming a venerated Fleshlight Girl and creating a BDSM line of toys with Stockroom. Joanna Angel is a self-made star who has made her mark on the industry, and this is only the beginning!